MW00618380

THE BITTER CHASE

Also by Cap Daniels

THE
BITTER CHASE
CHASE FULTON NOVEL #14

CAP DANIELS

ANCHOR WATCH
PUBLISHING
** USA **

The Bitter Chase
Chase Fulton Novel #14
Cap Daniels

This is a work of fiction. Names, characters, places, historical events, and inci-dents are the product of the author's imagination or have been used fictitiously. Although many locations such as marinas, airports, hotels, restaurants, etc. used in this work actually exist, they are used fictitiously and may have been relo-cated, exaggerated, or otherwise modified by creative license for the purpose of this work. Although many characters are based on personalities, physical at-tributes, skills, or intellect of actual individuals, all of the characters in this work are products of the author's imagination.

Published by:

** USA **

All rights reserved. No part of this book may be reproduced or transmitted in any form or by any means, electronic or mechanical, including information storage and retrieval systems without written permission from the publisher, ex-cept by a reviewer who may quote brief passages in a review.

13 Digit ISBN: 978-1-951021-24-5
Library of Congress Control Number: 2021911347
Copyright ©2021 Cap Daniels – All Rights Reserved

Cover Design: German Creative
Cover Photo: Cap Daniels

Printed in the United States of America

Dedication

This book is dedicated to . . .

My wonderful friend, Hancy "Hank" Deacon.

It would be impossible to compile a list of the indescribably fantastic things my writing career has brought into my life, but if I made an attempt to do so, it would, without question, start with a list of the life-changing people who've become dear friends as the direct result of these stories I dearly love to create. Very near the top of that list would be Hancy. Like most of the great things in life, I don't remember exactly how our friendship began, but I'll always be thankful it did.

Hancy is beautiful inside and out but will deny both, intellectually brilliant but will never admit it, and most of all, unshy about speaking her mind. She'll likely claim that last one with enormous pride . . . as she should. Hancy is quick to let me know when I'm screwing up, but equally quick with heartwarming praise when I accidentally get something right.

Although she and I have spent fewer than two hours together, we've built a beautiful relationship one email at a time. I treasure her friendship as if we've been lifelong pals. Her wit, wisdom, and honest endless love for the people in her life are treasures far beyond the bounds of measurement. I'm deeply honored to be one of the people she calls her friends, and I vow to never take that blessing lightly.

Thank you, my spectacular friend, for being the best of what we should all strive to be. I love you bunches, and I promise to keep writing phrases like "gosh darn it" because as you are quick to remind me, a great story is still a great story, even without the foul language.

Special Thanks To:

My Remarkable Editor:
Sarah Flores – Write Down the Line, LLC
www.WriteDowntheLine.com

Lehrkind Mansion Bed and Breakfast Inn, Bozeman, MT
Chris and John, our hosts at what became our base of operations
during research for this book.
https://www.bozemanbedandbreakfast.com/

The Bitter Chase
CAP DANIELS

Chapter 1
Toy Soldiers

March 2004

Clark Johnson, former Green Beret, wore the warrior's gaze as the web of his hand between the thumb and index finger slid up the dimpled grip of his Glock 19 pistol until he felt the familiar sensation of gripping the pistol exactly as he'd been taught and practiced countless times. With flawless execution of the programmed muscle memory, his thumb unlocked the retention device of the holster, freeing the weapon from its confinement. Rotating the muzzle toward the target the instant the front sight cleared the holster, the seasoned soldier pressed the weapon toward the intended victim with perfect, blinding speed. His left hand met the knuckles of his right as he gripped the 9mm. His right index finger pressed the custom trigger until he'd taken up eighty percent of the trigger's travel while raising the weapon to bear on his target. The instant his front sight touched the imaginary box covering his victim's heart, Clark's finger pressed through the trigger break, freeing the firing pin to strike the primer and send the projectile rifling through space and time, blindly following the orders of its master. Recoil sent the weapon upward and back, but the trained muscles of Clark's wrists, forearms, and hands returned the muzzle to its previous deadly alignment with its target's heart, and the weapon roared again, sending a second projectile through the air before the first had made deadly contact. Unblinking and without conscious thought, Clark raised the pistol, bringing to bear on the cartilage of the nose directly between his victim's eyes. The third round left the muzzle at 1,250 feet per second on its torturous, lethal mission. What the first two rounds had done inside the victim's chest cavity would be reproduced inside what remained of the target's brain, sending him lifeless and melting to the floor. With the immediate threat eliminated, Clark's next movement was the quick and highly efficient scan: left, right, rear, and back to the front. Finding no additional targets, he holstered the weapon, which was still smoking from the perfect implementation of its designed use.

"And that's how it's done," I said to Disco, the newest member of our team. "I guess they don't teach A-Ten drivers to shoot like that, huh?"

The seasoned combat pilot stood, staring into the three holes in the paper target. The two holes in the heart looked more like one enlarged wound. "I'm not sure I'll ever be able to do that."

Clark pulled the plugs from his ears. "Anybody can do that to a paper target, but doing it when the target starts shooting back? Now, that's the tough part."

Disco stepped to the line, and Clark faced him from his right side. "We start from the interview position with both hands held comfortably between your chin and solar plexus. On the command of 'Threat,' your right hand moves to the pistol grip. Try to make contact about eighty percent of the way up the grip, and continue sliding your hand until it seats perfectly in the web. Give that a try."

Disco practiced the motion several times until he could consistently hit the spot and establish the perfect grip to draw the weapon.

Clark held Disco's hand in place on the pistol. "Now, press your thumb against the retention release, and draw the weapon upwards about an inch."

Disco mastered the release, and class continued until he could draw the weapon, marry his hands just after rotating the muzzle toward the target, take up the slack in the trigger, and present the weapon to the target.

Clark said, "Good, let's do it by the numbers. One . . . grip. Two . . . release retention. Three . . . draw. Four . . . marry the hands. Five . . . present the weapon and take up eighty percent of the trigger press. Six . . . align the sights and complete the trigger press. Remember, we press triggers. We don't pull them. Pulling leads to missed shots, and missed shots lead to the wrong guy getting dead. Namely, you."

Disco slowly progressed through the procedure several times before Clark ordered, "Lock and load. Put one round in the heart, and take your time. We're in no hurry. Slow is smooth, and smooth is fast."

Our chief pilot did exactly as Clark had taught and drilled hole after hole through our target's paper heart.

"Well done. Holster up, and let's try the T-box drill I demonstrated earlier. Imagine the letter T formed by the eyes and nose of your target. That's where your third shot should find its home. Two to the heart, and one to the T-box, nice and slow. Trust me, the speed will come."

Disco shot the T-box drill until both Clark and I were satisfied he could consistently make the shots, even under the clock.

I gave the order, "Unload, and show clear."

The three of us unloaded our pistols and visually inspected the chambers of each.

"All right, gentlemen," I said. "Stow your weapons. It's time for us to have some fun."

We placed our pistols in the floorboard of my brown VW Microbus that had once belonged to my favorite psychology professor and former Cold War clandestine operative, Dr. Robert "Rocket" Richter.

I opened the silver case and handed out realistic-looking replicas of the Glocks we'd been shooting all morning.

Disco rolled the weapon in his hand, studying it thoroughly. "What's this?"

I tossed him a helmet. "This is how we make the targets shoot back, and Clark and I are the targets."

We donned our helmets and gloves and headed back to the range. I held up my pistol. "These work just like your Glock, except for two important differences. There's no lead and no gunpowder. Instead, there's compressed air and plastic pellets that sting like a hornet when they hit unprotected skin. That means cover up or prepare to nurse some wounds."

Disco holstered his pistol with a satisfied nod. "Far out."

I looked up. "Far out? Really? Are you seriously that much older than us?"

He threw up his hands. "Just wait. If you're lucky, you'll get old one day."

"Never!"

After a couple of shots to get Disco comfortable with the unrealistic recoil of the weapon, I said, "We'll make the first one simple. I'll move toward you, and you'll draw just like we taught you. After you've correctly made the draw and presentation, I want you to put one round anywhere on my body above the waist. I won't shoot back, this time, but I will be advancing on you. Shoot me before I get to you. Got it?"

"Sure. Sounds simple enough. Let's do it."

I stepped off twenty yards and turned to face our student. "Ready?"

He gave me a sharp nod, and I started moving forward in a fast walk. Disco's hand flew to his pistol, and his draw and presentation were perfect, but I've never loved looking down the business end of a pistol barrel, even if it's only loaded with plastic beads.

As Disco brought the weapon level in front of his face, his sight alignment was perfect, so I ducked my chin in preparation for the sting of the pellet, but instead of pressing the trigger, he froze, eyes wide and finger well clear of the trigger.

"Shoot him!" Clark demanded.

I continued my approach, but Disco didn't budge. It was as if he were frozen in place.

"Shoot him!" Clark barked again.

It was time to play psychologist, so I said, "Okay, cut. Holster your weapon, and let's have a chat."

Disco did as I ordered and pulled off his helmet.

"Why didn't you shoot?" I asked.

He stared down at his hands as if they were foreign to him. "I don't know. I just couldn't do it."

"What do you mean, you couldn't do it? All you had to do was press the trigger. You did everything else beautifully."

"I don't know. It just felt too real. For some reason, I couldn't make myself pull the trigger."

"Did you hesitate to pull the trigger in the Warthog when you rolled in on a column of Iraqi tanks?"

He shook his head. "No, but that was a lot different. Those tanks were a mile away and didn't have human faces."

"But they were full of human faces and asses and elbows," I said.

"Yeah, but they were intent on killing the troops on the ground."

I laid a hand on his shoulder. "I pray the day never comes, but if you're ever on the ground beside me in a gunfight, you can rest assured that guy coming at us means to do you and everyone behind you deadly harm. If you hesitate, he wins . . . every time. When you draw that weapon, do so with the absolute intent to end the life of the bad guy in front of you. We're not toy soldiers. We're warriors, and you're one of us now. Every member of this team has to know you'll pull that trigger every time it needs to be pulled. Otherwise, you're a liability to yourself and every member of your team."

His Adam's apple rose and fell as the reality of our existence washed over him.

I placed a hand in the center of his chest and pushed him backward a few strides. "Watch Clark."

I trotted back to the twenty-yard mark, drew my pistol, and charged. Before I'd taken two strides, Clark drew and put two in my chest and one in my face.

I hit the dirt as if the live T-box drill had worked its magic, and Clark took a step toward Disco. "Pretty good reaction time, huh?"

Our pilot looked up. "Yeah, you could say that. I don't know how you do it."

Clark leaned down and pulled at a fold in his shirt, and a white plastic bead fell from the cloth. "It wasn't fast enough. Chase put one in my chest before I could get out of the holster. That's how fast it happens. Hesitation is surrender. Now, get on your feet and shoot me before I shoot you."

He trotted away a few yards and turned to see Disco pressing the trigger. Clark took a knee, and I drew my pistol and demanded, "Drop your weapon! Do it now!"

Without hesitation, Disco put one in my thigh, one in my shoulder, and one directly in my T-box.

I holstered. "Sadly, that's the reality of the world in which we live. I'm not going to intentionally put you in a gunfight, but I can't stop someone else from bringing the fight to you. We have to train to a gruesome standard—one in which we rack up a higher body count than the bad guys."

We ran the drill three dozen more times, switching up the scenario every time. Disco only won when we let him, but his reaction time decreased with every iteration, and his hesitance to press the trigger vanished.

When we'd all had enough, we tossed our helmets back into the Microbus and guzzled bottles of water.

Clark, always ready to train, ran his fingers through his beard. "So, Disco, how are your knife-fighting skills?"

Before Clark could bring a knife to a gunfight, the sound of hoofbeats thundered toward us. I inherited four horses, along with Bonaventure Plantation, a two-hundred-acre parcel of land situated on the North River in St. Marys, Georgia, with a stable, a small home I liked to call the hermitage, and one massive antebellum brick house. The property had been in my mother's family since the birth of America and had fallen to me after the death of my great uncle, Judge Bernard Henry Huntsinger. The historical house burned to the ground at the hands of an arsonist, but I rebuilt, leaving the exterior virtually unchanged while making a few minor upgrades to the interior.

I loved everything about the property except the horses. I'd rather roll around with rattlesnakes than get near a horse. Every encounter I'd ever had with an equine left me hoping I'd never have another. Suspecting the galloping horse was coming for no other reason than to torture me, I turned to see which one of the foul beasts it was. To my surprise, it was Pecan, the horse I hated the least, and on his back sat the woman I loved most, my wife, Penny.

I poured the last few ounces of water from my bottle into my mouth and stood. "Hey, I didn't expect to see you out here. What's up?"

She pulled Pecan to a halt a few feet away. "I think you should come up to the house. You're never going to believe who Skipper found."

Chapter 2
The Prodigal Daughter

Having accomplished everything we'd hoped on the range, Clark, Disco, and I loaded our gear into the Microbus and followed Penny and Pecan along the river's edge. The mast of *Aegis*, my fifty-foot, custom-built catamaran, came into view long before the chimneys of Bonaventure, but soon, we were parked beside the first set of hardened doors leading to the armory beneath the house.

"If you guys don't mind, I'm going to run inside and see what's going on with Skipper, but I'll be back out to help you unload the gear."

Clark gave me a shove. "It's always the same with you, College Boy. You'll do anything to get out of the real work."

"Yep, that's me, but what can I say? Rank has its privileges."

Clark held his nose. "If by *rank* you mean how bad you smell, then I'd have to agree."

Disco shook his head as he hefted a pair of ammo cans from the back of the van. "Does it ever stop?"

Clark stopped whatever he was pretending to do. "Does *what* ever stop?"

"The banter between you two."

Clark turned to me and scratched his head. "What's he talking about?"

I shrugged and laid my gun belt inside the van. "It's not banter, Disco. It's love. Stick around long enough and you'll get some on you, too."

Clark keyed in the access code for the armory's outer doors and scanned his thumbprint. The electromagnetic locks clicked, and he pulled the doors to their stops as I rounded the house toward the back gallery.

As I climbed the wooden stairs that were built to look original to the early-nineteenth-century house, I paused to study the corner of the top step. It was charred, weathered, and ragged, but it made me smile every time I saw it.

Penny and I were married on the steps of the original house, and the corner of the step on which I'd knelt during the ceremony was the only piece of Bonaventure to survive the arsonist's fury. I would always see that burnt piece of oak as the indestructible foundation on which my marriage, and ultimate happiness, was built.

Penny slid from Pecan's saddle and left the beast standing by the gazebo. "Are you coming?"

"Yeah, I'm coming. I was just taking a little stroll down memory lane."

She followed my line of sight and tapped the charred timber with the toe of her boot. Sliding her hand into mine, she said, "Yeah, I do that, too, but I don't think you want to miss what's going on inside."

I pulled open the screen door and followed her through the kitchen to the base of the curved staircase leading to the second floor. She motioned up the steps. "You take the elevator, and I'll take the stairs. The winner gets an hour of anything they want from the loser."

I jammed a thumb into the button, stepped inside the elevator car, and entered the access code to the third floor—a floor that hadn't existed when the original house was built in 1804. When the doors opened into the foyer of the operations center, I strolled across the Oriental rug and took a seat in one of the wingbacks poised beside the double doors leading into the new center of my universe.

Penny's bare feet pattered up the stairs, and when she rounded the newel post, she waggled an accusing finger in my direction. "You cheated. You didn't tell me about the cipher lock on the second floor."

I checked my watch. "How could I cheat? You set the rules. I just played your game. Oh, yeah, and I won. I have high expectations for that hour you owe me."

"Cheaters don't get rewarded in this house. Now, come on. I think you're going to find this even more interesting than that hour you think you're getting."

We stepped into the secure communication center, and Penny pulled up the videophone on the main screen covering most of the wall at the west end of the room.

"What's this all about?" I asked, waiting for the screen to come to life.

"Just wait. You'll see."

Soon, the image of the best operational analyst I'd ever met filled the screen. "Good afternoon, Skipper. Penny tells me you've made an interesting find."

"Hey, Chase. You might say that, but more accurately, I didn't make the find. I'm the one who got found."

"Okay, I'm intrigued. Let's hear it."

Elizabeth "Skipper" Woodley was the daughter of my college baseball coach at the University of Georgia and practically my little sister. She'd studied under an analyst I knew only as Ginger and quickly became a prodigy. No matter what I needed, from intel to an exfil from a hot LZ, Skipper never wasted any time making sure I had it.

Without preamble, she stared directly into the camera in her office in Silver Spring, Maryland. "Anya is in New York City."

Anastasia "Anya" Burinkova was an enigma wrapped inside a *Russkaya zagadka*. She'd been trained by the KGB before the Wall came down, and she was quickly absorbed into the SVR, the Russian Foreign Intelligence Service. With a knife in her hand, she had no equal as an assassin, but her loyalties hadn't always conformed to Soviet standards. She was dispatched to find, interrogate, and flip me—and she managed two out of three—but instead of flipping me, she defected to the United States and became a member of my team of operators. The skill set she brought to the team was unmatched, and her intimate knowledge of Eastern Bloc tactics was a bottomless well of intelligence for a team of American covert operatives. Despite her position on my team, she vanished into thin air immediately following an operation in Saint Augustine, where she left a pair of bad guys sliced into unidentifiable pieces. Since her disappearance, even Skipper had been unable to determine where she'd gone or if she were still alive.

I leaned toward the screen where Skipper held my full attention. "How did you find her?"

"I told you, I didn't find her. She found me. And that's not all. Brace yourself. She's working for the Justice Department on an undercover assignment against the Russian Mafia."

"What? How did that happen?"

Skipper pulled a sheet of notes from her desk. "They apprehended her after that thing in Saint Augustine and gave her a choice. She could either go to prison for life or go to work for them."

I was still leaning forward and more interested than ever. "Why didn't she let us know?"

"Lean back," Skipper said. "You're freaking me out. Your face looks like a Cabbage Patch Kid or something when you get that close to the camera. Anyway, she didn't let us know because that was part of the deal. She could have no contact with anyone from her former life."

"Still, though, that's not like her."

"Maybe not, but it doesn't matter now. She was in a mess in D.C. and called me for help."

I ignored her instructions to lean back. "When did this happen?"

"A couple of days ago."

"A couple of days ago?" I roared. "And you're just now telling me?"

"Calm down. It all happened faster than I could process it, and I'm telling you now. Obviously, you've not talked to Mongo."

I finally leaned back as I pondered what the news would do to our gentle giant. Mongo was, by far, the largest member of my team at just over 6'8" and 300 pounds. He and Anya had struck up a relationship that no one really understood. The supermodel looks of the Russian against the gargantuan size of Mongo made the two an unlikely pair, to say the least.

"No, I've not heard from Mongo. As far as I know, he's still looking for Anya down in Miami."

"Not anymore," Skipper said. "He's probably somewhere licking his wounds right now. Anya kissed him goodbye on the telephone yesterday."

That sent me back into my chair. "Oh, boy. I guess I should call him, huh?"

Skipper sighed. "Yeah, I think you should. I don't know how close the two of them got, but despite how he looks on the outside, he's a real softie. I'm sure he's pretty upset."

"I'll call him as soon as we get off the phone. What else can you tell me about Anya?"

"Like I said, she's working with the feds to mess with the Russian Mafia. I hate to give the Justice Department any credit, but honestly, Anya is probably the perfect weapon for that job. Believe it or not, she's the one who busted Leo, The Lion, in Miami last month, and apparently, she's working some fake diamond case in New York."

I tried to take it all in, but there was too much about Skipper's story that left me with nothing more than questions. Articulation abandoned me, so my first question came out. "How long?"

"How long what?" Skipper asked.

"How long does she have to work with the feds to stay out of prison?"

She took a bite of a granola bar. "I don't think that's your real question. I think you really want to know how soon she'll be rejoining the team."

"She's never *really* been part of the team," I said.

Penny huffed, and Skipper said, "Maybe not the way the rest of the guys are, but she's put in plenty of hours knocking down bad guys with all of you."

I traced invisible circles on the surface of the table. "I meant she's never had the team mentality it takes to stay alive when everything goes to crap."

"Yeah, but she comes in handy when it's time to get nastier than the bad guys."

"Okay, I'll give you that, but do you know how long it'll take to get her out of the feds' hands?"

"Based on what she told me when I took her back to New York, she doesn't even know. I gave her a cell phone, so if they let her keep it, we've at least got a number we can call."

She gave me the number, and I saved it in my phone.

When I finished, I looked up at the camera. "Is there anything else?"

"Yeah, there's one more thing. Call Mongo. He could use a friendly voice about now."

I closed the call and turned to my wife. "What do you think?"

Never hesitant to express an opinion, she said, "I think Skipper's right. Anya probably is the best person for the job."

I gave her a smile. "Of course you'd feel that way. You just don't want her back on the team."

She reached across the table and took my hand. "No, I'm over that. I know she brings skills to the team that you wouldn't have without her, so I'm always in favor of anything that will keep you and the guys safer. I kinda like having you come home to me. You know, it's that soldier-home-from-war thing. I think it's hot when you come home all scraggly and scuffed up. When you shave the beard and put clean bandages on the wounds, it's like you're stepping between worlds—the one where you have to save all humanity, and the one where I get to pretend you're home for good."

"I know this isn't the life you expected. I'm not exactly the white-picket-fence kind of guy." I motioned around the room. "But I built you an ops center. How many women can say their husbands did that?"

She squeezed my hand again. "I wouldn't change a thing, Chase Fulton. Besides, if I wanted a white picket fence, I'd build it myself."

"I know you would. Now, get out of here. I have to call Mongo, and I'm not looking forward to it."

She pulled the door closed behind her as she left the ops center, and I stared down at my phone, trying to write the speech I would deliver. Before I could dial Mongo's number, his name appeared in the center of the tiny screen of my phone.

"Hey, Mongo. I was just about to call you."

His deep baritone poured through the earpiece. "Yeah, I thought you'd be calling soon. I guess you've heard the news about Anya, huh?"

I took a deep breath. "I just got off the phone with Skipper. It sounds like Anya is okay, but how about you?"

A long, cold silence followed, and I waited patiently, as I could almost hear my friend's heart breaking on the other end of the line.

"I'm going to be all right. She called me, more or less, to say goodbye, and I'm taking a little time to put my feet in the ocean and pull myself together. That girl has a way of . . . well, I guess you know as well as anybody."

Before I could piece together something meaningful to tell my enormous friend, Clark and Disco came bounding through the door. The look on Clark's face said he wasn't coming to get help unloading the Microbus. He motioned toward the phone pressed to my ear. "Is that Mongo?"

I nodded, and he ordered, "Put him on speaker. We've got a mission."

Chapter 3
A Bigger Phone Booth

It was going to take some time for the whole team to learn the capabilities of our new ops center. Putting Mongo on speaker through my cell phone in our state-of-the-art facility would be like building a fire in an electric oven. In seconds, I had not only Mongo, but also Hunter, Skipper, and Singer on the secure line. Skipper was back on the screen, but the others were voice-only comms.

Clark scanned the room. "Where's the microphone?"

Skipper laughed. "It's everywhere, you caveman. Just talk. The whole room is wired for sound."

Clark gave the room a second appraising scan. "Okay, if you say so. Is everyone where they can talk freely?"

Hunter, the former Air Force Combat Controller, said, "I'm with Tina, but we're in my truck."

Singer, our Southern Baptist sniper and de facto spiritual advisor for the team, reported, "I'm headed up to the monastery to see my brother, but I'm alone for now."

Mongo's response was a little more somber. "Yeah, I'm all alone . . . again."

Clark sent a look of concern toward the disembodied voice of the giant and whispered, "Is he okay?"

I gave him a shake of my head and mouthed, "No. Anya dumped him."

He gave me a knowing nod and turned to the screen. "Okay, Skipper, put him through."

Our analyst stroked a few keys, and the face of a man I'd never seen filled half of the screen beside her with a thin black line separating the two. The man wore the wrinkles of a life spent worrying about the lives of others and bearing the weight of the world on his shoulders. I examined his face for any hint of familiarity, but nothing about him rang any bells.

The stranger in our midst poured a long drink from a crystal tumbler and sighed. "Gentlemen, the briefing I'm about to give is one we all prayed would never leave our tongues."

He paused as if expecting a response, so I gave him one. "Sir, I'm afraid you have, at least, me at a disadvantage. It would appear you know us, but I'm afraid I've not had the pleasure."

The man took another sip. "Under normal conditions, none of you would've ever seen my face. My name is Gardner, and I represent the Board."

The Board was the center of my professional universe. Every official mission my team and I were handed came from that mysterious entity. Until that moment, I'd never directly heard any of their voices, and I'd certainly never seen any of their faces. Whatever was about to happen was a leap into a realm none of us were capable of predicting.

Gardner continued. "Men, I'm about to ask you to volunteer for an assignment unlike anything you've ever undertaken. As you know, we go to great lengths to ensure none of our teams ever cross paths. There are several reasons for this, but the most crucial of these reasons is to protect the identities of our operators. Men like you live in a small world, and keeping you apart is never easy, but it is, unfortunately, essential."

Hunter's voice filled the room. "Are we going to fish or just cut bait all afternoon?"

Gardner either couldn't hear him, or he ignored my partner. "We have a team that's suffered a fate worse than death. The team has been compromised by a mole who's leaking operational details, organizational structure, and capabilities. These moles stand to destroy us if they are not stopped."

"Which is it?" I asked.

"I'm sorry, Chase, but I don't understand your question."

I cleared my throat. "You first said, 'a mole,' then you used the plural. Which is it, *a* mole or *multiple* moles?"

"That's why you're our first choice for this unorthodox mission," Gardner said. "You and your team represent a collection of skill sets unmatched within our organization. The diversity of your backgrounds, training, and individual perspectives make you the only reasonable choice, but what we're asking is something no operator ever wants to do."

I leaned forward in an effort to recreate my Cabbage Patch Kid appearance on Gardner's screen. "Exactly what are you asking, Mr. Gardner?"

He drained the remaining contents of his tumbler. "I'm asking you to investigate another team, find the mole or moles, and stop our organization's bleeding."

I suddenly wanted a tumbler of my own, but instead, I pulled out a pad and pen. "Where's the other team?"

"Billings, Montana."

"How large?" I asked.

"Six men."

Without looking up, I made notes as we continued. "How long has this been going on, and how did you discover it?"

"That's classified."

That stopped my pen and boiled my blood. "Classified? Are you serious? You want my team to crawl around inside the lives of another team of operators who are, likely, just as dangerous as we are, and you've got the gall to tell me something is classified?"

Gardner straightened himself in his chair. "Chase, I want to know why you're asking the questions instead of your handler, Mr. Johnson."

I opened my mouth to answer, but Clark held up a finger. "Chase is doing the talking because he's the team lead. He'll be the one whose butt is going to be hanging out when we find your mole—or moles—and you start raining down retribution on some of our fellow operators. If Chase has a question, and you're not willing to give an answer, especially on a mission like this, then we're not the team you're looking for."

Gardner said, "Let me stop you right there, Mr. Johnson."

Clark never hesitated. "No, I won't be stopped right there by you or anyone else. You're asking us to investigate another team of tier-one operators solely on your word that there's a mole. No offense, Mr. Gardner . . . No, on second thought, I'm okay if you're offended. For all we know, you've given this same spiel to a dozen other teams before calling us. If you want us to take a serious look at this mission, you'll give us every drop of every piece of intelligence you have on this rogue team. Anything less, and you can keep making calls, but you're not going to be able to sell this crock of crap to any team who's worth their salt. Now, I'm finished, and you're welcome to answer Chase's questions."

Gardner seemed to chew on Clark's admonition for a few seconds before saying, "That's why you're the first team I called and the only team we want on this mission. Here are the details as we know them."

I held up a palm. "Before we go any further, I want to make something crystal clear. That's the first and final time you'll play games with me. My team and I will listen, and we'll tell you if we can accomplish the mission. It's not about whether we want the mission. It's about whether we're capable of completing it, so no more games. Give us all you have, and you'll get our honest response."

Gardner asked, "Does everyone have clearance and an NDA?"

"Stand by," I said. "Hunter, we need to get Tina out of your truck for the briefing. Can you make that happen?"

"Sure. No problem. She has some shopping to do anyway, so I'll drop her off in a second."

After some commotion on the line, Hunter was back. "Okay, Chase. It's just me now. Let's get to it."

I turned back to the camera. "Mr. Gardner, everyone on the line has clearance, a need to know, and a signed non-disclosure agreement, so let's have it."

With pen, once again, in hand, I waited, and Gardner finally continued. "We believe the leak has been happening for approximately twenty months. It was discovered when another team of operators from the Pacific Northwest walked into an ambush during what should've been a milk run."

"What kind of ambush?" I asked.

Gardner said, "No shooting. It was a vehicle ambush that left two of our operators dead and a third burned nearly to death in the resulting fire."

I looked away from my legal pad. "And you think that was the work of the team in Montana?"

"No, but I think it was the result of a leak from the Montana team. I don't think they were directly involved, but by all indications, someone from the Montana team tipped off the bad guys that we were coming after them."

"Who were the bad guys?" I asked.

Gardner bit his lip. "That's where it gets sticky. Our target was the Chinese, or at least operatives working with the Chinese."

A groan rose from my team, and a cannonball landed in my gut. "The Chinese?"

"Yes, I'm afraid so, but that's not the worst of it. Of the last four missions the Montana team worked, none were completely successful. In each case, some critical element of intelligence was compromised, or a piece of vital technology, somehow, escaped being recovered."

I laid my pen across my pad. "We're going to need dossiers on each of the operators on the Montana team, including financial workups. How long will it take for you to get that information to us?"

"It's already been sent to your analyst by encrypted email. I'm sure she'll have it ready for dissemination within minutes of the close of this briefing."

"That's a good start," I said, "but we're also going to need a full report detailing the actions of the team members that you and the Board believe are the potential moles."

Gardner said, "That's all included in the email."

I scanned the room for signs of questions, but everyone was stoic. "I have just one more question for you, Mr. Gardner. When will we have access to the additional members of the Board for interviews?"

"I'm afraid that won't be possible, Chase. The anonymity of the Board is paramount."

I leaned back in my chair and threw my right ankle across my left knee. "Let me get this straight. You want my team to investigate another team on the word of one member of the Board. We may not be detectives, Mr. Gardner, but we're also not fools. For all we know, you could be the rogue operative, and the Montana team is on to you. You could be sending us in to eliminate a threat against you. We'll look at the intel, but we won't commit without a conversation with the remaining members of the Board."

Gardner stared at the floor, age and weariness rippled across his forehead. "Okay, Chase. Look at the intel, discuss it with your team, and we'll meet again tomorrow morning at eight a.m. via teleconference."

"It sounds to me like you're in a hurry. Why the sudden urgency if you've been watching the Montana team for nearly two years?"

He grimaced. "Let's just say the team stands to unleash a great deal of havoc on the American intelligence community if they're not stopped soon."

I turned to Skipper. "Cut Gardner's feed, but I want you and everyone else to stay on the line."

Gardner's face disappeared from the screen, and Skipper doubled in size in front of us.

Mongo was the first to speak. "I guess it's time to turn into Superman and fly home, huh?"

I laughed. "There's not a phone booth in Miami big enough for you to change into your cape and tights."

"In that case, I'll hit the road without my cape and be there in five hours or so."

It was Singer's turn. "I guess my brother and the monks will have to wait. I'll be there in a couple of hours."

Hunter said, "We're in Jacksonville, but I'll grab Tina and head that way. Give us an hour or so."

With the three of them off the line, I turned back to Skipper. "Have you glanced at the email from Gardner yet?"

"Do you really have to ask? You should hear your printer come to life any minute. I sent six copies."

As if on cue, the printer hummed, and pages magically appeared. "I'd like for you to be here for this one, Skipper."

She leaned forward and lifted a backpack into view. "Bag's already packed, and reservations are made. I'll be there before sundown."

Skipper signed off, and Disco stood. "Something tells me I'm not needed at this point."

I said, "It's not that you're not needed, but I do have something to discuss with Clark."

Our pilot wasted no time surrendering the room, and suddenly, it was time to have the talk I'd been dreading since leaving the Gulf of Aden.

Chapter 4
The Guessing Game

Clark Johnson, the man who'd spent four years of his life teaching me to stay alive in situations that would kill most everyone else, stood and pulled an inch-thick stack of paper from the printer. "All right. Do you want to start with the dossiers or the background?"

I motioned toward his chair. "That can wait."

He waved the stack of papers. "This is the very definition of something that *can't* wait."

"Actually, when you hear what I've got to say, I think you'll understand what I mean."

He tossed the printouts onto the conference table and reclaimed his chair. "This ought to be good. Should we figure out some way to turn off the microphones in here?"

I pointed at a panel of lights and switches near the door. "Take a look at that big red light at the bottom of the panel. When that light is on, the mics are on, but as long as it's off, this place might as well be Fort Knox."

"It's going to take me a while to get used to all of this high-tech gadgetry."

"Yeah, me too," I admitted. "But what I've got to tell you is old-school tradecraft. I'm sure you remember when things calmed down in the Gulf of Aden."

"Sure, we were playing shoot-the-duck carnival games with the Israelis while you were chatting it up with Rabin."

"That's what I need to tell you. As you know, Rabin is the deputy director of Mossad."

Clark's jaw dropped. "No, I didn't know that, but that guy sure can mix it up in the field for an admin puke."

"I think Rabin is still a knuckle-dragger behind his necktie, and he seems to know a lot more about us than he should. He told me there's someone close to me who isn't what I believe them to be."

Clark seemed to absorb the words and let them dance around inside his mind before showing any reaction. "What do you think he meant by that?"

I shrugged. "I don't know, but I can't stop thinking about it. I've run everybody in my life through the wringer a dozen times since Rabin told me that, and I can't come up with a single person who isn't what they claim to be."

Clark held up a finger. "If what you told me was a quote from Rabin, he didn't say what they *claim* to be. He said what you *believe* them to be. Those are two very different things."

I replayed the moment in my mind. "You're right. He definitely said believe."

Clark drummed his fingertips against the surface of the table. "So, let's go through what you believe about the people close to you. Maybe it's not as sinister as it sounds."

"All right, let's start with you."

He held up a palm. "Hang on. What you think of me is none of my business, so let's start somewhere else."

"Whatever you say. My first thought went to Disco, but I've since abandoned that one. He's not been around long enough to be considered close. I don't have anything against him, and I'm glad he's with us, but I can't imagine he's who Rabin was talking about."

Clark bit his bottom lip. "I agree, and I'll confess, my first thought was Penny. I mean, who's closer to you than her?"

I traced the swirls of wood grain on the surface of the table. "Yeah, I know what you're saying. She's the one who's stuck at the top of my list at the moment."

Clark snapped his fingers. "Focus. If we're going to figure this out, we've got to look at it analytically and keep emotion out of it. Tell me what you think Penny is."

My mouth went dry. "I'll admit, I didn't know much about her at first, but that's true of most relationships. I don't know much about what she's actually doing in California with the movie, but I don't really need to know the details of that mess. Honestly, I don't want to understand it."

The look on Clark's face told me he was suddenly invested in my situation. "Forget about the Hollywood stuff. None of that is real, anyway. Let's focus on what you believe about her."

"I believe she's my wife."

"Yeah, I think we can chalk that one up in the known category."

"I believe she loves and trusts me. I believe she's a caring, kind, honest person."

He nodded slowly. "How about her folks? That whole thing was a mess."

"It was, but now that all of it is out in the open, I don't have any concerns about any of that."

Clark inspected his nails. "There is that whole fugitive-from-justice thing, but I don't think the feds are spending too much time worrying about Carla Thomas."

He leaned in. "Don't get the wrong impression. I love Penny, but I'm just trying to give you something to think about. When you met her, she was living aboard someone else's sailboat and constantly on the move. After that, she was living on your boat and still constantly moving around. Sometimes, people who have something to hide tend to move around a lot. Again, don't shoot me, but it is something to think about."

I ran a hand through my hair and examined the ceiling. "I've already thought about that, but we did a thorough background check and even got clearance for her. What could she be hiding that we didn't find?"

"The only thing that doesn't show up in one of *our* background checks is the stuff you've *not* been caught doing . . . yet."

"Oh, boy. That's one way to look at it."

"It sounds funny, but it's the truth. Who's next on your list?"

"I guess it has to be Hunter," I said.

Clark balanced a pen across his knuckles and made a show of his performance. "Maybe it's me. I'm starting to think I should be in the circus with skills like this."

"Yes, that's the perfect place for you . . . the circus. They're always looking for clowns."

"Maybe I could be a lion tamer. How hard can it be?"

"I'll start calling you a Ringling Brother if it'll make you feel better."

He flipped the pen into the air and caught it with the skill of a drunken juggler.

"Nice job, Big-Top Clark. Now, let's get back to work. Tell me about Hunter."

He pocketed the pen. "He's as solid as they come. Too many people in the Special Warfare community know him, and nobody has a negative word to say. If I could've handpicked a replacement for me, it would've been Stone W. Hunter."

I tried my hand at pen balancing and discovered it wasn't as easy as Clark made it look. "So, it's not Hunter, and Anya is way too obvious. I'm already leery of her."

He wrinkled his forehead. "Singer?"

"No way. He's the best of us. What could he possibly be hiding?"

"There you go again," he said. "We're not looking for someone pretending to be something else. We're looking for somebody who isn't what *you* believe them to be."

"I believe Singer to be one of the best snipers on the planet and practically a saint . . . when he's not killing people."

Clark rocked in his chair in subconscious agreement. "I've known him a lot of years, and the only things that have changed about him are his ability to make shots nobody else would even risk taking, and his singing has gotten better."

"I trust you more than anybody on Earth, so if you're as confident as I am about Singer, I can't imagine him being the one Rabin was talking about. I think it's safe to toss him out of the running."

"That brings us to Mongo," Clark said.

"Yes, it does. On the surface, Mongo appears to be a colossal giant drifting through life and ripping trees out of the ground, but that perception couldn't be more incorrect. He's probably the smartest and most sensitive of all of us. Sure, he *can* rip trees out of the ground, but he can also explain photosynthesis and how those trees use sunlight to make food for themselves. Right now, though, the sensitive part of him is bigger than the physical part. Inside his head, he's a train wreck in a swamp."

Clark examined the wall across my shoulder. "How do you think it'll affect him if we take the Montana op?"

"I was thinking about that earlier. I think it'll be good for him. His brain needs something to do other than think about the Russian." I glanced toward the doors and lowered my voice. "Trust me, nobody knows better than me how that girl can mess with a man's head. I don't know anything about their relationship, but as you know, I didn't just *fall* into that honey trap. I jumped in with both feet."

Clark gave the doors a glance. "It wasn't your feet, College Boy. Mongo is older and wiser than you were seven years ago, but all men occasionally do their thinking with . . . their *feet* . . . and he's no different. You're the educated one in this equation, but from my perspective, Mongo believed he finally found someone who looked past his exterior and saw the man he really is behind that giant façade. Maybe he thinks that's what he lost and may never find again."

I leaned across the table and pulled the stack of paperwork toward me. "Who knows what women think? Especially Russian women . . . But I thought that's how Anya felt about Mongo. She'd finally found a man who could see past her physical appearance and find something to love other than her body."

Clark peeled off one complete set of documents from the stack of six and thumbed through it. "I guess none of that matters anymore as long as Mongo can get back in the fight. I've seen a lot of good warriors lose their heads over women, and, without fail, that always translates into poor focus, lousy performance, and often the death of people around them. We can't let that happen with Mongo. If he's not mission-ready, you can't put him back in the field."

I pulled my set of documents from the stack. "Me? What do you mean I can't put him back in the field? You're our handler. *You* make those decisions."

He looked up with cold determination in his eyes. "No, Chase. I'm *your* handler. You run the team. I just run you."

Ignoring the most important documents in my life at that moment, I leaned back in my chair. "Yeah, and just how did that happen? The only uniform I've ever worn as an adult had my last name and the number twenty-one on the back and University of Georgia Bulldogs on the front. How does that qualify me to run anything except a baseball field?"

He leaned forward and planted his elbows on the table. "Let me tell you something you don't know about you. I could bring every member of your team in here, one by one, and ask each of them the same question. If you had to dig a foxhole and fight off a hundred men, who would you put in that foxhole beside you? Without hesitation, every single member of your team, including me, would have the same answer—I'll take Chase. That's what qualifies you to run the best team of operators I've ever seen, and don't you ever forget that."

We spent the next hour committing the dossiers of the six Montana operators to memory and scouring their financials. After watching Clark nod off for the seventh time, I slammed my palm on the table, sending him jumping out of his skin. "No sleeping in the foxhole, Master Sergeant Johnson! I think we could use a pot of coffee."

Chapter 5
Not a Democracy

By nine o'clock that evening, once again, my team had morphed from a scattered collection of misfits into one big happy family gathered around the kitchen table. Actually, the table was two floors above the kitchen, and instead of plates of Maybelle's handiwork, each of us had a stack of dossiers and case history in front of us.

I made the decision to give Penny a seat at the table for two specific reasons. First, I wanted her to understand the operation well enough to function as the manager of the ops center while the rest of us were in the field. Second, I had gone to great lengths in the past to separate my profession from my marriage, and it was time for that to end. If Penny was going to be the most important person in my life, that life couldn't be divided into portions that did not include her.

Clark called the meeting to order in his typical gentle fashion. "All right. Everybody shut up and listen."

The small talk ceased, and every eye turned to face *my* handler.

He shook his stack of paperwork. "Has everyone read through this pile of garbage at least once?"

Heads nodded, and hands instinctually reached for their packets.

"Good. Chase and I have been over the files line by line all afternoon. It took four pots of coffee, and that still couldn't keep us awake. Personally, I didn't see anything impressive in the dossiers. Did any of you?"

I believed Mongo would sit in silence for the duration of the meeting, but I was wrong.

He flipped several pages into his packet. "Take a look at the financials for this guy named Brown on page eighteen." We flipped to the page and scanned while Mongo continued. "Three years ago, he was broke, and now his net worth is just under three million."

I examined Mongo's face and saw nothing except professionalism. "So, does that mean Brown is your suspect number one?"

The giant shook his head. "No. That scratches him off my list of suspects. Unless he's an absolute idiot, any operator on the take would go to enormous lengths to hide his sudden influx of cash. Brown's not hiding anything, and judging by his service record, he's definitely no idiot. His résumé is pretty impressive. Scout/ sniper, Ranger, SF, and Delta Force. Four Purple Hearts, a Silver Star, and a DSC."

Penny's eyes met mine, and Mongo noticed.

He paused and turned to Penny. "That's the Distinguished Service Cross, the second-highest award the U.S. military can issue. They're usually awarded when the Medal of Honor can't be justified, but they're always awarded for a single act of valor or heroism during one event. Usually, that event is a single battle. The citation for the DSC isn't in my packet." He turned back to face Clark and me. "Do you have a copy of the citation? I'd love to know what he did to earn the Cross."

Clark shook his head. "I don't have it. Maybe Skipper can . . ."

Without looking up from her keyboard, Skipper said, "Already on it, boss. Give me thirty seconds."

In less than half the requested time, our analyst slid her glasses up her nose and cleared her throat. "The president of the United States of America, authorized by Act of Congress July ninth, nineteen eighteen, takes pleasure in presenting the Distinguished Service Cross to Master Sergeant Alvin J. Brown, United States Army, for extraordinary heroism in connection with military operations against an armed enemy as a member of a joint-forces unit. On or about the seventh day of July, two thousand two, in a classified operation, acting on direct orders of the president of the United States, Master Sergeant Brown distinguished himself by rescuing six United States Marines from a burning armored personnel carrier at a classified deployed location, having fallen victim to an ambush by forces superior in number, armament, support, and position. With his left leg severed below the knee, Master Sergeant Brown fashioned and applied a field-expedient tourniquet while returning fire against enemy forces. Disregarding his wounds and his own personal safety, Brown exposed his position while maneuvering over two hundred yards across mountainous, rugged terrain toward the overturned and burning APC. Before reaching the vehicle, MSG Brown suffered numerous wounds from a seemingly endless barrage of small arms fire. Upon reaching the vehicle, MSG Brown tried, without success, to open the hatches of the deformed, battle-damaged APC. While severely wounded and continuing to return enemy fire, he placed and detonated a pair of explosive charges, freeing the hatch and allowing the otherwise doomed Marines their freedom. During the subsequent battle, MSG Brown, six Marines, four Special Forces operators, and two civilian contractors fought bravely, ultimately defeating the superior force, killing no fewer than thirty-three enemy aggressors while suffering no American losses. MSG Brown subsequently lost consciousness after the engagement due to blood loss and shock from the trauma he endured. MSG Brown's exceptional valor and bravery under fire not only prevented American casualties, but also reflect great credit upon himself, the United States Army, and the Nation."

My team sat in reverent silence for several moments, and I caught the glisten of a single tear in the corner of Penny's eye.

Mongo tapped a finger against Brown's dossier. "He's definitely not our bad guy, but he may be our best way in."

Clark stared at the ceiling. "Two thousand two . . . Can anybody think where that little gunfight may have occurred?"

With the exception of Penny's confused gaze, smiles and nods filled the room.

I turned to my wife and mouthed, "Afghanistan."

"All right," Clark said. "That rules out one and leaves us with five to go. Who's next?"

Preferring her laptop to printed pages, Skipper scrolled through the files. "The one anomaly I keep coming back to in the financials is this guy, Aaron Copeland."

We all flipped through our packets and settled on Copeland's dossier and financials.

I said, "I don't see anything special about him. What am I missing?"

Skipper stroked a set of keys and brought Copeland's financials up on the big screen. "It's not what you're missing. It's what *he* is missing. His net worth remains virtually unchanged, despite earning a more-than-comfortable living. These guys aren't earning what we are, but then again, we are the best. I'm curious where his money is going, though. The team as a whole has been paid a little over ten million bucks in the past twenty-four months. If they split it evenly—which I doubt because they aren't as generous as our fearless leader—that's just under two mil apiece. There's no reason why anybody's balance sheet should stay the same when he's making that much money. Either I've lost the ability to do math, or there's something fishy in that equation."

Everyone silently pored over Copeland's file.

When I'd come to the same conclusion as Skipper, I asked, "Does anyone disagree?"

Six heads all shook in unison, but Disco held up a finger.

"Yeah, what is it?" I asked.

Disco closed his packet and screwed up his face. "I know I'm the new guy here, and I'm not trying to gum up the works, but did we already vote to take the job and now we're on to mission planning?"

I leaned back and smiled for the first time since Clark called us to order. "You are the new guy, Disco, and because of that, I'll take a minute to bring you up to speed on how things work around here." Suddenly, I had everyone's attention. "Typically, Clark is handed an assignment package from the Board, then he briefs me on the package. I then make the call. If I want the job, I say yes, and I bring the rest of the team in for the initial briefing. After that briefing, if anyone is not on board, they are under no obligation to gear up and hit the trail with the rest of us."

Clark caught my attention as he rose from his chair and turned away from the table.

"Is everything all right?"

He waved me off with a dismissive hand. "Yeah, everything's fine. Carry on."

I turned my attention back to Disco. "So, back to the mission brief. If a member, or members, of the team protests and makes a compelling argument why we shouldn't take the mission, I will, sometimes, call it off and tell Clark we're out."

My handler returned to the table with a bottle of Gentleman Jack, a bottle of water, and eight tumblers. I paused, amused by his demonstration. He poured two tumblers a quarter full of the golden Tennessee sipping whiskey and slid one to me. Then he rolled the plastic bottle of water across the table to Singer, our Southern Baptist teetotaler sniper. With a nonchalant effort, he slid empty tumblers around the table and slid the Gentleman Jack to Hunter. The bottle made its way around the table, and each of the team poured a finger or two into their tumblers, with the sole exception of Singer, who poured water into his glass.

I touched the rim of my glass to Clark's and enjoyed a sip of the smoothest whiskey to ever flow out of Lynchburg, Tennessee. "You see, Disco, this isn't a democracy, and it's not about rank or seniority. Everyone at the table is welcome to drink our whiskey— or not, in Singer's case—but you have to pour your own. It's the same with missions. You're never obligated, but if you choose to come along, you have to pull your own weight. We're taking the Montana mission. The only question is, how many butts are going to be on the plane when we go?"

From the other end of the table, he raised his glass. "I'm in, but I call dibs on driving."

Skipper raised her glass. "I'm in, too, although my butt won't technically be on the plane. It'll be right here in the ops center."

Hunter, Singer, and Mongo added their tumblers to the raised collection. "We're in."

I raised an eyebrow at my beautiful wife. "How about your butt, Mrs. Fulton?"

She shot looks around the table. "What do you mean? I can't go with you."

"No, you can't, but what you can do is work hand in hand with Skipper to man the ops center. The poor girl has to sleep sometime."

Her beautiful smile lit up the room, and her tumbler joined the others. "In that case, you can count my butt in with everyone else's."

I turned back to our chief pilot. "See there, Disco. That's how it works, so no more stupid questions out of you. Got it?"

Everyone except Disco laughed. He instead chose to drink, and we followed suit.

Skipper tapped on the table with a little more energy than necessary. "Hey, before this gets out of hand, we still have four team members to study and an initial deployment plan to develop."

We briefly discussed the remaining members of the Montana team, and I said, "They all look clean from two thousand miles away. I say we put our boots on the ground and take an up-close and personal look. Does anyone disagree?" I didn't give them time to answer. "Good, I thought so. Now, all that remains is Skipper finding us a place to sleep and picking a wheels-up time."

Skipper made a show of striking a key on her laptop. "Nope, you're wrong again, Chase. All that remains is to pick a wheels-up time because I just procured a six-bedroom, seven-bath house in West Yellowstone, less than a three-minute drive from the Yellowstone Airport. We've got the house for sixty days, with an option for a thirty-day extension."

I scanned the room. "Does anyone need more than forty-eight hours to be mission-ready?"

Hunter frowned and shook his head as if he'd been attacked by a swarm of . . . something.

I watched in amusement. "Are you okay?"

"Yeah, I'm fine," he said. "But why would any of us need more than forty-eight minutes to be ready to go?"

Mumbles of agreement rose from the table, so I motioned to Clark. "Are you going or staying?"

He lowered his chin. "You told Disco to stop asking stupid questions, and now you're asking them. Of course I'm going. We'll take Gardner's zero-eight-hundred meeting in the morning and hit the friendly skies as soon as we give him the good news."

"Speaking of the friendly skies," I said. "You have to choose a cockpit. Are you going with Disco in the Citation or with Hunter in Caravan?"

He scoffed. "Why are you taking the Caravan?"

"Because there's about a billion acres of pristine mountain lakes in Montana, and I intend to land on every one of them."

"Whatever, College Boy. You and Hunter can have all that low-and-slow stuff you want. I'll ride in style with Disco."

Chapter 6
Low and Slow

Seven a.m. found Clark, Skipper, Penny, and me in the ops center with precious little sleep in our wake. Clark was the first to yawn, but it soon became "the wave," making its way around the table.

Following my yawn, I gave an exaggerated stretch. "I guess I'm not the only one whose brain wouldn't shut up last night."

"Mine rarely shuts up," Skipper said. "I wish I had a switch to turn it on and off."

Clark said, "Not me. I can function at my peak on just a few minutes of sleep."

"Yeah, right," I scoffed. "You're like a cat in the afternoon sun. I think you need more sleep than the rest of us combined."

He ignored the jab. "What are we going to do if Gardner doesn't produce the rest of the Board this morning?"

"Oh, he'll produce bodies. I have no doubt about that. But how are we going to know if those bodies are really the members of the Board?"

Clark lowered his eyes as if in deep thought, then he pulled a small, leather-bound book from his pocket and tossed it onto the table in front of me. I reached for the book, but his palm landed on it before I could pick it up.

With his hand still firmly anchoring the book to the table, he twisted in his chair so he could see the panel by the door. "Good. No light. No microphones." He lifted his hand and flicked the book toward me with his fingertips. "If you ever tell another living soul you've seen that book, I'll have you drawn and quartered. What you'll find in there is more classified than the aliens in Roswell."

I felt the worn, smooth leather between my fingers and stared up at my handler. "So, the aliens are real?"

He motioned toward my hands. "Just open the book."

I did as instructed, and I couldn't believe my eyes. The first several pages were telephone numbers to every decision maker inside the federal government. The center section of the book offered even more telephone numbers, but those were the numbers to world leaders across the globe, not just inside the good old USA.

I shot a glance at Clark, and he motioned for me to keep flipping. The final seven pages each held a small, black-and-white photograph and a short bio on each of the seven members of the Board—the oracle of our existence as covert operatives. I studied each page carefully, committing as much information as possible to memory. When I came to the page bearing the only familiar face, I said, "So, his name isn't really Gardner."

Clark slowly shook his head. "No. Gardner is his call sign because that's what he does. He plants seeds, and then he waters and fertilizes them and watches them grow. You and I are two of his potted plants. He handpicked both of us before we knew people like us existed."

I grimaced. "But I thought Dr. Richter picked me out of his psych class at UGA."

Clark grinned. "Yeah, and I thought I impressed the CIA at Delta selection . . . until I knew the truth. Dr. Richter was only a small tooth on a huge cog that plucked you from polite society and stuck you in the fertile ground Gardner provided. You and I took root and grew and produced fruit, but most seeds don't grow. Who knows why some people fail while others thrive? Things like that are above our paygrades. Now, give me back my book."

I hesitantly slid the worn relic back across the table. "Did you get that from your dad?"

"Yep. He passed it down to me just like I'll pass it down to you someday when you get too old and crippled to dig foxholes and kick down doors."

I held up both hands. "Don't put that evil on me. I drive boats, fly airplanes, and pull triggers. That's the extent of my capabilities."

"You just keep thinking that, and someday you might convince somebody of it, but everybody in this room knows the truth about you. You're a lot more than you pretend to be, and way more than you're willing to admit, but everybody who knows you, sees the truth."

I cast my eyes toward Skipper. "Have *you* seen Clark's little book?"

"No, but I'd give a million dollars to take a peek."

Clark put on his world-famous crooked smile and slid the book back into his pocket. "Thankfully, a million bucks wouldn't change my life very much, so I think I'll keep this thing tucked away until I get desperate for cash."

One by one, the remaining team members filed into the ops center and took their seats in the same chairs they'd occupied ten hours before.

I noticed the seating decisions and said, "Singer must be rubbing off on you bunch of heathens. Just like good Baptists, every-body's chosen their own personal pew. Pretty soon, we'll be passing the collection plate to take up a love offering for some-body."

I let a few groans and grumbles bounce off me while Skipper set up the comms for the meeting. At precisely eight a.m., our own version of a jumbotron sparked to life, and the screen divided itself into seven equal boxes, six of which contained torsos beneath pixelated heads. The seventh box held the clearly focused upper body and face of the man I'd known only as Gardner.

He kicked off the meeting. "Good morning, team. Forgive me for hiding the faces of my colleagues, but I'm sure you understand the necessity."

I started to speak, but Clark beat me to it. "Of course we understand, and we appreciate each of you taking the time to show your . . . well, torsos. We're prepared to move on the operation, but I'm deeply disappointed that you left out one extremely important bit of intel. If we're going to pull off the operation, there can be no October surprises. We have to know everything up front, and I mean absolutely everything. We're not junior deputies with plastic badges down here. We're a team of badass operators who'll stand in line to fight a circle saw, but we're not going to operate in the dark."

Gardner licked his lips. "Mr. Johnson, what you need to understand is—"

Clark cut him off. "Oh, this team and I understand full well everything we need to understand, but what you don't seem to understand is that we're smarter than you give us credit for being, so we're signing off so we can go to work. If the information you've been holding back shows up in our analyst's email inbox in the next fifteen minutes, we'll be on our way to Montana ten minutes after that, but if it doesn't, we're going deep-sea fishing, and your mole—moles—will remain *your* problem." He turned to Skipper and made a slashing motion across his throat.

She instantly cut the connection, and the screen went black. Everyone sat in stunned disbelief.

"What was that all about?" I asked. "What are they holding back?"

Clark shrugged. "I have no idea. In fact, I don't even know if they *are* holding anything back. But if they are, now they believe we know, and they'll jump through their asses to get it into Skipper's email box in the next fifteen minutes."

I chuckled. "Are you saying all that was a bluff?"

Before he could answer, Skipper's laptop chimed, and she clicked her mouse. She read with laser focus for several seconds before looking up at Clark. "How could you have known?"

"It's what I do," he said. "I drink good whiskey, and I know things. Put it up on the big screen."

A few keystrokes later, the one-paragraph email appeared in front of us.

Hannah June Meriwether is deeply involved and possibly being held against her will within a religious cult operating from a compound near the town of Gardiner, Montana, northwest of Yellowstone National Park.

I read those thirty-three words twice and laid my head in my hands.

Skipper was the first to speak. "What is it, Chase?"

I looked up to see every eye in the ops center focused on me and confusion consuming the room. "Hannah June Meriwether is the former president's niece."

Clark assumed my recent position of face in hands. "Oh, boy. I guess we've stepped off in a puddle that's way deeper than it looked."

"When do you think they were going to spring this on us if you hadn't pushed Gardner?"

He didn't remove his face from his palms. "I don't know, but I don't like it."

Hunter said, "I guess that makes this a rescue operation?"

Disco chimed in. "Isn't that what the FBI's HRT is for?"

I fielded that pop-up. "It *would* fall to the FBI Hostage Rescue Team if it were an overt operation, but the federal government can't be seen storming another compound like they did in Waco, just to pluck out the former president's niece, who is most likely there of her own free will. America won't stand for another tank ramming its way into another Branch Davidian–style compound, and the White House knows it."

"Instead, we get to do it quietly in the middle of the night, under the guise of investigating another team of operators on American soil. Sometimes it sucks to be me."

"Hey, handler. Remember that time I asked if you were staying or going and you said, 'Of course I'm going'? In fact, I think you scolded me for asking stupid questions." I gave Skipper a wink. "I'm pretty sure we had the mics on and recording when you said that. Skipper can play it back if you don't remember."

Clark finally looked up and sighed. "Yeah, yeah, you've made your point. Let's get in the air. We've got a mole to exterminate and a niece to liberate. It's just a walk in the park. What could possibly go wrong?"

We convoyed to the airport and towed out the Citation and our amphibious Caravan. We loaded the weapons and ammo aboard the Caravan because it seemed impossible to overload the old workhorse. If we could cram it through the doors, the 208 would carry it. The Citation, although it had an enormous speed advantage, was far too fickle about weight and balance.

With Hunter in the left seat, doing the flying, we blasted off into the wild blue yonder, headed for the wilds of southern Montana with a thousand pounds of guns and bullets behind us. The Caravan lumbered through the air on the climb-out and settled into cruise flight at twelve thousand feet, making 160 knots. With the autopilot set and all systems in the green, our headsets filled with Clark's voice from the cockpit of the Citation somewhere above and well ahead of us. "You boys wanna race? Last one there buys the first round."

I pulled the boom to my lips and keyed the mic. "Sure, we'll race, but the finish line is the Madison Arm of Hebgen Lake. If you think you can land the Citation on that lake before we glide on, Hunter and I will gladly buy the first round."

Chapter 7
A Different Kind of Crash

On Black Tuesday, October 29, 1929, the stock exchange crashed in horrific fashion and drove home the final nail in the coffin of the American financial system. That event was the genesis of one of the most horrific periods in American history. Over the coming decade, the world followed the United States as it circled the drain. Fortunes were destroyed, millions of homes were foreclosed upon, and unemployment skyrocketed. The extravagance of the Roaring Twenties, greed, and the refusal to heed the warning signs in place since the fall of the Roman Empire were to blame. But just as it had done during every crisis in its history, the great experiment in democracy rose from the ashes, Americans went back to work, fortunes were reestablished, and once again, there was a chicken in every pot . . . just in time for Adolf Hitler to turn the world inside out.

To those of us who consider airplanes to be magic carpets, the final October 29th of the 1920s is not remembered as the day the world fell apart; instead, we celebrate it as the day on which Clyde Cessna's DC-6 was certified, giving birth to one of the world's greatest aircraft manufacturing companies.

Clyde fled Enid, Oklahoma, when the local bankers turned off the credit tap for the fledgling aircraft designer, and he set up shop in Wichita, Kansas, with a new partner, Victor Roos. Nobody remembers Victor because only one month into the partnership, he abandoned Mr. Cessna, dissolving their partnership. Like most American businesses of the day, Cessna Aircraft fell victim to the Great Depression and closed its doors in 1932, but that was not the end of the company. The magic carpet beneath my butt was living and flying testament to that. Clyde's nephews, Dwane and Dwight Wallace, bought the company from their uncle and re-opened the doors in 1934. The nephews went on to produce a massive collection of some of the world's most iconic aircraft, of which I owned three: the 182, the Citation, and of course, my beloved amphibious 208.

For those and a million more sentimental and nostalgic reasons, I took the controls from my friend, partner, and practically brother, and flew a low approach over Cessna Aircraft Field with the floats of my airplane only inches off the deck. The air traffic controllers in the tower at McConnell Air Force Base were kind enough not to have us shot down as we climbed out practically over their parallel runways just southwest of Cessna Field.

I surrendered the controls back to Hunter, and he let the wheels gently kiss the pavement at Wichita's Dwight D. Eisenhower National Airport, where we emptied our bladders and filled our fuel tanks.

Hunter gave the Caravan an abbreviated pre-flight inspection and checked his watch. "I'm sure the rest of the guys are already on their second round of cocktails in Montana."

"Maybe so, but they didn't get to do a flyover at Cessna Field."

He started up the ladder toward the elevated cockpit and gave me the thumb and index finger pistol. "There is that. Now, let's see if this old thing will start."

It did, and we lumbered our way back to altitude with the propeller pointed northwest—next stop, West Yellowstone . . . or maybe Hebgen Lake.

Cessna Aircraft Company, in its infinite wisdom, decided they wouldn't pressurize the Caravan. Instead, they installed an on-board oxygen system that made our almost direct route possible. The Rocky Mountains just south of Casper, Wyoming, was the first obstacle that sent us higher than we ever flew the 208 down south.

Hunter pulled his oxygen cannula from the hook over his head and threaded it over his ears and beneath his nose. "Unless you need a nap, you might want to breathe a little compressed gas for the climb."

I pulled down my cannula. "We'll both need a nap by the time we make Montana."

The oxygen kept our brains operating in the green at altitude as the Rockies passed beneath our floats, and eleven hours after the wheels left the ground at Saint Marys, Georgia, they chirped their way onto the asphalt at West Yellowstone Airport.

We ran the shutdown checklist and climbed from the cockpit.

Hunter groaned as if he'd been shot as he stepped onto the portside float. "You didn't tell me it was still winter up here."

"It's Montana," I said. "Winter is subject to break out any minute, any time of the year."

We added jackets to our attire and stepped to the parking apron where piles of snow still stood, bordering the pavement. To our surprise, a brown Chevy Suburban rounded the FBO and approached.

Hunter shot me a glance as his right hand slid toward his concealed Glock. "Are we expecting a welcoming party?"

I put a few hundred pounds of aluminum float between myself and the approaching SUV as my hand went the way of Hunter's and gripped my pistol.

Through the open sunroof of the SUV, Mongo's head, massive shoulders, and torso rose into the frigid evening air. "Nice reaction time, losers. If we were the bad guys, you two would've been meeting your maker by now."

I reseated my pistol in its holster. "Great. That's what we need after an eleven-hour flight—a smart-ass version of the Hulk."

Clark brought the Suburban to a stop, and the team formed a bucket brigade, pulling gear from the plane and depositing it into the back of the SUV.

Clark looked up. "Is that everything?"

I stepped from the float. "I believe so. How's the house Skipper booked?"

Clark shared a knowing look with the rest of the team. "Oh, I think you'll approve. She's never let us down yet."

Not only had Skipper delivered again, but she'd done so in spades. The house was an enormous, three-story, alpine mountain mansion. After stowing our gear, I followed my nose into the kitchen. "What do I smell going on in here?"

Disco looked up from the indoor grill. "It'll be elk steaks and potatoes unless you'd prefer a PB and J. What took you guys so long?"

I watched the steaks sizzling. "A PB and J sounds good, but I don't want to hurt your feelings by not eating one of your steaks. And we took the scenic route. That high-speed, high-altitude stuff is for pilots who aren't good enough to fly close to the ground."

He ignored the abuse. "You can have your steaks any way you want them, as long as they're medium rare. The bar's open, too, so kick your feet up, and I'll ring the dinner bell in ten minutes."

I poured three fingers of my old friend, Jack, over a few cubes of ice and strolled onto the deck, where I found Singer admiring the scenery.

The most observant person I'd ever met gave no indication of having noticed me until he said, "Sure is pretty, isn't it?"

"It certainly is. But what are you doing out here all by yourself?"

He never took his eyes off the mountains. "I'm just admiring a little piece of God's creation I've never seen before and thinking about the mission."

I took a sip of my whiskey and set my tumbler on the rail. "What do you know about the cult that's holding the former president's niece?"

For a moment, I wondered if he'd heard my question, but after several seconds, he reached for my cocktail, lifted it from the rail, and stuck it beneath his nose. A smile came across his face, and he handed the drink to me. "Have a smell and tell me how it makes you feel."

I'd grown accustomed to our Southern Baptist sniper's unique perceptions of the world around him, but I couldn't imagine what lay along the path he was about to guide me down.

I took the tumbler from his hand and did as he instructed. "It smells like oak and grain to me."

He closed his eyes as if disappointed. "I asked you to tell me how it made you *feel*."

I considered what he asked and lifted my glass back to my nose. "It makes me feel like I'm in an old familiar place."

He slowly nodded. "Yep, that's how I feel about what's coming, Chase, but for me, that old familiar place is some cold, wet hole, while looking at the world in front of me through the scope on top of my rifle. I love the beauty of the world, my friend, but I hate the way it looks with my crosshairs over it. That always means I'm about to separate another soul from its earthly body, and every time I do that, a little bit of me dies, too."

Singer had long been my spiritual advisor. He understood matters of faith at a level I'll never fathom, but when he turned to me in search of relief from his demons, I was left without words.

All I could say was, "Maybe this mission won't require those crosshairs."

He turned back to the mountains. "Maybe so, my friend . . . Maybe so."

My ice cubes turned to water, and the honey-colored whiskey turned lighter and softer as the ever-darkening night sky surrendered its brilliant blue to a blackened vastness with ancient stars scattered like infinitely tiny holes in a black velvet veil.

As if triggered by the appearance of the stars, Singer said, "They all have the same things in common."

"Who?" I asked.

"Cults. They all display zeal and commitment to their leader like nothing you've ever seen. Your men love you, Chase, but even for us, there are limits. Within these cults, there are no limits to which the faithful will go to please and ingratiate themselves to their leader."

I ran my finger around the rim of my glass. "That sounds a lot like Hitler's Nazis."

"You're not too far off the mark there. The Nazis meet most of the qualifications of being a cult."

"So, there are qualifications to being a cult?"

"Sure," he said. "For the most part, all cults punish dissent or doubt. They usually perform some kind of mind-altering practice like meditation, chanting, or terrible work schedules. That's bad enough in itself, but here's the kicker. Without fail, the leader of a cult will dictate exactly how members should think, act, and feel."

"What draws people to such things?"

He rubbed his hands together as the night air grew colder by the minute. "That's your department, psychologist, but there's no one particular personality type that is drawn to cult life. Everyone from professional athletes to homeless veterans end up inside these compounds, but if I had to pick one common thread that seems to run through the followers, they're all looking for something that's missing in their lives, and the cult finds a way to temporarily fill that void. There's a certain elitist mentality within most cults that makes people believe they are privy to some precious secret no one else knows. Most of the time, they believe their leader is on a mission from God to save humanity but that the world is too evil to recognize and accept their help. That leads to an us-versus-them mindset that builds an even bigger wall between the members of the cult and the outside world, including their friends and family."

I sighed. "It's terrifying to think about. Chasing terrorists, and even separating their souls from their bodies, as you put it, makes sense to me, but I'll never understand a cult."

"It gets worse. One of the biggest issues I have with the cult mentality is that the leader is viewed as a messiah and isn't accountable to any authority."

I finished my drink. "It certainly sounds like this local group checks all the boxes for being a cult."

He held up a finger. "Yes, they do, but there is one area that's a little odd."

"What's that?"

"In most cults, the group is absolutely obsessed with recruiting new members and stockpiling money, but this gang of idiots up here isn't doing that. They're just living their lives inside that compound and leaving the rest of the world alone."

"Maybe that's a good thing."

"I don't think so," he said. "It's too sinister for me. What are they doing in there? Are the followers safe, healthy, and for that matter, still alive? It's impossible to know. They've cut off all communication with the outside world."

"You make it sound like it's not going to be easy to worm our way inside."

Disco stuck his head through the door. "Dinner's ready."

The sniper laid a hand on my shoulder. "You can take one thing to the bank, for sure. It's a whole lot easier to get in than it is to get out."

Chapter 8
Latin Lessons

My first taste of an elk steak made the five-thousand-dollar jet fuel bill worth every penny.

"Nicely done, Disco. Who knew a caribou would taste so good?"

Clark said, "You're an idiot, Chase, but that's why we love you."

I dropped my knife and fork. "Okay, Green Beret, let's hear it. What's the difference between a caribou and an elk?"

Clark sat in stunned confusion, trying to piece together an answer.

Mongo came to his rescue. "Everybody knows the elk is a *Cervus Canadensis* and much larger than the reindeer or caribou, which is obviously the *Rangifer tarandus*."

Clark pointed toward the giant. "Yeah, see? Everybody knows that."

I turned to Mongo. "How do you know this stuff?"

He held up his palms. "I'm *not* just another pretty face."

"No, you certainly aren't," I said. "But speaking of pretty faces, has anyone checked in with Skipper and Penny?"

Clark swallowed a mouthful of grilled *Cervus Canadensis*. "We checked in when we got here . . . about eight hours before you and

Hunter finally showed up. Skipper was compiling background on Hannah June and said she'd email it as soon as she was fin-ished."

I locked eyes with my handler. "Which mission is primary? Hannah June or the moles inside the other team?"

"I'm starting to think they may be one and the same." Suddenly, Clark had everyone's attention, and the eating ceased. "Obviously, the Board sent us up here to rescue the former president's niece, even if sweet little Hannah June doesn't want to be rescued. We know that much for sure, but the fact remains that a tactical team has been compromised. I'm not exactly sure why I feel this way, but something tells me they're *Togetherus Linkedus*, as they say in the original Latin. Right, Mongo?"

The big man chuckled. "Whatever you say, boss."

Clark gave him the thumbs-up. "Either way, we have to run ISR on both situations before we make any moves. If they're linked, we'll find where their paths cross."

I drummed my fingers on the table. "Intel, surveillance, and reconnaissance won't give us all the answers, though. Sooner or later, we'll have to get inside."

Clark nodded. "You're right, but we have to know what we're getting into. I'm okay with the idea of fighting our way out of a cult compound. We'd have a better-than-good chance of surviving that skirmish, but if we get ourselves into a gunfight with another tactical team, we're going to have our hands full. We have to assume they're at least as good at gun-fighting as we are."

I cleared my throat. "I'm not trying to step on your toes, but we need to establish a command structure. Is this your op or mine?"

He took another bite and started talking before he'd gotten it down. "I knew you were going to bring that up, so I've already got an answer . . . and that answer is both. We're going to run two ISR teams. I'll take one, and you'll take one. We'll work from both ends and pray we don't meet in the middle."

"Fine by me," I said, "but I'm not taking Mongo. He's impossible to hide."

Our human oak tree stuck out his bottom lip in feigned sensitivity.

Clark said, "I'm good with that. Having him on my team reduces our chances of losing a fight if it comes to fisticuffs."

Hunter held up his fork. "Where did that phrase fisticuffs come from anyway?"

Instinctually, everyone turned to Mongo, who wiped his mouth with the corner of a paper napkin. "It started in the early seventeenth century. That's the sixteen hundreds for you knuckle-draggers. It's a combination of the word *fistic,* which means relating to the fists, and the word *cuff,* which, as everyone knows, means a punch. Most lexicographers believe the term was originally two words—*fisty cuffs*—but later morphed into *fisticuffs.*"

Singer shook a steak knife toward Mongo. "You know, having you around is like having our very own Cliff Clavin from *Cheers.* You just don't drink as much beer as he did."

"All right, knock it off," Clark ordered. "It's time to pick teams. Obviously, I've got Mongo, and I'll also take Disco, so that leaves you with Hunter and Singer. Are you okay with that?"

I shoved another bite of elk into my mouth and nodded. When the bite found its way to my stomach, I asked, "Who takes the cult, and who gets the other tac team?"

He pointed at me with his fork. "You choose."

"All right. Since I've got Singer, we'll take the cult, and you guys can deal with the other shooters."

Clark shot glances toward Mongo and Disco, and they gave him a nod. "We've got to talk R-O-E." Forks and knives froze as my handler continued. "The rules of engagement are simple on this one . . . at least for the ISR portion of the operation. Do not shoot! Run, hide, jump in the river, or do whatever you have to do to avoid engagement. We will not shoot unless there's absolutely no other option. Got it?"

Mumbled understanding poured from the table, and Clark continued. "As for the tactical team, we'll find them and watch them one by one. We have no way of knowing how they behave off the clock. If they're like us, they spend a lot of time together, even when they're not on a mission, but until we get on them, there's no way to know. Does everyone still have their packets Skipper gave us?"

Heads nodded, and Clark said, "Good. I want you to go over the dossiers tonight and commit them to memory. Study the photographs, too. It's not like we can walk up to these guys and say, 'Hey, aren't you a double-naught spy?'" Nervous laughter rose and quickly fell. "Have you got anything, Chase?"

I laid down my fork. "Things will be a little different with the cult. If they're as closed up as Singer says they are, we're probably never going to see any of them outside the compound."

Singer raised a finger.

"Yeah, what is it?" I said.

"What I meant was, none of the *peons* will leave the compound. The senior leadership doesn't live by the same rules as everybody else. They'll come to town and do all sorts of things the rank and file isn't allowed to do. And you know what they say . . . When the cat's away, the mice will play."

"I like it," I said. "If we can get an observation point established so we can watch what happens inside the compound while the senior weirdos aren't home to enforce the rules, we might get a glimpse into real life inside the walls."

With our appetites satisfied, I stood from the table and collected plates. "You guys get some rest. Clark and I will clean up the kitchen."

When the rest of the team had made their way somewhere else, I said, "What makes you think the team is connected with the cult?"

"I don't know. It's just too convenient. What are the chances of two missions popping up within fifty miles of each other without a connection?"

"I don't know. That's your department. I just pull triggers."

"Yes, College Boy, of course that's all you do."

I opened the dishwasher and filled the silverware basket. "What if the other team is clean and the only real mission is Hannah?"

"I guess that'll reveal itself as we watch, listen, and learn what these idiots are doing."

"What do you expect to find?"

"I don't know," he said. "But I know what I *hope* we find."

"What's that?"

He dried his hands. "I hope we find out the other team are all good guys and we don't have to kill anybody. And I hope we find Hannah June and she's willing to walk out the front gate with us, hand in hand."

I laughed. "You're not hoping for much, are you?"

"Okay, here's the truth. I think there's probably a pair of moles and we're going to have to confront them. When that happens, I'm afraid seven Spanish angels are going to take another angel home."

"Is that what we're doing now, quoting Willie Nelson lyrics?"

He threw down the towel. "It seemed appropriate."

"Maybe so," I admitted. "But honestly, I don't see the thing with the cult working out much better. The difference is, we know what we're up against with the other team. Who knows if those maniacs behind the fence can even spell the word *gun*?"

We wrapped up the kitchen chores and rounded up the team in the living room. Clark took a seat on the enormous stone hearth in front of a fireplace big enough to dance inside. He pulled a piece of firewood from the stack beside him and opened his pocketknife, whittling as he spoke in true Jed Clampett style. "Wheeew doggies, if this ain't a mess, it'll do 'til one gets here. Does anyone have anything they want to talk about before we head off to bed?"

Singer said, "If you wouldn't mind, I'd like to say a little prayer before we get too deep into the mud of this whole thing. You don't have to hold hands and get down on a knee. I just thought it wouldn't be a bad way to start this crazy mission—or missions— whatever it turns out to be."

No one objected, and Singer talked to God like an old familiar friend. The beliefs, doubts, and faith of my team were none of my business, but even if they didn't share Singer's faith, seeing them bow their heads during a ritual so dear to our sniper made me feel more like a family than coworkers.

When Singer finished, a soft round of "Amen" came from the hearts of every man in the room.

I gave him a nod. "Thank you, Singer. That means a great deal to all of us, I'm sure."

Every head nodded in silent agreement.

The world into which we stepped when our real work began was one of uncertainty and mortal danger around every corner. No matter what we believed about what comes next after more of our blood is outside our body than in, we all recognized the inescapable truth that doing our jobs long enough meant certain death. But even in the face of that reality, we still pulled on our boots every morning and stepped between what was behind us and the enemy in front of us, vowing to give our last breath defending those who depend on us and those who can't fight for themselves.

The somber nature of the moment left a bitter taste in my throat that I couldn't ignore. "If you don't mind, Clark, I've got something to say."

"The floor's all yours."

I licked my lips and choked back the trepidation I felt. "There's been something on my mind since we got home from Djibouti, and it's not fair to any of you that I keep it to myself. All of you remember Mr. Rabin, the Mossad officer on the gunboat . . . Well, he's a lot more than just a case officer. He's the deputy director."

That sent eyebrows raising, and I suddenly had everyone's undivided attention.

"He told me something before he put us on a plane back to the States. He said there's someone close to me who isn't what I believe them to be. That's been haunting me every waking minute of every day since we got home. I'm telling you this because you have the right to know what's going on in my head. If any of you were preoccupied with something heavy like this, I'd want you to come to me about it. That's why I'm laying it all on the table for you. I trust every one of you with my life, and I know you feel the same about me. If you didn't, you wouldn't follow me all over the world starting fights."

A few nervous chuckles helped dissolve the weighty feeling in the room.

"It's important that each of you knows I'm not accusing anyone of anything. I have no idea who or what Rabin was talking about, but if anyone has doubts or wants out, this isn't a cult. If it's not for you, no one will hold it against you, and our respect for you won't change. I don't want the Board to send another team to spy on us. We're better than that."

"You've got that right," Mongo growled.

I gave the big man a nod. "I don't know if Rabin was talking about one of you or somebody outside the team, but if your loyalties lie somewhere else . . ."

Singer spoke up. "Whoever it is, he ain't one of us, Chase. Everybody in this room, except Disco and Hunter, owe our lives to you. We'd have never made it off the Khyber Pass if you hadn't come to get us. I can speak for every one of us when I say that we would stand toe to toe and spit in the devil's eye for you."

Groans of agreement filled the air, and Hunter said, "You can add my name to that list, too. I've fought beside you, and I never would've made it out of a few of those fights if you hadn't been there. There's nobody on Earth I'd rather work for and with."

A lump rose in my throat. "I appreciate your faith in me . . . all of you. And even though Disco is the new guy, I have no reason to doubt his integrity. I want all of you to know that even though Rabin planted that seed in my head, I have enormous confidence in each of you, and I would never let that seed affect my loyalty to the team as a whole and to every one of you individually." I surrendered the floor to Clark.

"Well, all right. I didn't think this was going to turn into confession and a prayer meeting, but if anybody else has some heavy stuff they want to lay on us, apparently now is the time."

The air felt suddenly thick, but Disco broke the mood. "I'll say this. You dudes are a trip, and I'm proud to be the new guy."

Sincere laughter replaced the earlier nervous chuckles, and Mongo said, "You may be the new guy, but as far as I'm concerned, you're the cook. That dinner was out of this world."

Hearty reinforcement followed, and Clark had to break it up. "That's enough, you bunch of animals. Hit the sack. I know it's early, but we've got jet lag to sleep off. Well, except for Chase and Hunter. They've got prop lag."

"Hey!" I protested. "The Caravan may have a prop, but it's still a jet."

Disco jumped in again. "You know, a wolf and a lapdog will both eat table scraps, so just because you burn jet fuel like the big dogs doesn't make you a wolf."

Chapter 9
Heigh-Ho, Heigh-Ho

I've watched thousands of sunrises over salt water from almost every continent, and I fell in love with every single one of them. The majesty of the life-giving light blooming across the eastern horizon has always been mesmerizing for me, but watching it happen over the snow-covered, jagged peaks of the Rocky Mountains took my breath away. The beauty of the ocean is balanced precariously against the horror of the devastation the sea can wreak upon humanity as well as nature; likewise, the magnificence of our closest star rising above one of the world's most spectacular mountain ranges is set against the deadly winds, plummeting temperatures, and soul-stealing isolation awaiting anyone who dares to face the mountain peaks unprepared and alone. In many ways, that's precisely how I felt deep within my heart on that frigid morning: unprepared and alone.

A team of some of the most elite warriors on Earth slept, or perhaps, milled about, completing their morning rituals just behind me while I stood in the freezing air of the deck, cradling a steaming mug of coffee. Every member of that team had worn the uniform and drawn fire in parts of the world most people never know exist. All of those men were exceptionally well-trained operatives with the battle scars to prove it. I was a former baseball player with a few months of paramilitary training at the Ranch under my belt and a dozen operations in my wake. Nothing about me qualified me as the leader of that group of men, but for reasons I'll never know or understand, every one of them would turn to me for direction, instructions, and orders every time duty called. Taking that responsibility lightly would never be a mistake I would make.

"Good morning, College Boy. What are you doing out here in the cold?"

I turned to see the man I considered to be my leader.

Clark Johnson stood in the doorway with a cup of coffee in one hand and a waffle iron in the other. He held up the appliance. "Do you know how to work this thing?"

I couldn't contain my laughter. "It's a pretty complex machine. I think you plug it in, pour in the waffle batter, and close the lid, but I could be mistaken."

He rolled his eyes. "If I wasn't still half asleep, I'd beat you senseless with this thing. I meant, do you know how to make waffle batter?"

"That may have been what you meant, but it's not what you asked. You're the one married to one of the world's greatest chefs. Why are you asking me about waffle recipes?"

He growled. "I'm sleepy, hungry, and now I'm mad at you. Get in here before you freeze to death, and let's figure this out together."

I followed him to the kitchen, where Disco was pouring his first cup of caffeine for the day. He took inventory of Clark's possessions. "Oh, good. You found the waffle iron. Plug it in, and I'll make us breakfast."

I gave Clark a poke to the ribs. "See, I told you plugging it in was step one."

To my surprise, he ignored the verbal jab and set up the machine for Disco.

"Is everybody up?" I asked.

Disco said, "Yeah, we're all up and moving. The rest of the crew are showering. They'll be down when they smell the bacon and coffee."

He was right. The aroma brought my team out of the woodwork. Everyone was dressed in layers and ready to face the Montana air.

Disco's breakfast was almost as big a hit as the previous night's elk steaks.

"Why didn't you mention being able to cook when we interviewed you?" I asked.

He gave a chuckle. "Being able to cook is like being able to fix cars or computers. You really don't want anyone to know. Otherwise, you'd never do anything else."

Bellies full and coffee gone, Clark said, "It'd be good if we're all singing from the same sheet of music, so let's brief the op order. I'll go first."

Everyone leaned in, including Hunter and Singer, who'd be with me all day.

Clark began. "We'll start with verification of the addresses we have on file, and we'll try to snap a picture or two so we can update the dossiers. We'll make no intentional contact. Everything is fifty meters today. Once we know where everyone is, we'll slowly initiate a few"— he made air quotes with his fingers—'accidental brushes.' That's it for my briefing. What have you got, Chase?"

Every eye turned to me. "I plan a flyover this morning to identify an observation point and get the lay of the land. The compound should be easy enough to find, and the bird's-eye view will give us a solid understanding of the layout. We'll shoot some film and try not to arouse any suspicion. I touched base with Skipper while the rest of you lazy bums were still asleep, and she's arranged for another Suburban to be waiting for us at the Gardiner Airport when we finish our airborne surveillance. We may leave the truck up in Gardiner and use the Caravan to commute back and forth since the drive takes a couple of hours, but we'll make that call later today."

Clark clapped and rubbed his hands together. "Does anybody have any questions?" No one spoke up. "Okay, I've got one more thing. Let's plan ops-normal calls at eleven, thirteen, and again at fifteen hundred. Do them on the satellite phones. There's probably not much cell coverage in those canyons." He paused, maybe for dramatic effect, and then said, "Anything else?"

"If not, heigh-ho, heigh-ho, it's off to work we go!"

We piled into the Suburban and headed for the airport, where we found my Caravan still on the ramp where we parked it the evening before. A lineman was pretending to be busy, so I called him over.

"Yes, sir. What can I do for you?"

I pointed toward my airplane. "I paid for a hangar for the Caravan, but it's still on the ramp."

He pulled the radio from his belt and called someone who I presume worked behind the desk, where the temperature was a balmy seventy-two. "Hey, control, it's Jimmy. This guy out here with the amphibious Caravan says he paid for a hangar. Do you know anything about that?"

The woman's squeaky voice came through the radio. "Oh, yeah, it's going in the big hangar with the Citation that came in yesterday, but we didn't have anybody to run the tug last night. Can you take care of that, Jimmy?"

The man looked up at me and shrugged. "Ah, what are you gonna do? I'll get the Citation pushed back into the corner and make room for this thing. I'm sorry about that. I just live a mile away. I don't know why she didn't call me last night."

I examined my frost-covered airplane that hadn't spent a night outside in a long time. Something inside me wanted to apologize to the old girl, but instead, I ordered up a little attention for her. "We're going to use the plane today, but if you'll de-ice her, we'll call it even for leaving her on the ramp."

"No problem, sir. I'll get the truck and have her thawed out in no time. Do you want me to top it off, too?"

"Yes, top it off with Jet-A with Prist. My card is on file inside."

Jimmy no longer had to pretend he was working. Between de-icing and refueling, he might've even broken a sweat. With the preflight inspection complete, we climbed aboard, and Hunter had the Pratt and Whitney PT6 turbine spinning the propeller seconds later.

We pulled our headsets in place and did an internal comms check.

Singer said, "You're loud and clear, Chase, but what was that thing you asked for with the jet fuel?"

"I think he means the Prist," Hunter said.

"Oh, Prist is a fuel additive that keeps the jet fuel from freezing. We don't always need it down south as long as we don't do any high-altitude flying, but up here, I thought it was probably a good idea."

The sniper huffed. "Well, I guess you learn something new every day."

Checklists complete, Hunter lined up on the centerline of the runway and gently added power. The turbine engine dragging us down the runway was the primary reason the Caravan was such a workhorse. No one would ever call that engine underpowered.

If the scenery had been breathtaking from the ground, to see it from the air was more than the human eye could take in. As badly as I hated cold weather and snow, there was a magnificent beauty about it that seemed to fill an emptiness I never realized I harbored.

Fifteen minutes later, Hunter said, "We're coming up on Gardiner. I can keep flying around till we run out of gas—and Prist—if you want, but I'd like to get a little help spotting that compound."

Hunter and I pressed our faces to the windows in search of anything that looked like it could be a fenced-in asylum for the zealots.

I said, "Follow the road northwest out of Gardiner. It's supposed to be about twenty miles out, just beyond the ninety-degree bend in the road and river."

"Here we go," Hunter said to no one in particular as he rolled left and followed the meandering river and highway.

Snow covered most areas except for the few places that were exposed to the sun for more than a few hours every day. The steeply rising mountains on either side of the river valley kept most of the Earth in shade except for the brief period when the sun was directly overhead.

Singer had the best eyes of anyone I'd ever known, but as we neared the bend in the river, he said, "It won't be easy to pick out with everything so white down there. Why couldn't we do this in July?"

Hunter said, "At the rate we're going, it may be July before we finish."

I unplugged my headset from the console and slid from the right front seat to join Singer and Hunter on the left side of the airplane. We scanned the valley below while Hunter kept his head on a swivel looking for other air traffic and those granite peaks in every direction.

Singer pointed beneath the left float. "There's the bend. The compound should be just to the north."

Hunter said, "We're about a mile north of the bend. There's enough room between the mountains to make a slow three-sixty if you want."

Singer nodded. "Yeah, do it, Hunter. I think I see it, but I can't be sure."

As Hunter brought the airplane about, the angle of the sun revealed the perfect outline of a walled compound with a plowed road leading from the gates to the main road.

I followed his line of sight. "Good eyes, Singer. That has to be it, but why would they plow the road if they're isolationists?"

Singer asked, "Can you get us any lower without hitting a rock?"

"I can, but not in this three-sixty. I'll fly up the canyon until it widens enough to turn around, and I'll descend as low as I can. I'm comfortable with that maneuver to the south. I know there's room to climb out down there."

I liked Hunter's aeronautical decision-making skills. With every hour he spent in the cockpit, he grew more capable and confident.

"Here comes our chance to make the turn and descent, but it's going to be steep. Hang on."

There are airplanes specifically made to roll upside down and perform mind-boggling feats in the sky. The Caravan was not such an airplane. She was slow and heavy, but Hunter made her feel like a stunt plane as he pointed the left wingtip toward the ground and pulled off the throttle. The nearly seven-thousand-pound hunk of aluminum obeyed with glee.

Singer sent his hand to his stomach. "How about a little warning next time? My gut wasn't ready for that."

"I did warn you, you big baby. Get on the other side. I need to stay over the highway, so the compound will be off the right this time."

Singer and I moved to the starboard side and glared down the canyon. He said, "You watch the compound. I'll find us a nice little hidey-hole where we can camp out and keep an eye on those fruitcakes."

I picked out the compound and made the distance calls.

"There it is. One mile . . . Half a mile . . . Quarter mile . . . Over the target."

We banked hard to the left and started a climb.

Hunter looked over his shoulder, "Did you see enough, or do you want another run?"

"Let's do at least two more passes," I said. "I'll run the film this time. Can you get us down to five hundred AGL?"

"Sure, let me get this thing turned around, and I'll take us down to five hundred above the ground. Hey, Singer, try not to throw up on the nice upholstery back there. Here we go!"

Another steep descending turn pointed us back up the canyon, and I brought the aerial camera online. Cotton Jackson, our mechanic, had installed a state-of-the-art camera in the tail of the Caravan for occasions just like this one, and I was anxious to put it through its paces.

As we overflew the compound again, the nose of the airplane shot toward the heavens, and we banked hard to the right, pinning Singer and me to the windows. The maneuver was so erratic I thought we'd been hit by one of the extreme updrafts of wind so common in mountainous terrain.

Hunter's near-panicked voice roared in our headsets. "Brace! Brace! Brace! This is going to suck!"

Chapter 10
I Have the Controls

My desire to be at the controls of an airplane had never been stronger, but I was pinned to the window and fighting against too many Gs to pull myself free and dive for the cockpit. Even if I could have, I'd never make it in time to resolve whatever was happening up front. I shot a hard stare toward Singer and saw the eyes of the Southern Baptist sniper completely at peace. There was no fear, no anxiety, and no panic. He stared back at me and saw exactly the opposite.

Outside the windows, the granite face of the vertical canyon wall loomed ever larger, filling the air with certain death and no means of escape. Everything moved in ultra-slow motion, and the world turned silent with the singular exception of the stall warning horn blaring like an air raid siren.

At least one wing of my Caravan had exceeded the critical angle of attack and could no longer produce sufficient lift to keep the heavy airplane and its occupants aloft. We were going down. The only remaining concerns were whether we'd hit the canyon wall or come to rest on the valley floor less than five hundred feet below.

As the nose fell, the view outside the window changed little. Patches of snow crept into view as we fell through the air, approaching the canyon floor. I prayed Hunter would continue pushing the nose over to build airspeed. Even a few knots of forward speed would be better than hitting the highway—or the riverbed—in a vertical fall.

As time continued at a snail's pace, the decisions of my life played out like a slideshow in my mind's eye. Leaving Hunter alone in the cockpit instead of sending him back to scan for the compound was the opening scene. Maybe I could've avoided whatever had sent my airplane plummeting to the Earth. Second was the unforgettable face of my beautiful wife. Every emotion I felt for her suddenly overtook me and left me furious for putting myself in a position to separate the two of us forever. A thousand scenes played out until the show ended with me standing over home plate in Omaha, Nebraska, in 1996, in the final game of the College World Series. If I had stepped aside and tagged the runner instead of lowering my head and daring him to plow into me, my right hand never would've been destroyed. I would've played professional baseball for the Atlanta Braves. I never would've met the remarkable men who'd become my team—my family—and I never would've known the pride and honor of defending the way of life we Americans hold dear. Looking back, I wouldn't have changed a thing.

The G-forces pinning Singer and me to the windows subsided, and we slid to the seats beneath us. Finally able to look ahead, I stared into the cockpit and saw Stone W. Hunter with one hand on the yoke and the other on the throttle, doing what a competent pilot should be doing: flying the airplane until every piece stopped moving. The wings were level, the throttle was full forward, and the airspeed indicator was climbing. I tore my focus from the instruments and stared out the windscreen, hoping to see bright blue sky, but instead, I saw only earth—snow-covered and unforgiving.

With my line of sight back to the controls and instrument panel, I watched Hunter apply just enough back pressure on the yoke to raise the nose a few inches. Airspeed continued to build, and the scenery through the windscreen slowly turned from our demise to a cold, snow-lined river. The Yellowstone River stretched out in front of us in one of its few long straight courses. Most of the river wound its way around bends and turns every few feet, but what I saw was nothing short of a gift from God. A quarter mile of straight, flat, calm water lay in front of us like an oasis. There wasn't enough river to get the airplane airborne again, but Hunter was more than capable of getting the floats on the river and getting us stopped before we hit anything hard. It would take a crane to get us out of the river, but I'll take a crane over a coffin any day.

My relief turned from gratitude to terror in an instant when I saw Hunter press his palm against the throttle. Instead of pulling off the power and letting us settle into the shallow water of the Yellowstone, he was making the critical mistake of trying to keep an airplane flying when it wanted to land. We were low, slow, and doomed, but there was no time for me to intervene. Instead of lunging for the cockpit, I yanked the seatbelt from beneath me and shoved the buckle together. The only hope of surviving the coming crash was to keep as much of my body securely in the seat as possible. Hunter had been right. This was definitely going to suck.

The ordeal likely lasted a few seconds but felt like hours. I couldn't look away from the scenery beyond the spinning propeller.

Singer laid a hand on my shoulder. "What's he trying to do, Chase?"

The sound wasn't the crisp, tinny voice so typical of electronic comms. It was loud and choppy, which left me confused and concerned until I realized we'd lost our headsets in the melee.

I looked back at the sniper. "I don't know, but it's going to hurt. Strap in."

He didn't hesitate. Almost before I finished the command, he was strapped solidly into his seat. At the same instant, the metal buckle clicked into place, the man of enormous faith closed both eyes, and his lips began to move in silent prayer. I wondered what he was asking for. Did he wish to go quickly without pain, or was he asking for a miracle to lift us out of the riverbed and back into the sky? I believed I'd never know the answer to my question, but I was wrong. Regardless of what he'd asked God, a miracle is what we got.

Hunter kept the throttle fully open and accelerated toward the frigid water. Despite the massive turbine spinning out front, we didn't have the speed or power to climb out of our descent. Through sheer determination and some of the best flying I'd ever seen, Hunter let the keel of the floats kiss the surface of the water, momentarily stopping our descent. The floats instantly became turbine-powered canoes as Hunter patiently let the airspeed build with the floats racing across the surface of the river. As the speed increased, my partner nursed the flying machine back into the air, and we climbed out over the rising terrain in a lazy, standard ascent until we were a thousand feet above the highest peaks in the area and configured for straight and level flight.

Hunter set the autopilot, shucked off his headset, and laid his head back against the headrest in relief.

I gave Singer a wink and unbuckled my seatbelt. Winding my way into the cockpit, I ruffled Hunter's sweaty hair. "You picked one hell of a time to practice your touch-and-go landings. What happened back there?"

He pulled a water bottle from the bag beneath his seat and emptied it down his throat. "That chopper came out of nowhere. I can't believe we didn't hit him."

"What chopper?" I asked.

"You didn't see it? He popped up in the windshield as soon as we rounded the bend over the compound. Please tell me you had the camera running."

We pulled our headsets back on, and I said, "Oh, for the record, I have the controls."

He let out an exhausted sigh. "Yeah, you definitely have the controls."

Hunter climbed from his seat and staggered into the back. I moved from the right seat into the left and meticulously ran through the aircraft systems to determine what survived and what didn't. The engine instruments were in the green. The landing gear cycled correctly, and the prop cycled. I leaned as far as I could, pressing my face to the side windows to examine the floats and exterior structure. Everything seemed to be shipshape, so I checked my watch. It was almost eleven and time to make the ops-normal call to Clark, but nothing had been normal about our operations for the previous hour.

I plugged the sat-phone into the comms panel and dialed the number.

"Hey, College Boy. How's it going?"

"Oh, it's just another day in paradise up here. We spotted the compound, did some aerobatics, did a touch-and-go in the Yellowstone River . . . You know, just a normal day."

"What?"

"Hunter was doing the flying, and a helicopter popped up out of nowhere and tried to fly through the windshield."

"It's always something. Is the plane and everybody okay?"

"I believe so. Everything's in the green, and we're okay. Hunter's a little shaken up, but that was fighter-pilot stuff he pulled off. I've never seen anything like it."

"You should probably get the airplane back to West Yellowstone. You don't want to have to abandon it up there in Gardiner if you find something wrong after you land."

"That's good thinking," I said. "We'll make one or two more photo runs and head home. Hunter probably needs to change pants."

Clark laughed. "No doubt. Our morning isn't as exciting as yours. We found two guys so far, and they're just doing normal guy stuff. We're going to try and find the other four this afternoon, just to get eyes on them. We'll meet you back at the house before sundown."

"Perfect. We'll see you there. But go ahead and make the next two calls this afternoon so we'll know you're okay."

"You got it."

The line went dead, and I disconnected the autopilot. "Do you guys have your headsets on?"

Singer said, "I've got mine, but Hunter's still recuperating. Hang on. I'll hand him a headset."

Seconds later, my partner said, "I think I've finally caught my breath. What's the plan?"

"We're going to make at least one more pass on the compound to get some good footage, but we'll head home after that to inspect the airplane. She's been through quite an ordeal this morning."

"You can say that again," Hunter said. "If you don't mind, I think I'll just stay right here in this seat."

"Make yourself comfortable, Chuck Yeager."

I looked over my shoulder to make sure nothing was rolling around the cabin after our adventure, and everything was in its place. "Hey, Singer. Make sure the camera's rolling. I'm going to stick our nose back in that canyon."

He shuffled his way to the rear compartment and checked the panel. "It's still running, Chase. I can't wait to see the footage of what we just went through."

I pulled the throttle back and nosed over for another run down the canyon. Even though I hadn't seen the helicopter Hunter spotted, that didn't mean it wasn't still out there buzzing around. I brought the radar system online, hoping it might pick up the chopper and give me enough warning to avoid a repeat performance of our earlier excitement.

Back down at five hundred feet above ground level, the compound came into view, and I froze the controls. I wanted the highest quality video we could produce, so flying a stable pass was crucial.

No helicopter jumped in our way, but I never stopped looking out the window. I climbed away from the cult's hidey-hole and made a hundred-eighty-degree turn over the Gardiner Airport.

Hunter yelled, "There he is!"

Thinking I was on a second collision course with the chopper I'd never seen, I said, "Where?"

"On the ground by the fuel pump. Let's get down there and have a little heart-to-heart with that SOB."

In an effort to play moderator, I asked, "Exactly what was that guy doing wrong that we weren't also doing?"

"We didn't try to kill anybody," Hunter said.

I chuckled. "From his perspective, we may have been trying to kill him. I'm sure an eyeful of Caravan floats got his attention, too."

"That doesn't stop me from wanting to kick his butt."

"We'll save that for another day," I said. "Let's stay on mission and make one more pass. Singer, is there anything else you need to see?"

"No, I've picked out a few spots that'll make great observation points. A compound in a valley is a terrible tactical decision because every direction has high ground. I certainly wouldn't want to trade places with them."

"Sounds good to me," I said. "I'm going to slow us down as much as possible and make one more solid, stable pass, then we'll head for home." I pulled the throttle back and deployed the flaps as I began the northwest run.

The second pass almost went off without incident.

As we flew directly over the main house, Singer said, "It looks like we woke them up. A trio just ran out the front door with their eyes on the skies."

"Were they armed?" I asked.

"No, they were just lookers, not shooters . . . so far."

I tried to turn my head far enough to get a look at the three men, but even at ninety knots, we'd put too much distance between us and them for me to get a glimpse. "Do you want to make another run to see if they'll shoot?"

In unison, Hunter and Singer said, "No, thank you."

Bringing the flaps up, I added power and climbed away from Gardiner, Montana, and the Temple of Truth encampment with the thought of the former president's niece being tied to a bedpost some-where beneath us.

Chapter 11
Everybody Needs a Hobby

The flight back to West Yellowstone was uneventful except for one unexpected request. As I leveled off at the top of our climb and pointed the nose to the south, Singer asked, "Chase, would you mind if I came up front?"

"Sure, come on up." I moved from the left seat back into the right, and slid the left seat all the way back, making it easier for him to climb into.

He timidly eased himself across the controls and onto the seat. "I was thinking it might be a good idea that I learn a little about what goes on up here in the driver's seats . . . just in case."

"I think that's a good plan, my friend. Slide your seat forward until you can reach the rudder pedals comfortably, and we'll start your first flight lesson."

He was overcautious with every movement.

"Don't be afraid," I said. "There's nothing you can touch that'll kill us . . . despite Hunter's circus this morning."

Singer slid the seat into position and held the yoke with both hands.

I reached over and moved his right hand from the yoke. "Let's fly with just one hand. And you can relax. It's not going to bite you."

"That's easy for you to say. I've been watching you guys do this stuff for years, and you make it look easy."

"It is easy. It's just like making a thousand-yard shot with no wind."

He shot me a look. "I don't think so."

I returned his look. "Think about it. For you, a thousand-yard shot is a piece of cake, but most people could spend a thousand bucks in ammunition and never get near the target."

"Yeah, but that's because they've not been taught how to shoot."

I gave him the thumbs-up. "You're right. The same is true in an airplane. If I could find a monkey who spoke English, I could teach him to fly." I motioned toward the back. "Even Hunter can do it."

He chuckled and returned both hands back to the yoke.

"Nope," I said. "Just one hand. Relax and follow me through the controls. We're going to make a couple of turns." I gave the yoke a gentle pull and roll to the right. "Now, add some right rudder pedal as we turn. That'll coordinate the turn and keep us from sliding sideways through the air."

He moved with me as I reversed the direction of our turn.

"You have to add just a little back pressure on the yoke as we turn. We have to compensate for the loss of lift we experience when we exchange the vertical component for a horizontal component in a turn. Make sense?"

He nodded as tiny beads of sweat formed on his brow. "Yeah, I guess, but it's not like driving a car."

"No, definitely not, but it is fun once you get over the I'm-about-to-die feeling."

"How long does that take?"

I removed my hands from the yoke but kept my feet on the rudder pedals. "You give it a try now. Nice and easy to the right."

He rolled the yoke to the right, and he even remembered to step on the right pedal, but the nose fell as we made the turn.

I said, "Not bad, but don't forget to give a little pull in the turn. Now, do one back to the left."

He did as I instructed, but he got a little bit excited about pulling, and the nose came up about fifteen degrees. Realizing he'd done *something* wrong, he shoved the yoke forward to stop the climb. Ten seconds later, he was chasing the airplane all over the sky with both hands and both feet. I'd never seen him nervous, and I'd certainly never seen him scared, but we checked both of those boxes in a matter of seconds.

I expected him to give up at some point and simply let go of everything, but that didn't happen. He kept reacting to everything the airplane was doing as the scenario worsened by the second. The pitching and yawing weren't nearly as bad as it must've appeared to him, but I kept my hands near the controls to prevent another airshow like Hunter had flown earlier.

Then the light came on for the sniper.

Solve one problem at a time. That's how it's done in the cockpit, and that's exactly what Singer figured out . . . the hard way.

He rolled the wings level, eliminating the turning tendency, centered the rudder pedals, eliminating the yaw, and finally lowered the nose to the horizon, returning the airplane to relatively straight and level flight.

I relaxed and programmed the GPS to take us directly to the West Yellowstone Airport. "Now, just follow that magenta line and tell me when you see the airport."

Singer made a show of approximately doing what I said, but the closer we got to the airport, the smaller the corrections became.

"Any luck spotting that airport, eagle eye?"

He sighed. "Oh, yeah, I was supposed to be looking for an airport. There's a lot to this flying stuff."

"It's okay," I said. "This isn't the best training airplane in the world, but when we get back to Saint Marys, we'll get you some time in the One-Eighty-Two, and you'll do fine."

He smiled. "I think I'd like that."

"Me, too. And by the way, that's the airport right there off the nose. I have the controls."

I flew a nice, long final approach leg so Singer could get a good look at the airport. Once his eyes knew what to look for, I was confident he'd never miss another one.

My landing wasn't stellar, but it was better than Singer's would've been, and I taxied to the hangar where the Citation rested.

Jimmy, the lineman, rolled up in the tug and waited for the propeller to stop spinning. "Welcome home. I moved the Citation all the way back into the corner. I don't know when the owner will need it again, so I may have to move your Caravan a few times."

I glanced inside the hangar. "I bet the guy who owns that big thing is a real jerk."

Jimmy shrugged. "Couldn't say, but it sure is a nice airplane."

"Thanks, Jimmy. I appreciate that."

He shot several looks between me and the Citation. "Wait . . . what? Is that yours, too?"

"It is, and we won't need it for a while, so it's fine back in the corner. We'll probably use the Caravan every day for a while, so I'd appreciate you not blocking us in."

"Sure thing. I'll leave it just inside the door. Oh, and in case I'm not around or Cynthia isn't smart enough to call me at home, the tug doesn't have a key. Just throw it out of gear and push the starter button. I suspect you can run a tug if you can fly both of these babies."

I slipped him a piece of legal-tender appreciation and pulled out my phone.

A few rings later, Skipper picked up in the ops center back at Bonaventure. "Hey, Chase. How's it going out there?"

"Everything's going fine. How about down south?"

"My student and I are doing great, and she's learning like a champ."

"I've picked up a new student, as well. Singer got his first thirty minutes in the front seat this afternoon, and he did great . . . for a sniper."

"Good for him," she said. "Are you just calling to chat, or do you have anything to report?"

"Ah, I'm just checking in for now. We found the compound and got twenty or thirty minutes of film. We'll go over the footage, and I'll email you a report later. Clark's team put eyes on two of six, and he thinks they'll be able to find the other four this afternoon. I'm sure he'll have plenty to report in a few hours."

"That's great news. It sounds like you're taking it slow and keeping the excitement to a minimum, for now."

I glanced at my partner, whose knees still seemed to be shaking. "Yeah, you could say that. Excitement is overrated. I do need a favor, though."

"A big favor or a common one?"

"Just an ordinary, run-of-the-mill favor," I said. "Why?"

"Then make that request with your wife. It can be her first official duty as a trainee analyst."

I heard the digital click of Skipper opening comms with Penny's headset. "Go for Penny," Skipper said.

"Hey, sweetheart. I hear Skipper's really putting you through your paces."

"I'm sorry, field operator. This line is for official business only, and *sweetheart* is inappropriate for the workplace. In fact, it could be considered sexual harassment."

"Oh, so that's how we're playing it, is it?"

She giggled. "I'm sorry, but I couldn't resist. It's good to hear your voice. I bet you're freezing to death out there. We checked the local weather for you this morning, and it was twenty-two degrees. I know how much you love the cold."

"It's definitely not my favorite, but it is beautiful country. We should spend some time out here when we get a break."

"I'd love that," she said. "Now, what's the favor?"

"We need another vehicle. Another Suburban would be great, but anything four-wheel drive with six seats will do."

I could hear her fingers already rattling the keyboard. "Where and when?"

"ASAP, either at the West Yellowstone Airport or the rental house."

"Stand by." After twenty seconds, she said, "Done. It'll be waiting for you at the airport in thirty minutes."

"Nope. You're wrong. I'm telling your trainer."

She stammered. "Huh? I mean . . . what are you talking about?"

"It won't be waiting for me. I'll be waiting for it. We're at the airport now."

She groaned. "I guess we're even for the sexual harassment thing, huh?"

"I guess we are. Skipper tells me you're learning quickly. This is going to be a challenging operation for a teaching moment. We're essentially running—"

"Side-by-side operations, I know. We've already been talking about that. The plan is for me to focus on the cult side of things, and she'll handle the other team. Of course, she'll technically be handling everything. I'm just tagging along."

"I'm really glad you're doing this. I like you being part of the operation."

"Yeah . . . me, too. So, when do I get a gun?"

"You know the armory code and your thumbprint works, so make a run downstairs and pick one."

"You're funny," she said. "Do you need Skipper again?"

"No, just tell her to expect a report in about six hours."

"Will do. Oh, and for the record, you can call me *sweetheart* anytime you want."

Jimmy gave us a wave as he motored away from the hangar on the antique tug.

I flagged him down. "Is there a good A and P mechanic around?"

"There is," he said. "His name is Myron Beavers, but don't call him that. Just call him Ratchet, and the last hangar down there is his. He's always there. Is there something wrong with your airplane?"

I squinted against the sun. "Really? Myron Beavers. His mother must've been a cruel woman."

He chuckled. "No doubt. But like I said, call him Ratchet. Otherwise, you're not going to like the results."

"Good enough. Ratchet, it is. And no, I don't think there's anything wrong with the plane, but we put a little excess stress on it this morning, and I'd like a good mechanic to have a look before we take it back up."

He looked toward Ratchet's hangar. "You'll be in good hands with him. He used to work in Alaska, so he's got a lot of experience on floatplanes."

"Thanks, Jimmy. Have a good afternoon."

Hunter and I gave the airplane a thorough inspection, and we took Singer through the basics of aircraft systems and structure. We didn't find anything that looked out of place, but the collision with the river was enough to rattle my teeth, and it's always better to be safe than sorry when it comes to flying machines.

I glanced toward the terminal, hoping to see a Suburban pulling up, but no such luck. "Why don't you and Singer head up to the FBO and wait for the truck while I go meet Myron Beavers."

Hunter gave a mock salute. "Don't call him that, boss. You heard the man. You won't like the result."

I shrugged. "Maybe I'll risk it just for fun."

"Then maybe you better wait for Mongo to get back before you go down there."

"Oh, all right. I'll mind my manners this time, but don't expect it to become an ongoing thing. Come back and get me if the truck shows up."

"Will do."

I was pleased to find Myron "Ratchet" Beavers kneeling on the wing of a de Havilland Twin Otter on amphib floats. "That's a good-looking airplane," I yelled toward the wing.

Ratchet made no move to look down at me. "Yeah, she is on the outside, but the kids they've got flying her are hell on these tur-bines. Can I help you with something?"

For a reason I can't explain, I stood on my toes. The extra four inches the maneuver gave me did nothing to overcome the height difference between my head and the Otter's wing some twenty feet in the air. "I hope so. I've got a Caravan on floats, and I'm afraid we may have overstressed her a little this morning. If you've got time to take a look, I'd appreciate it."

The man still didn't look at me. "It's a hundred or a hundred and eighty. It's up to you."

"I don't understand," I said.

"What's there to understand, mister? If you want to get in line, it's a hundred bucks an hour, but if you want me to look at it now, it's a hundred and eighty."

"I'll take the see-it-now price."

He slid from the back of the wing and landed on the float like a cat. He looked older than his gymnastic maneuver made him appear, but the nature of his work and the environment in which he did it wasn't easy on body or mind.

"I'm Chase," I said, sticking out my hand.

He didn't take my hand. "Name's Ratchet. Where's your Caravan?"

I motioned across the ramp. "It's in the big hangar up there."

"So, am I coming to you, or are you bringing it down here? It's an extra twenty an hour if I come to you. All my tools are here, so I prefer to work out of my own shop."

"I just need you to look at it. Hopefully, she won't need any repairs. If you don't mind, I'd prefer you come to my hangar."

"Suits me," he said as he checked his watch. "Let's go."

I led the way across the ramp without another word with Myron Beavers.

When we arrived at the hangar, I motioned toward my Caravan. "There she is."

He stood, looking up at the airplane, but he didn't move.

I waited for a long, uncomfortable moment before saying, "Feel free to get started anytime."

He checked his watch again. "I've already started, but I can't inspect it without a flashlight."

"No problem," I said. "I've got a flashlight in the cockpit. Let me get it for you."

"Okay, but there's a hundred-dollar surcharge for using your tools instead of mine. You want me to go get my flashlight or use yours?"

"I've got an idea," I said. "Why don't I pay you a flat fee of a thousand bucks, cash, and you do the inspection with the flashlight of your choice?"

"Suits me. Do you want the inspection put in the airframe logbook? 'Cause if you do, there's a twenty-five-dollar documentation fee."

I laughed. "If it needs repairs, we'll log the repairs. Otherwise, just take a look."

He stuck out his hand, palm-up, without saying a word, so I climbed the boarding ladder and pulled the flashlight from its bracket. When I got back to the hangar floor, I handed him the light, but instead of taking it in his outstretched palm, he snatched it with his left hand, leaving his right still in the outstretched position.

I said, "I'm sorry, but I don't know what you want."

"The thousand bucks."

I counted out ten one-hundred-dollar bills and slapped them into his palm. He counted them twice and turned to leave.

"Where are you going?" I demanded.

"Back to my hangar. I'll be back on Tuesday afternoon or maybe Wednesday morning after I finish the Otter. The flat fee doesn't qualify for jumping the line."

I'd reached my limit. "Look, Myron. I'm not interested in playing games with you . . ."

He pressed his lips together as if he were suppressing a smile.

"Just inspect the airplane for overstress damage, or give me back my thousand bucks."

Ratchet had apparently reached his limit, as well, and the suppressed smile became uproarious laughter from both him and Jimmy the lineman, who revealed himself from behind the hangar door.

"You guys sure have some sense of humor out here in the Rockies."

Ratchet pulled the folded bills from his pocket and returned nine of them to my palm. "Sorry about that, but everybody needs a hobby, and mine and Jimmy's is messing with transient pilots. Let's have a look at your airplane and see what you broke."

Chapter 12

If It Ain't Broke

Myron "Ratchet" Beavers pressed the button on *my* flashlight and crawled the length of both floats on my amphibious Cessna 208 Caravan, presumably looking for damage from contact with the Yellowstone River and any rocks that may have been too near the surface of the water. The groans and grumbles coming out of his mouth were either the physical manifestation of the pain associated with a life spent working on airplanes or bad news for the keel of my floats.

After a crescendo of popping knees and old-guy noises, Ratchet was back on his feet with questions in his eyes. The first of these questions came at the same instant his butt landed on top of the portside float. "Just how fast were you going when you hit the river?"

My answer left me feeling less than meaningless. "I don't know."

His eyes filled with a new set of questions. "You don't know? How could you not know?"

"I wasn't in the cockpit," I admitted.

His questioning face morphed into a face of utter confusion. "Your airplane flew itself into a collision with the river? I think you may not completely understand the limitations of the autopilot system on your airplane."

Hunter and Singer pulled up in the promised Suburban right on cue.

I wanted to have a little fun at the mechanic's expense, but I rose above my childish desire to get even. "I wasn't doing the flying." Motioning toward Hunter as he dismounted the vehicle, I said, "He was."

Ratchet gave the flashlight a twirl. "Here's hoping he knows there's no auto-land feature on this airplane."

"Hey, Hunter, meet Ratchet, the A and P mechanic. He wants to know how fast we were going when we hit the water."

My partner extended a hand, and Ratchet shook it without standing up. "Our airspeed was around one ten to one fifteen, but if we did any damage, it was our vertical speed that's to blame. We were sinking pretty hard, maybe five hundred feet per minute."

Ratchet sucked part of his mustache between his lips. "No, I don't think we can blame the vertical speed for all the damage, but I have to get it up on some jacks to know how extensive the damage is."

"So, there is damage?" I asked, afraid of the coming answer.

"Oh, yeah," he said. "For starters, the linkage on both water rudders is damaged. Did you hit the water with the rudders down?"

Hunter studied the sky. "I don't think so, but we'd gone through some extreme altitudes leading up to the touch-and-go on the river. The rudders could've come down without me realizing it."

Ratchet said, "They were definitely down, but that may have happened when you hit the water. There's not much you can do to twist this airplane around enough in the air to get them to fall on their own. More than likely, they came down on contact with the water, especially if it was as hard as you say."

"What will you be looking for when you jack it up?" I asked.

He let his heel bounce on the side of the float above the main landing gear. "I can see the right-side squat switch got knocked loose, and it looks like you may have partially separated a seam just aft of the step on this side. I'm afraid we'll have to move her to my hangar after all. She needs more love than I can give her away from tools."

Hearing the initial diagnosis left me heartbroken but thankful the workhorse had gotten us home safely. "I guess that means she's not airworthy, huh?"

Ratchet shook his head. "If you mean legally, not even a little bit. Obviously, she was healthy enough to get you in the air and back here without falling out from under you, but now that you know at least the preliminary diagnosis, she has to stay on the ground until repairs are made or a ferry permit is issued by the FAA. I hate to be the bearer of bad news, but if an airplane ain't broke, I don't fix it. But this airplane is definitely broke, and somebody has to fix it."

I ran my hands through my hair and sighed. "I guess all we can do is get Jimmy out here with the tug and drag her down to your hangar."

Ratchet slid his glasses down his nose and looked at me over the frames. "I don't think you understand. I don't have room for anything this big in my hangar until I get two or three airplanes out of the way. But that's not all . . . I don't have room in my schedule to take on a job this size for at least another six weeks."

"Six weeks? Can you get it in sooner if I'm willing to pay an expedition fee?"

"I'm sorry. I don't do that to my customers. I'll break away from a job to look at another airplane, but it wouldn't be fair for me to completely pull off of one man's job to start another. I've built a career on doing what I say I'll do in the time I say I'll do it, and if I changed that now, the extra you'd pay me wouldn't feed me for long when my word stopped being any good."

"I respect that," I said. "The world could use a million more just like you, but I'm between a rock and a broken airplane here. Have you got any suggestions?"

He cast his gaze on the Citation in the back corner of the hangar and wiped his face on the arm of his shirt. "If you had the bankroll the owner of that jet has, I'd have some suggestions, but short of that, you're going to have to deal with a busted airplane until a good mechanic can fit you in. Notice I said a 'good mechanic.' You're looking at structural damage, so don't settle for just any old wrench-turner. You want somebody who understands seaplanes."

It was my turn to let my eyes explore the Citation. "Let's say I do have the identical bankroll as the guy who owns that jet. What would your suggestions be?"

One long breath later, Ratchet motioned toward the Citation with his chin. "That's yours, isn't it?"

I gave him a silent nod, and he hopped down from his perch on the float. "Then I'd suggest hiring the Cessna folks from Wichita to come ferry this thing back to the factory where it was built and arrange for a short-term lease of an equivalent airplane. I get the feeling you guys aren't out here to go fly fishing and take guided tours of Yellowstone, so whatever your mission is, you can lease an airplane that'll do it while the best mechanics in the world are putting yours back together. And if you don't believe the boys at Cessna are the best in the world, just wait until you get their bill."

I palmed another hundred-dollar bill and shook Ratchet's hand. "Thanks for taking a look and for the suggestion. Now, give me back my flashlight."

He slid the bill from my hand and tossed the light toward me. "If you need me, let me know. For now, I'll put you on the books right behind the seven airplanes I'm already committed to work on."

"Thanks, Ratchet. Before you go, would you mind telling us how you got that nickname?"

He stared at the floor. "Oh, it's just a nickname I picked up from working on airplanes all these years."

"Something tells me you're not being totally honest with us," I said.

He twisted the toe of his boot against the concrete. "Ah, the truth isn't always worth telling."

Singer spoke for the first time. "Actually, the truth is the *only* thing that's *always* worth telling."

Ratchet gave Singer a long look and then turned to me. "I guess he's the type who doesn't say much, but when he speaks, people tend to listen, huh?"

I smiled. "You'd be exactly right about that. He's the only one of us with any real wisdom."

"In that case," he said, "the truth is, a long time ago in my misspent youth in Alaska, I caught a fellow stealing avgas out of the tank that belonged to the company I was working for. I grabbed my rifle from my truck and headed for the door with the intention of ending that guy's thieving days. One of the old mechanics snatched the rifle from my hand on my way out the door, so I picked up the closest weapon I could find. It turned out to be a breaker bar, which isn't technically a ratchet, but by the time they pulled me off the guy, he had several imprints on his skull that looked just like the business end of that breaker bar. The guys in the shop started calling me Ratchet after that, and it stuck. When the whole thing shook out, the thief was the nephew of the guy who owned the company I worked for."

A round of appreciative laughter came from the three of us, and Hunter said, "I guess it's good you didn't shoot the guy."

"Actually, the owner of the company told me he wished I *had* shot the guy. It would've saved him a lot of money over the long haul."

Our respect for our new friend rose exponentially, and he ambled back to his hangar to continue through his backlog of broken airplanes.

I pulled out my phone and dialed Skipper. She answered almost before I heard it ring. "Ops Center."

"Hey, Skipper. It's Chase."

"Didn't we just talk a few minutes ago?"

"Yes, but the situation has changed a great deal since then. We had a mechanic look at the Caravan, and he found quite a bit of damage. I need you to get on the phone with Cessna and arrange for a ferry pilot to come fly it back to Wichita and deliver us an equivalent lease airplane while they're repairing the damage."

"Ouch. That's going to sting the checkbook," she said.

"Yes, it is, but I'd also like for you to get on the phone with the insurance company and tell them . . . On second thought, I'll call the insurance company. They'll have questions about the accident, for which you won't have answers."

"The insurance company won't be the only one with questions. You didn't tell me about any airplane accidents. Spill it."

"It's nothing, really."

"If it were nothing, we wouldn't be lining up ferry pilots, insurance agents, and leased airplanes, so spill it."

I took her through the adventure, play by play. She gasped several times and insisted on knowing if everyone was okay more times than I could count.

Twenty minutes later, I hung up the phone, and Hunter shot me a look that felt a lot like the "Spill it" Skipper had commanded.

I said, "The good news is that insurance will fully cover the repairs, and the ferry permit is in the works."

Singer nodded. "Those are good things, but that tone of yours means there's also bad news."

"You know me too well, Singer. The bad news is there are no equivalent airplanes available for lease. That leaves us stuck with the Citation and three Suburbans."

"Maybe Ratchet knows somebody who'd rent us an airplane for a while."

I pointed to my partner. "Now, that's why I keep you around. Occasionally, a great idea will fall out of your mouth."

A jog to the maintenance hangar turned into a race, but I wouldn't let a sniper and a PJ outrun me.

Ratchet watched us jog to a stop just inside the hangar door. "What are you guys in such a hurry for?"

I waved a dismissive hand toward Singer and Hunter. "These guys like to believe they can outrun me, but so far, it hasn't happened. I took your advice, and Cessna is sending up a mechanic and a ferry pilot. The second half of your suggestion is leaving us a little stumped, though. We can't find another Caravan on floats to lease. We thought you might know somebody with an airplane we could rent while we're here."

Ratchet looked away then finally said, "I'm not sure there'll be a lot of people willing to lend you a million-dollar airplane since you crashed yours."

"I didn't crash it," Hunter protested.

Ratchet laughed. "Incidental contact with the Earth at high speed that leaves an airplane unusable is pretty much the definition of a crash."

"Okay, you may have a point there, but we need an airplane, not a commentary on my flying."

Ratchet scratched his head. "I know a couple of guys up in Alaska who might have something, but I don't think they'd like your recent record—no matter what you call banging into a river."

"Thanks. If anything comes to mind, give us a call. We really need something to fly."

The mechanic looked through us and across the airport. "Are you guys any better at flying helicopters than you are at keeping airplanes in the sky?"

I suddenly liked where the conversation was headed. "We've got two helicopter instructors on the team, so, yeah, we can fly a chopper. What's on your mind?"

Ratchet closed one eye and pointed across the ramp. "See that Bell Four-Twelve over there?"

The three of us turned on our heels and peered across the airport. "Yeah, I see it."

The mechanic pulled off his hat. "I just put a new PT-Six turbine twin-pac and a set of blades on that thing, and the owner died of a heart attack before he paid me for it. The widow is trying to sell it, and if she gets it done, I'll get paid. Here's her number. I'm sure she'd love to talk with you about adding it to your fleet."

Chapter 13
If the Phone Doesn't Ring

My watch reported one o'clock—time for an ops-normal call from Clark's team. I checked my sat-phone to ensure it was powered up and had comms with at least enough satellites to ring when my handler called. The phone was doing everything it was designed to do . . . except ringing.

Four minutes passed, and still no ring. I waved the phone at Hunter. "How long do you think I should wait?"

Hunter double-checked the phone, I suppose, in an effort to make sure I had it turned on. "He's the one who's operational right now, so it's his responsibility to make the calls. He may be in a sensitive situation and—"

The plastic brick vibrated, and Clark's number appeared on the black-and-white screen. "It's about time. Is everything all right?"

"It is now," Clark said. "But it was touch and go for a few minutes. I didn't think I was going to make it."

"You didn't think you were going to make it? What are you talking about?"

"Thankfully, Disco found a Texaco station with a relatively clean bathroom before I destroyed a good pair of pants."

I couldn't avoid a least a little chuckle. "Well, I'm happy to hear the crisis was averted. How's the *actual* mission going?"

"Now that we avoided having it hit the fan—almost literally—it's going better than I expected. We put eyes on five of the six, but we're having a little trouble finding the missing link."

"Who's missing?" I asked.

"Douglas Callaway, their sniper."

"That's not good."

"Nope. He's definitely not the one I want to be missing. If he's anything like Singer, it makes me a little nervous to think about him hiding out on one of these ridgelines with me in his crosshairs."

I turned to my favorite sniper. "Do you know Doug Callaway?"

Singer sighed. "I've been thinking about him and running that name through my skull for a few days, and I keep coming up empty. That doesn't make sense. His dossier said he was a Coastie, but I'm not so sure about that. Maybe we should continue this chat this evening when we're all together."

I gave him a nod and returned to the phone call. "Singer doesn't know him, but he's suspicious. We'll explore that tonight over dinner."

"Sounds good. We're going to give this another hour or so and then head home."

"All right, but if you're . . . indisposed when the next ops-normal call is due, hand the phone off to Disco or Mongo."

"Will do," he said.

"Oh, and before you go, I need to brief you on the damage to the Caravan."

"Damage? I thought you said it was okay."

"I did say that, but I was speaking out of school. We had the local A and P look her over, and there's quite a bit of damage to the main landing gear, the water rudders, and there's possibly at least one parted seam in the portside float."

"Ouch. How long, and how much?"

"That's the bad news. The local mechanic can't get to it for several weeks, so I made arrangements for a ferry pilot to come pick it up and get it back to Wichita so the Cessna crew can put it back together."

"Cotton is going to kill you," he said.

"I'd love to have him and his toolbox out here, but if it's as bad as the local guy says it is, I think it's best that she goes back to Cessna. I know it's bad, but that's not the worst of it."

"I probably don't want to hear what's next, do I?"

"You probably don't, but I'm telling you anyway. I can't find another seaplane to lease, but there's a tiny ray of hope here at the airport."

He let out a long sigh. "This sounds expensive."

"It may be," I admitted. "There's a Bell Four-Twelve for sale with new engines and a new set of blades. The owner passed away, and his widow is trying to sell it so the mechanic who did the work can get paid."

"How much?"

"I don't know yet, but we're going to look at it now. I'm sure it's out of my price range, but since you're the boss and we're doing the Board a big favor here, maybe they'll be willing to write a check."

"Maybe," he said. "Check it out and take it flying if it's airworthy. It sounds like you at least met the mechanic. Find out what he says about it, and we'll have a powwow when we get back."

"All right. We'll do it. That's all I have, so we'll see you in a couple of hours."

The helicopter was far from new, but it appeared to be solid. The panel was full of steam gauges and old radios, so an avionics upgrade would be in her future, regardless of who bought her. With new engines and blades, if the airframe turned out to be in good shape, the old bird would make a nice addition to the hangar back in Saint Marys.

I climbed out of the cockpit and saw Ratchet ambling across the ramp. When he finally made it to the helicopter, the inquisition began.

"I know you said the engines and blades are new, but how are the bones?"

He ran his hand along the edge of the windshield. "She's a good helicopter. I've done all her maintenance, repairs, and annual inspections for ten years or so. There's nothing wrong with her except that panel. She's in serious need of something digital up there. The owner was a retired Vietnam-era Huey pilot, so he was right at home behind that old panel."

"How much?" I asked. "And can we fly it?"

He patted his pocket. "That's what kept me. I just got off the phone with Mrs. Templeton. She said I could let you fly it as long as I went with you, and she doesn't know how much it's worth."

I sucked air through my teeth. "I hate deals like that. I'd much rather know a starting price than to be asked for a blind offer."

"I can give you my opinion, and we can get an appraiser out here to take a look, but let's take her for a spin first."

After a thorough preflight inspection, the four of us climbed aboard.

Ratchet said, "I'm not a pilot, so don't expect any help from me. I can light the fires, but that's where my abilities end."

I pulled on a headset. "I think I can figure it out. Just don't let me get us lost. I'm not sure I can find my way home with a pair of forty-year-old radios and an ADF receiver."

"In that case," he said, "maybe we should keep the airport in sight."

I brought the turbines to life and let them warm up while I ran through the systems checks. Everything was in the green, so I checked the wind and scanned the area for traffic. We appeared to be alone on the ramp, so I rolled on the throttle and pulled enough pitch to bring us to a low hover.

The machine was heavy, but she came off the ground nicely and even rewarded my efforts to hover her as close to motionless as possible. Everything felt right, so I announced our position and intentions on the common traffic advisory frequency.

A minute later, I put the civilian version of the military Huey into a high-speed taxi down the centerline of the runway. The speed built as it should, and everything looked good.

"Let's go flying," I said.

Ratchet laughed. "We're already flying."

"Let's fly higher."

And we did. The chopper climbed, turned, cruised, and descended just as the handbook said it should. I put enough distance between us and the Earth to perform an autorotation, and she seemed to enjoy stretching her legs. I couldn't find anything the old girl wouldn't do. I flew two approaches to a full stop each time, running the machine through her full operating range, and she seemed to want to keep flying.

After hover-taxiing back to the ramp and shutting down, I said, "Okay, let's hear your number."

He pulled off his headset and hung it on its hook. "One point six to two."

I grunted. "That's a lot of money and a big range."

"This is a lot of airplane," he said. "The new engines and rotors were almost a million bucks before we ever took them out of the shipping crates." He looked around, perhaps searching for prying ears. "Just between you and me, Chase, she'd probably sell you the thing for the price of the engines and rotors."

"How much does Mrs. Templeton owe you?"

He looked down as if ashamed to answer. "Just over ten grand."

"She could afford a million dollars' worth of parts, but she can't write a ten-thousand-dollar check? Something's not adding up."

"It's a long story, but here's the nuts and bolts. The owner made an arrangement with a couple of logging companies to do some flying for them, and they agreed to front the money for the engines and blades. He was going to work off the cost over the next few years, but the heart attack beat him to the finish line."

"Is there a lien against it?"

"No, I don't think so, but the loggers are getting antsy, and I could use the ten grand."

I turned and looked over my shoulder. "Did you guys feel anything you didn't like?"

Singer said, "My stomach didn't like some of those steep turns, but if felt like every Huey I've ever been aboard."

Hunter nodded. "I didn't hear anything creaking or cracking that shouldn't. How did it feel up there?"

I scanned the outdated panel and worn controls. "It felt like an old workhorse who was happy to be back in the field."

Hunter's eyes lit up like a kid at Christmas. "Can we take her home with us, Daddy? Please?"

Ratchet joined the laughter. "I still don't know what you guys do, but you must be good at it."

"We just get lucky . . . a lot," I said.

He stepped from the chopper and tied it down. "If you're serious about it, I'll talk to Mrs. Templeton and come up with a real number."

I pulled the checkbook from my hip pocket. After writing ten thousand dollars and no cents on the line, I handed him the signed check. "We're serious enough to pay your bill now. Talk to Mrs. Templeton, and let's reconvene later."

Chapter 14
Lost and Found

We pulled into the driveway of our rented chalet as the clock struck three, and simultaneously, my sat-phone vibrated. I pressed the button and stuck the hunk of plastic to my ear. "Nice timing. I guess you didn't have any more bathroom emergencies."

"Nope, it's been an unproductive afternoon on that front, as well as the secondary mission locating the rest of the team. We're still missing one pesky little sniper. Did you fly the Four-Twelve?"

"We did, and other than needing an avionics upgrade, I couldn't find anything wrong with it."

"How much?" he asked.

"We don't know yet. The mechanic said one point six to two million."

Clark let out a long, low whistle. "That's a lot of money and a lot of price range."

"That's what I told the mechanic. I guess great minds really do think alike."

He chuckled, "I don't think you want to chunk your mind into the same category as the gray matter I lug around. Is it worth two million?"

"I don't know. Maybe. But we'll have Skipper do some shopping. Ratchet, the mechanic, is going to talk to the owner for us.

He did say he thought we could probably steal it for the cost of the engines and blades, but I don't feel good about ripping off a widow. If we buy it, we should do so at fair market value."

"You and your morality."

"Yeah, well, just ask Singer. We have to answer for our sins one day, and I don't need to add any more check marks by my name in the Great Book for pulling a fast one on a widow."

He said, "We'll be home in less than an hour. Try to have dinner on the table when we get there, darling."

"I'll darling you," I said. "You took the chef with you. Come to think of it, you always take the chef when you leave. First it was Maebelle, and now Disco. The rest of us are going to starve to death if you keep this up."

"It's always something with you. I'll see you in forty-five minutes."

My next call rang on the third floor of Bonaventure Plantation back in Saint Marys.

Skipper clicked a key. "Ops center."

"Hey, Skipper. I've got a preliminary report for you. Advise ready to copy."

"Send it," she said.

"Team one—that's Clark, Mongo, and Disco—located five of the six local team members . . . everyone except their sniper, Douglas Callaway. They're en route back to the house now, but go ahead and do a little digging on Callaway. It makes us nervous having a sniper running around on the loose. Those guys aren't exactly harmless."

"Okay, got it. Let's hear your report."

"I had Hunter and Singer. We located the compound and ran some video. I've not looked at the footage yet, but I'll do that before we convene for our official brief in a few hours. As you already know, we had an incident with the airplane, leaving it crippled."

She said, "We've already dealt with that, but I still haven't been able to find anything to lease that has the capability of the Caravan."

"We may have solved that problem on the ground. We found a Bell Four-Twelve with new engines and blades. It's for sale, so we're sort of in negotiations to buy it."

"Sort of? How does that work?"

I explained the situation, and she said, "I'm on it. I'll have you some price comps when you call back. Do you have anything else?"

"I'd like to talk to my wife, and I'd like for you to order us a bunch of pizzas. It's apparently my turn to cook."

Without a response, she clicked off, and Penny's voice took the place of Skipper's. "Hey. How's it going out there?"

"Just another day in paradise," I said. "The real work won't start for another day or two, but we laid some pretty good groundwork today. Skipper will cover it with you, and I'm sure you'll be listening in on the full briefing later tonight. How are things there?"

"My head is about to explode," she huffed. "I don't know how Skipper remembers all this stuff. I'm learning, but I'm taking a lot of notes." Her tone softened to barely above a whisper. "I had no idea Skipper did so much work when you guys are out on a mission."

"Her job is a lot harder than ours. We'd be lost without her."

"I can see that . . . now. It's crazy, but I'm enjoying it. I really like being involved. Oh, speaking of being involved, the movie is finished and in editing and post-production. There will be a private airing by invitation only in Hollywood, and I'd really like for you to come with me."

"I wouldn't miss it for the world. When is it?"

"I don't know yet. They've not set a date, but I'll let you know as soon as they do."

"There is one more piece of official business I forgot to tell Skipper," I said.

"Hang on. I'll get her."

"No, that's not necessary," I said, trying to catch her before she clicked off. "I can just tell you."

"I'm ready . . ."

"Skipper's working on price comps on a fifteen-year-old Bell Four-Twelve with new engines and blades for me. When she pulls the comps, remember to factor in the new parts."

"Wow, okay. Are we buying a helicopter?"

"Maybe. It depends on a lot of factors, but I think we can justify the expense, especially if we can get the Board to pay for it."

"I'll remind her about the new parts for the comps. Is there anything else you need?"

"Just that for now, but we'll talk again soon."

When I glanced at the phone before shoving it in my pocket, I noticed a message from Skipper. When I clicked on the icon, a list of local pizza delivery joints filled the screen, and the message read, "I'm an analyst, not a waitress."

Touché.

I placed the pizza order for delivery and ignored the kitchen.

As my laptop came online, I inserted the aerial camera's memory card from our near collision with the helicopter. A few clicks later, the video was poised for a private showing, just like Penny's movie would soon be. My curiosity drove me to play the video before the rest of the team arrived.

I sat silently watching the terrain of southern Montana pass beneath the lens of the camera in smooth, predictable motion at two miles per minute. Although my eyes were searching for the Temple of Truth compound—and the former president's niece—the beauty of the landscape was impossible to ignore. Rising spires of granite jutted skyward as if clawing for the floor of Heaven as crevasses wound their way through the stone and earth and melting snow like talons stretching for the ceiling of Hell.

Lost in my concentration for the compound and nearly mesmerized by the terrain, it happened—abruptly and violently. The view raced forward, doubling its speed and peering up the canyon with the highway and shallow river now out of frame and out of mind. A flash of black metal beneath the blur of a spinning rotor materialized on the edge of the picture, but for no longer than an instant. The view became a flurry of stony canyon wall followed by empty, distant sky, moving too fast for the lens of the camera to react and focus. As the scene played out on the screen, I flashed back to the view outside the window of the Caravan during the chaos. I'd never forget that view, nor the feeling in the pit of my stomach.

Finally, the camera reclaimed its grasp on the world below as the highway and river and crevasses and treetops grew ever larger in the frame. I relived the agonizing seconds passing beyond my control inside the airplane as the video replayed the captured scene in silent, terrifying definition. The moment of Hunter's decision to sidestep the certain destruction of the asphalt road with its graveled shoulders and banks of darkened, piled snow, shone in brilliant relief as the flight path of our rapidly descending magic carpet abruptly aligned with the sunken, meandering bed of the Yellowstone River. The snow-kissed, jagged banks of the river disappeared to the left and right of the frame as the bubbling flow of water consumed the screen. The water rose with heart-stopping speed until the keel of both floats contacted the surface, sending bone-jarring shock through the airframe and camera mounts. Spray from the icy water turned the screen white and streaked with the foamy combination of water and violent energy from the plummeting three-ton airframe.

Had that energy been transferred to the road less than fifty feet away, there would've been no hope for the survival of the airplane and only slightly more for the survival of its passengers and crew.

The rushing torrent of water beneath the camera's lens gave way to smooth, uninterrupted flow as the propeller dug into the air, accelerating us across the surface until finally the floats separated from the water and we traded forward motion for vertical energy to climb. Trailing water diminished as we climbed away from the river, but the left float continued to pour a steady stream far longer than the right. Ratchet had been correct. The float had separated at a seam, allowing river water to see a portion of the pontoon it should've never viewed: the inside.

I clicked on the two vertical bars, pausing the scene, and turned to see my partner standing only inches behind me and peering over my shoulder.

He swallowed hard. "I guess we're lucky to be alive, huh?"

"It wasn't luck, my friend. It was some of the best aeronautical decision-making that's ever been done. Your ability to remain calm and put that airplane exactly in the only position we could've survived is the reason we're alive. You're a hell of a pilot, Stone Hunter, and I'm thankful we're on the same team."

He laid a hand on my shoulder. "You and Clark made me the pilot I am, and I'm not arrogant enough to take credit for what happened out there today. The only explanation is the prayer of our sniper."

"Speaking of our sniper . . . Where is my favorite choir director?"

"He's out back on the deck, I think."

I moved the computer from my lap to the coffee table in the center of the living room and headed for the deck. The same instant I turned the knob, opening the door to join Singer, he ordered, in a stage whisper, "Stop!"

That froze me in my tracks and made me want to open the door even more.

"Don't come out here," he said. "Back away from the door, and turn off the lights."

I did as he said, but my curiosity gnawed at me, leaving me barely able to stay inside the house.

Hunter watched me abandon the door and extinguish the lights. "What's going on?"

"I'm not sure," I admitted. "But I think Singer must see a bear or something. He told me to stay inside and go dark."

That brought Hunter to my side, his curiosity obviously as piqued as mine.

Two minutes that felt like two lifetimes later, Singer walked through the door as if nothing happened. He strolled past the two of us. "Follow me."

We obeyed and gathered by the fireplace.

"What's going on?" I demanded.

"I found our missing sniper."

Chapter 15
Used Car Salesman

The doorbell rang just as Clark, Disco, and Mongo pulled into the driveway.

I started for the door, but Singer put his hand in the center of my chest. "No. Stay right here, and don't move. That goes for you, too, Hunter. I've got the door."

Hunter and I held our position, still uncertain of what was happening around us, and Singer headed for the door. He shot a quick glance through the door light, planted his foot twenty-four inches from the threshold, and opened the door inward. The four pizza boxes hit the floor seconds after Singer yanked the delivery guy through the opening and planted him against the wall.

His eyes turned to beach balls, and his hands flew toward the ceiling. "Look, man. I got like forty bucks, but it's yours. Whatever you want. This job ain't worth dying for."

Singer shot a finger to his lips. "Shhh. Be quiet. What kind of car are you driving?"

"A ratty old Jeep, but you can have it. Just don't hurt me. I'm just a delivery guy trying to pay my kid's college tuition. I got no beef with you. You don't even have to pay for the pizzas."

"Forget about the pizzas," Singer said. "How much is your Jeep worth?"

Confusion melded with terror on the delivery guy's face. His eyes darted between the dropped boxes and our sniper. "I don't know. Maybe three or four thousand. I've never thought about it."

Singer loosened his grip on the man's jacket. "Relax. Nobody's going to hurt you. Just don't move."

The man nodded nervously but made no effort to bolt.

Singer said, "How much cash do we have, Chase?"

"Plenty. Why?"

"Have we got five grand?"

"Yeah, sure we do, but what's going on, Singer? You're acting crazy."

"I'll explain in a minute. For now, get me the cash. I'm renting a Jeep with the option to buy."

I pulled fifty one-hundred-dollar bills from my pack and handed them to our previously rational sniper.

He turned to the pizza guy and shoved the cash into his hand. "Here's five grand. I need to borrow your Jeep for the night. If I don't bring it back, you keep the cash. If I do bring it back, you can have it back and keep the money. Do we have a deal?"

The baffled man stammered, "Is this some kind of . . . I mean . . . Are you messing with me? You're freaking me out, man. You've got to tell me what's going on."

Clark walked through the door with his pistol at low ready. "Is everything okay in here?"

Singer waved him off. "Everything's fine. I'm just making a deal with this guy. You can put the gun away."

The man's expression of fear and bewilderment grew even more animated. "Look, man. I don't know who or what you guys are, but I just want to get out of here. I don't want your money or any part of whatever this is. Just keep the pizzas and let me go, okay?"

Singer held up a finger. "Listen to me, and listen closely. No one is going to hurt you. We just need your Jeep for a few hours.

Call your boss and tell him you broke down and you need someone to come pick you up. You can come back tomorrow, and if
your Jeep is in the driveway, you can hop in and drive away five
thousand dollars richer. You're not a party to anything illegal, but
your Jeep may not survive the night. I need to climb a mountain."

Clark stared at me for reassurance that our sniper hadn't
flipped his lid, but I wasn't sure enough to give him what he
needed.

Disco slipped through the door and behind Clark, while wearing an expression almost as baffled as pizza boy.

Finally, the delivery man gave in and took the money. "Okay,
fine. Whatever you say. But I need to get my stuff out of the Jeep
and call my boss."

He shoved the cash into his pocket and scurried out the door,
bouncing off the belly and chest of our resident Jolly Green Giant
standing on the porch. He shot another terrified look up at
Mongo, sidestepped him, and ran for his Jeep. With one final look
toward the house, he jumped into the Jeep and reached for the ig-
nition. He was going to run.

At least that's what he *thought* he was going to do.

Mongo stepped through the door and tossed a set of keys to
Singer. "It sounded like you wanted that Jeep, so I nabbed the keys
so he couldn't bolt."

Singer caught the jumble and removed a single key from the
University of Montana ring. He jogged down the steps, and I followed, pulling my credential pack from my pocket as we went.
When we reached the Jeep, the man was frantically pulling items
from inside and shoving them into a backpack.

I held up my Secret Service credentials. "It's okay, really. You're
in no danger. We just need your Jeep overnight for official business."

He looked up and locked his eyes on my badge and I.D. "You
guys are feds? Secret Service?"

Singer laid the keyring in his hand. "You're in no danger, and we don't care about the pot you just shoved into your bag. We're not those kinds of cops. Now, come inside and call your boss. Everything's going to be fine. I'm sorry for scaring you."

I pocketed my cred-pack and led the way back inside. We got the pizza guy calmed down enough to make the call and get a ride on the way, but Singer was still the only one of us who knew what was really going on.

Pizza guy squinted and peered through the window. "There's my ride. I'm out of here, guys. This has been way too weird for me. You can keep the Jeep. And do me a favor, will you? Order pizza from somewhere else next time, okay?" He sprinted from the house and dived into the passenger seat of a Toyota Camry. Seconds later, he was gone, and I turned to Singer. "It's time to tell us what's going on."

He motioned toward the deck. "I was out back thinking and clearing my head when I caught a glimpse of something shiny on the hillside. Whatever it was, it wasn't there yesterday."

I lowered my chin. "You mean you memorized every detail of the mountainside?"

"No, not every detail, but I'm a sniper . . . and a pretty good one. I notice when things change in my environment, and that shiny thing wasn't there yesterday."

Clark spoke up. "Something shining on the side of a mountain could be anything."

"Yes, it could," Singer admitted, "but nothing natural flashes like that on a hillside."

"Water does if the light hits it just right," Hunter said.

"You're right, but there's no source of continually flowing water on this side of that mountain. That means whatever reflected the light from the setting sun isn't natural. A human put it there.

My bet is it's a rifle scope, and if I'm right, we're going to need that Jeep to get close enough to hike in there before sunrise."

Clark squinted one eye and leaned in. "Taking a team on an overnight hike through some of the roughest terrain in the country on a hunch is a pretty big gamble."

Singer squinted back at him. "It's not a hunch. It's a reflection of something manmade that wasn't there this time yesterday."

Clark nodded. "Okay. You're the eagle eye. It's your op. Who are you taking with you?"

"I want you spotting with me, and I want Hunter and Chase out front. Are you okay with that?"

"Like I said, it's your op. Let's shove some calories down our face holes and gear up. It looks like we're going for a little off-road adventure in a borrowed Jeep."

Disco salvaged the pizza from the dropped boxes, and we devoured the meal.

In twenty minutes, we were dressed in layers for an overnight operation in subfreezing conditions on a slick, snowy mountain face.

Mongo said, "What do you want me and Disco to do while you're gone?"

"Watch the aerial footage from the flyover. It's queued up on my laptop, but you can ignore the first fifteen minutes. That's just an airplane crash . . . Pretty boring. After that, brief Skipper, and get some rest, but leave your phones turned on. If we get in trouble on that mountain, you'll be the only two people on Earth who know where we are."

"You got it, boss."

"There is one more thing," I said. "When we get back tomorrow, how about another breakfast like this morning's?"

Disco smiled. "Yeah, I think we can do that. And if you happen to see an elk while you're out there, I'm always up for grilling steaks."

Chapter 16
Hide and Seek

The National Geospatial-Intelligence Agency is one of those alphabet soup groups scattered around the nation's capital. Most people have never heard of the NGA, but in the intelligence business, they're one of the "Big Five," alongside their kissing cousins, the CIA, NSA, DIA, and NRO. When I was introduced to the NGA, they were still calling themselves the National Imagery and Mapping Agency, or NIMA, but thanks to some line item in an obscure Senate bill that ultimately wore the president's signature, NIMA received a new nametag and became the NGA in the fall of 2003.

I liked them better when they sounded like a nerdy group of cartographers meeting in the darkened corners of some library in Foggy Bottom, but alas, I was not consulted before the bill became law. I was, however, brought into the loop when the best operational analyst I know managed to gain access to the massive imagery database, stored on computers the size of school busses, in a lonely, electrically humming basement in Springfield, Virginia. I didn't ask any questions when Skipper loaded the software onto my laptop, but how she came to possess such software will forever remain a mystery. My theory is a combination of her intellectual brilliance and her dark brown eyes no Washington D.C. geek can resist. Regardless of how we came to possess a key to the castle, I wasn't afraid to stick it into the lock.

Ten minutes of scrolling and clicking granted us detailed topographical and photographic data on the hillside we were about to assault.

Singer studied every detail as if his life depended on absolute memorization of the area. After scouring the aerial photos for several minutes, he tapped his finger near the left edge of the screen. "There you are, you little woodchuck. You picked the wrong guy to play hide-and-seek with. I'll see you soon, Dougy Boy."

I laughed. "Woodchuck? Really? That's what we're going with?"

Singer continued tapping the screen. "Yep, that's what we're going with. You know the whole, 'How much wood would a woodchuck chuck' thing, right?"

I nodded.

"Well, some woodchucks bite off more wood than they can chuck, and our friend, Doug Callaway, is about to learn how that tastes."

Singer, Clark, Hunter, and I mounted our rented pizza delivery Jeep and set out for the mountainside. When we pulled off the paved road and onto a trail leading up the northwestern face of the mountain, Clark brought the Jeep to a sliding stop. Hunter and I leapt from the seats, drawing our Leatherman tools as we went, and we soon had the brake-light bulbs removed from behind their red, plastic lenses. Clark gave the interior bulb associated with the open doors the same treatment, and with our night-vision goggles in place and the headlights off, my handler navigated the steep, winding trail barely above a walking pace.

Clark's eyes were glued to the trail through the green, grainy image inside his NODs. "This trail looked a lot better on the satellite imagery. It's beginning to look way too much like Afghanistan."

"This is the *good* trail," Singer said. "Just wait. The rough part starts when we turn to the north."

Clark huffed. "I'm really looking forward to that."

Singer's prophesy came true after a thousand more yards. The turn to the north put us on a ledge that was barely identifiable as a trail. Six inches outside Clark's door, a vertical granite wall soared out of sight, while the view from my side plummeted to depths my NODs couldn't identify.

"I don't like this at all," Clark said. "Let's get the top off in case we have to bail out."

The weathered fabric top of the Jeep came down easily, but the doors put up a fight. We pried and pulled against the rusted pins until our fingers bled. I turned my Leatherman in my hand with the intention of hammering the pin free, but before I could strike the first blow, Singer grabbed my wrist. "Chase, don't! That'll make the wrong kind of noise."

"The wrong kind of noise? What are you talking about?"

He motioned through the valley. "We don't know how well sound will carry up here. Callaway will ignore vehicle sounds and write them off to traffic on the streets below, but nothing in this environment would naturally make a metal-on-metal banging sound, and our woodchuck friend would definitely notice you beating the crap out of that pin."

"You snipers pay way too much attention to stuff," I said.

"That's how young shooters live to become old snipers like me."

With no room for a foothold left or right of the Jeep, Singer climbed across the roll bar and windshield and onto the hood. Finally back on terra firma in front of the vehicle, he lifted the hood latches and reached inside, leaving the rest of us in the dark when it came to his plan. Back over the windshield he came, carefully protecting his left hand as he moved as quietly as possible. Back inside the Jeep, he held out his hand between Clark and me. "Try a little of this."

I shook my head in disbelief at the ingenuity of our sniper. The index and middle finger of his left hand were covered with grease from somewhere beneath the hood. A coating of Singer's gooey black gold on the door pins released them from their rust-induced captivity, and we soon had the doors stowed beneath the rear seat.

Clark shoved the shifter back into gear. "Remember, if we go over the side, jump uphill, not down. This thing doesn't weigh much, but we don't want it rolling over us as we race it to the bottom of the hill."

Moving at just below the speed of smell, we made our way along the ledge as the trail seemed to narrow a little more with every inch we moved forward.

Clark said, "We're running out of road, boys. I'm open to any suggestions here."

Singer leaned forward between Clark and me. "If we can make another hundred meters, there's a wide spot where we can dismount."

Clark white-knuckled the wheel. "The blade of my knife is a wide spot compared to what we're on now. We should already be on foot."

"That's easy for you to say, but you don't have to carry a thirty-pound rifle and fifty pounds of support gear up that mountain."

"If we roll off this ledge, somebody will have to carry two hundred pounds of *me* out of here."

Our painfully slow progress continued until the trail gradually widened into an area about twice the size of the Jeep. Clark enjoyed his first unlabored breath in half an hour, and we put our boots back on the ground.

Singer pulled his rifle from its bag and slung it over his shoulder.

I motioned toward his rifle. "That's not your Barrett."

He reached back and ran a hand across the stock. "No, it's the three-three-eight Lapua. This one is a little lighter than the fifty-cal, but still enough bullet to give somebody the worst day of their life."

I said, "I don't care what you shoot as long as it gets the job done. Now, how about briefing us on the plan?"

He took a knee, and the rest of us followed. "Clark and I will set up a nest about five hundred meters up that hill behind us. If I memorized the aerial shots as well as I hope, that'll put me in the best possible spot to get Callaway's attention with a well-placed headshot."

"How long will it take you to get in position?" I asked.

"Maybe an hour, but no more. Clark will be the limiting factor since he's old and crippled. I could do it in thirty minutes by myself, but having a spotter on an op like this is a little important."

"It'll take Hunter and me at least that long to get in position to close on Callaway. Let's do comm checks every fifteen minutes, and you can talk us in when we get close."

Singer glanced up the steep terrain. "Let's go to work."

Fifteen minutes later, my earpiece crackled. "Point One, Spotter."

I keyed my radio. "Spotter, Point One has you loud and clear. How me?"

"Loud and clear," came his response.

"We'll be in your line of sight at the next comms check."

"Roger."

Hunter and I moved as quietly as possible through the darkness, snow, and underbrush. The closer we got to the potential enemy sniper, the quieter we had to be. There was no trail beneath our feet, but the course to the sniper's nest was relatively level.

Before fifteen more minutes had passed, my earpiece came alive again. "Point One, Spotter has you in sight. Over."

"Spotter, Point One, roger."

Clark said, "We're in position, and we'll be operational in twenty."

"Roger."

Hunter and I continued our trek toward the target until we'd moved within two hundred meters of his position.

In a soft whisper, I spoke into my mic. "Spotter, Point One is in position two hundred meters out."

Clark's voice came through as clearly as if he were standing beside me. "Roger, Point One. We're operational and have you in sight. Can you close silently?"

"Affirmative. The terrain is clear, and there's a stand of trees protecting our approach."

"Roger," he hissed. "Callaway is dug in and bearing on the house. He's behind a fifty-cal, but I can't see his other armament."

"Roger," I whispered. "We'll move on your command."

"Start your move," he ordered.

We crept forward, placing every step as gently as possible. In the next twelve minutes, we moved just over one hundred meters with Callaway never looking our way.

The remaining ninety meters took just over twenty minutes, but when Hunter and I were within fifteen feet of the sniper, I clicked my mic twice, and Clark said, "Roger. Send the wind."

I clicked twice to acknowledge and estimated the wind at four knots from right to left. I gave the coordinating clicks to pass the wind speed and direction to our spotter and sniper.

Clark said, "Roger. Four knots, right to left. Stand by for shot."

I clicked twice and focused intently on Doug Callaway's skull as we awaited the coming projectile—a projectile that would pass over our heads with barely a foot to spare. I had no fear of Singer hitting us, but the shot he was on the verge of taking was one only a dozen other living snipers could make. I prayed Singer was as skilled as my faith in him deserved.

The whistle of the three hundred grain, three-three-eight round hissed through the air, and Hunter and I sprang into action.

An instant later, Singer's bullet hit its mark, and the target exploded, sending shards of glass, aluminum, wood, and steel flying in every direction. We hit our lights, illuminating the sniper's nest like the Fourth of July.

Doug Callaway's body twitched and lunged backward in an instant. The shock was so violent, he likely never noticed the flood of light we poured onto his position.

Hunter and I leapt into Callaway's nest with our pistols drawn and trained on the sniper's head. He shielded his eyes against our glaring lights with a bloody hand. What remained of his custom-built rifle and scope lay in splinters. "Sorry about the rifle, Doug. Our sniper planned only to hit your scope, but it looks like he missed. But from two thousand yards in the dark, I'd say that's not a bad miss. Now, how about getting those hands on the ground?"

He surrendered, both mentally and physically, and stretched his arms out in front of him. Hunter knelt with one knee on the back of Callaway's left hand and slid the steel-lined flex-cuffs around his wrists. As soon as he secured the cuffs, Hunter searched the sniper and relieved him of a Glock pistol, four magazines, two knives, a bandolier of now-useless rifle cartridges, a cell phone, and a set of NODs.

My partner rolled Callaway over and sat him up. Another pair of flex-cuffs fit nicely around his ankles, and I keyed my mic. "Nice shooting, Annie Oakley, but you blew the shot an inch low. Prisoner is secure. No casualties."

"Roger. We'll continue to cover while you interrogate."

"Roger."

I directed the beam of my light away from our prisoner's face and took a knee in front of him. "Normally, we wouldn't be quite this aggressive, but you were pointing a rifle at us, and that pisses us off. So, let's start with that. Why were you pointing what used to be a rifle at our house?"

He spat demolished rifle debris from between his lips. "I was just returning the favor."

Hunter pressed the muzzle of his pistol against Callaway's kneecap and drew up the trigger slack. "Since you seem to want to play games, let's play my favorite game—Glock, paper, scissors. How about I go first?"

The sniper stared at Hunter's finger pressing the trigger and let out an audible sigh. "What would you do if you caught another team of operators surveilling your team all day? Would you blow it off, or would you set up an O.P. and gather intel on them?"

Hunter held up the man's bandolier. "You weren't just surveilling. Based on your ammo load, you were planning to shoot."

Callaway said, "Ask that sniper of yours out there if he's ever gone on a surveillance mission without ammo."

I had to admire the man's fortitude. He didn't beg, yell, or panic. In fact, he tried to turn the interrogation around on us.

"What are you guys doing snooping around up here and spying on my team?"

Hunter pressed his pistol even tighter against Callaway's knee. "We're asking the questions, not you. And if you want your kneecap to remain airtight, it's time for you to come up with some answers."

He raised his knee against Hunter's pressure. "You're not going to shoot me. If you were, I'd already have a hole in me. I answered your question. *You* were spying on *my* team, so now, I'm spying on yours. It's that simple, so I guess paper covers Glock, and that makes it your turn."

Hunter holstered his pistol and grabbed Callaway's wrist. Pulling the wounded hand toward the light, he drew his med-pack from his belt.

Callaway yanked his hand away. "It's just shrapnel wounds. I'm guessing that was a three-three-eight because a fifty-cal would've blown my arms off. While I'm making guesses, let me try one more. You're here because the Board thinks we've got a mole, and you're here to find that mole—if he exists—and bring him in. How am I doing so far?"

I don't know how I expected Callaway to act when we pounced on him, but that wasn't it. I found myself on my heels, unsure what to do next. Singer's plan called for interrogation and release, but that interrogation should've lasted hours, not minutes.

I had more questions, but what I really wanted to do was open the tap and let Callaway talk.

I said, "What makes you think you've got a mole on your team?"

He shuffled on his butt in a wasted effort to find a more comfortable position. "I've suspected it for a while, myself. I knew this day would come, but I thought they'd send assassins and not investigators."

Hunter growled. "How do you know we're not both?"

Callaway motioned toward the remains of his rifle with his chin. "Because assassins don't shoot rifles. They shoot skulls."

"Dropping you wouldn't accomplish anything," I said. "It would just leave one fewer suspect."

The sniper nodded slowly. "I guess that makes you the dog who finally caught the FedEx truck. Now, what are you going to do with me?"

Maybe Callaway was the psychologist and I was nothing more than the dog chewing on the tire of the FedEx truck.

I turned to Hunter. "Keep him pinned down. I need to talk with the handler."

Callaway let out an audible chuckle. "You've got to go check in with Daddy, huh?"

"If he tries to get up, shoot him." I lit up the hillside and took thirty strides before keying my mic. "Spotter, Point One."

Clark replied, "Spotter."

"I'm a little lost over here. This guy isn't resisting. He says he was watching us because we were watching his team. I didn't say anything about the mole, but he did. He says he's been expecting someone to show up. I could use a little guidance over here."

"Interesting. Truss him up, and get him down to the Jeep. We'll take him home and get the truth out of him. Is he wounded?"

"He took some shrapnel in his right hand, but he won't let us work on it."

"Roger," he said. "Get him down here, but don't let him run off."

"We'll be there in less than an hour."

I made my way back to the sniper's nest. "Cut his ankles free, and let's get him back to the vehicle."

Hunter drew his knife and ran the tip into the catch of the flex-cuffs around his ankles and then roughly hoisted him to his feet. "Let's go."

Callaway pulled away from Hunter and did what I would do in his position. He leapt from the nest and onto the downhill slope, allowing his feet to slide and bounce down the grade.

Hunter looked up. "How far do you want me to let him go?"

"Catch him."

Less than a minute later, Hunter had the sniper pinned to the hill, facedown in the snow. "Run all you want, hot rod, but that's going to make this a long night for you."

My partner pulled a length of five-fifty cord from his pocket and fashioned a leash for our guest of honor. "Don't fall down, or you'll find it a little hard to breathe."

Moving across the snow-covered terrain was slower-going than it had been when Hunter and I were creeping in, but Callaway's level of fitness made for relatively good time. An hour later, the lights of pizza boy's Jeep came into sight, and our pace increased.

Clark watched us approach and slid from the hood as we drew to a stop a few feet from the Jeep. He stared down Callaway without a word, grabbed his wrist, and inspected the sniper's hand. "We're going to clean this up before it gets infected. You're welcome to remain conscious while we do, or you can wake up with a nasty headache and a bandaged hand. It's up to you."

Callaway didn't put up a fight. He relaxed his arm and surrendered it to Clark. A few splinters and a quart of saline solution later, his hand was clean and ready for the bandage.

The sniper watched Clark wrap and tape the dressing. "How long were you in the Ranger Battalion?"

Clark gave his hand a squeeze, causing Callaway's knees to buckle. "Your night will be a lot more fun for you if you let us do the questioning. But if you'd prefer a longer, uncomfortable night, feel free to keep asking questions we're never going to answer." My handler gave him a shove toward the Jeep. "Get him in the vehicle, and let's get off this mountain."

For the first time, Singer stepped in front of the lights and locked eyes with his foe. After a wordless moment, our man of God said, "Coast Guard, huh?" Callaway didn't respond, and Singer slid a finger beneath his flex-cuffs. "Are those too tight?"

Callaway stared into Singer's eyes. "Jimmy Grossmann . . . I should've known. Where were you when you took the shot?"

Singer motioned up the slope. "Up there, about five hundred meters."

"That would make it what, a twenty-two, twenty-three-hundred-yard shot?"

Singer said, "Just under two thousand."

"Not bad," Callaway said. "And yeah, the cuffs are too tight."

Singer smiled. "Good. Now, get in the Jeep."

Chapter 17
A Burning Ring of Fire

We remounted the vehicle, and Clark made quick work of turning it around. Hunter sat behind me, Singer was behind Clark, and Callaway rode the hump with his arms stretched over his head, gripping the roll bar.

With the risk of being seen no longer a concern, headlights made the trip back down the mountain only slightly less terrifying. The ravine still loomed only inches from the left-side tires, giving Clark a show of the scenery unlike what he'd seen on the ascent.

"Is this the way you guys came up the mountain?"

"Wondering why you didn't see or hear us?" Hunter said.

"Yeah, a little."

"We were blacked out, and the wind was in our face. The traffic noise from below drowned what little sound we made. These are the things you'd know if you'd been a real sniper."

To Callaway's credit, he showed no reaction to Hunter's assault.

As we rounded the sharpest turn in the mountain trail, an assault of boulders big enough to wreck our Jeep cascaded down the slope and across the trail. Clark hit the brakes, barely missing a three-foot falling rock. Hunter and I instinctually pulled down our NODs, drew our pistols, and scanned the overhead slope.

Singer followed suit with the muzzle of his rifle and night-vision scope.

Still scanning, I asked, "What do you see, Singer?"

"Nothing. Whatever it was, I don't think it was human."

Callaway said, "You guys are jumpy. There are rockslides on this mountain every ten minutes. Some of them are caused by big cats, some by bears, and others just happen. It scares the hell out of you the first time, but after three or four an hour, the noise just becomes part of the environment."

A bowling-ball-sized rock came to rest on the trail a few feet in front of the Jeep, and Clark stood in the seat to survey the hazard. "If I can't clear it, I can push it out of the way with the bumper."

He carefully inched forward and eased the wheel ever so slightly to the left. The stone didn't contact the bumper or the frame, so we continued at a snail's pace until a second wave of falling rocks began their late-night careening down the slope. Simultaneously with the rockslide, the left side of the trail collapsed beneath the left front tire. A massive rock hit the top of the windshield, demolishing the glass, then came to rest on the steering column. The Jeep started rolling to the left as the trail crumbled beneath us. There was no possibility of saving the vehicle, so we lunged from our seats toward the right side of the Jeep and what remained of the trail.

I landed on the stony ground and finished the shoulder roll just in time to see Hunter's body come to a stop a few feet away. My NODs were nowhere in sight, but Hunter's skittered across the ground like a child's toy. I scarfed them up and shoved them against my eyes just in time to see Singer exiting the rear of the Jeep with his rifle bound in his arms.

The lights of the Jeep cut through the black night air like daggers as the vehicle rolled down the slope flanked by tons of falling rocks, gravel, and debris. Singer managed to get an arm around the trunk of a tree and stop his fall.

It was impossible to tell if Clark and Callaway made it out of the Jeep, but there were no options other than to follow the vehicle down the murderous slope and pray they'd gotten out.

"Are you all right?" I yelled toward Hunter.

He pulled himself to his knees and brushed off the snow and dirt. "I'm okay. Did everybody get out?"

"I can't tell about Clark and Callaway, but Singer is out, and he looks unhurt. Let's get down there and see how bad it is."

Hunter and I slid across the ledge and started down the slope in a semi-controlled descent. The terrain was absolutely unforgiving, and the roar of the tumbling Jeep spelled unescapable death for anyone who didn't get out.

We reached Singer, and I managed to get myself stopped, but Hunter kept sliding.

"Are you hurt?" I yelled.

Singer groaned. "I just knocked the wind out of myself, but I'm okay. I think Clark was pinned in, but I don't know what happened to Callaway."

"Hunter and I are going down. Catch your breath and get moving. We may need you and that rifle before this thing ends."

I pushed off and accelerated down the mountainside the same instance I heard the Jeep collide with something solid and come to a crashing stop. Our chase had just created its own finish line, and I was terrified by the thought of what I might find when I reached it.

To my horror, I watched orange flames split the darkness beneath me and begin growing into spires of heat and light. The scene created its own spotlights, eliminating the need for the night-vision devices. Hunter's silhouette rose between me and the flames fifty meters away.

Another form took shape beyond Hunter, and from my precarious, sliding position, it appeared to be the lower half of someone sticking into the air from the body of the Jeep. The legs—if that's what they were—kicked and twisted as if trying to find purchase on a surface that would never be there.

I kicked and pawed at the slope in a wasted effort to slow my descent. A fallen tree lay twenty feet in front of me, and it represented my only hope to stop my slide. I laid back and let the bottom of my boots strike the tree, using my knees to absorb the shock. I carried too much energy into the collision, and instead of stopping, I catapulted across the tree and came to rest in a bed of snow, rocks, and broken limbs. Thankfully, none of the limbs were mine.

Shaking off the collision, I stumbled to my feet, trying to make sense of the scene in front of me. The Jeep lay on its side with the headlights beaming away from me. The vertical appendages were definitely legs, but I couldn't tell whose torso was attached to the flailing limbs. Hunter leapt into the air and clawed at the Jeep's frame as the flames from beneath the hood continued to grow.

Shaken by the realization that someone was going to burn to death in the coming inferno, I sprang forward and crawled over the tailgate and into the demolished, burning Jeep that was on the verge of becoming a fiery casket. My ears rang, and my flesh tingled from the heat of the rising flames. The chaos of the moment left me barely able to focus on what lay only inches in front of me. Clark's limp form lay awkwardly slumping to the left while Callaway held my handler's head and neck firmly in his hands.

"He's pinned in by the wheel! Stabilize his neck while I work on getting him free."

The voice was foreign, but confident and commanding. Unsure who'd given the order, I wedged myself behind Clark's body and wrapped his head in my arms. If he were alive, supporting his neck could mean the difference between him walking again and spending the rest of his days in a wheelchair.

The fire continued to intensify as the scene grew clearer to me. Hunter wedged himself against the windshield frame and held Callaway's thighs as Callaway hung upside down working to free Clark's lower body from beneath the crushed, twisted steering column.

Willing myself to remain calm as the life of my brother literally rested in my hands, I demanded, "Is the jack still attached to the Jeep?"

Singer's baritone rang back. "I'm already on it!"

Seconds later, Callaway wedged the jack between Clark's feet and positioned the neck against the demolished steering column. The fire continued to rage only feet away beneath the twisted, unidentifiable hood, but none of us allowed the inferno to diminish our determination to free Clark from the vehicle.

"I need the jack handle!" Callaway yelled.

Singer scampered about in a desperate search for the steel rod that would hopefully allow Callaway to move Clark's prison bars.

"It's gone," Singer said, "but this should work."

Callaway craned his neck to look up at my sniper with the muzzle of his rifle suspended only inches from Callaway's grip. Their eyes met in a moment of understanding only two brothers-in-arms could know, and he took the rifle from Singer.

The muzzle slid perfectly into the hole designed for the jack handle, and Callaway pumped furiously, using the full length of the rifle as leverage. Metal tore and snapped beneath the force, and the flames danced into the night sky like a countdown to the Grim Reaper's approach. Every click of the jack felt like the second hand of the countdown of flames.

A moment would come when I'd be forced to give the order to abandon the rescue to save our own lives, but nothing about my team made me believe they would obey. Giving the order while blood still pumped through Clark's body was something I'd never have the stomach to do. Holding his head perfectly still could be the key to his survival, but I was forced to slide a hand from beside his face to his neck, praying I'd feel a pulse. If there was no pulse, I'd give the order to abandon the mission and escape the flames. If our brother, our friend, and our teacher lay dead with his head cradled in my arms, sacrificing our lives to free a corpse made no sense. So, I probed at the flesh of his neck with two fingers, desperately feeling for even the faintest pulse.

Callaway labored on, pumping the make-shift jack handle, seemingly oblivious to the danger he was in. The flames forced Hunter from the windshield frame to the back of the seat as he wrestled with Callaway's legs, pouring every ounce of strength and will into holding the sniper in position to continue his work.

Suddenly, an explosion split the air, and flames shot two dozen feet into the sky. Callaway jerked but didn't abandon his life-saving toil. Hunter turned to face the towering flames, and Singer yelled, "It was just the front tire exploding!"

Perhaps it was the explosion or Callaway's violent motion, but I felt something in the tips of my fingers pressed tightly to Clark's neck.

The horrific reality of our decision seemed to consume each of us simultaneously, and every eye turned to me. Sweat, blood, and determination poured from Callaway's inverted face as his tortured eyes asked the question no one could put into words.

"I've got a pulse," I lied.

Perhaps there was a pulse, but if so, I hadn't felt it. The motion I felt had perhaps been Clark's death rattle or the Jeep settling in the snow, but it wasn't the rhythm of a heartbeat.

Renewed by my lie, Callaway pumped the rifle with every ounce of remaining strength and stamina his body held until a crack sounded as if it had come from the belly of the Earth beneath us. The deformed steering column moved the final millimeter, allowing Clark's legs to swing free from their entrapment.

Hunter gave a mighty haul and pulled Callaway from his inverted position, depositing his exhausted body in the snow. The sniper scampered away, fearing the coming explosion when the flames reached the gas tank, but Hunter and Singer did exactly the opposite.

They moved with unimaginable speed to my side as we pulled Clark from death's determined grasp. I continued to stabilize his neck as Singer and Hunter bore the weight of his body until we were well clear of the burning vehicle. We gently laid him on the ground and collapsed beside his motionless form.

Panting like animals, we sat in the dancing shadows of the growing fire as plumes of mist billowed from each of our noses and mouths as, one by one, we caught our breath.

Each of us knew the moment would come, and finally, it did. The flames reached the fuel, and what had been a furnace became a hellish beast of orange flames consuming the darkness and roaring like thunder from a thousand storms descending on us from beneath infuriated heavens.

We raised our hands to shield our faces against the heat. Dangling from Callaway's wrist was the torn flex-cuff, and dancing on the night air, just beyond Clark Johnson's lips, were tiny puffs of condensation from his shallow but steady breathing.

Chapter 18
Welcome Aboard

Singer's deadly skill behind a rifle was challenged only by his prowess as a combat medic. He meticulously examined every inch of Clark's supine body lying on a bed of virgin snow.

"Other than a nasty bump on the noggin, I can't find anything wrong with him. Even his legs are okay and don't appear to be broken. I think he's just unconscious from a shot to the head from the roll bar or maybe the steering wheel. He's probably got a concussion, but it looks like Callaway saved his life."

Hunter pulled his knife from its sheath and handed it to Clark's rescuer. Callaway took the blade and buried the tip into the catch on the plastic flex-cuffs, freeing the arm and releasing the strap from around his wrist. He wiped the blade against his pants to remove the small droplets of blood that had fallen from his hand and then offered the knife back to my partner, butt-first.

Miraculously, my sat-phone was still in the cargo pouch of my pants, and I pulled it free. The small black-and-white screen showed three missed calls, so I scrolled through the list and selected the last of the three.

Disco answered within seconds of my signal bouncing around half a dozen satellites and finally finding its way back to Earth. "Are you guys okay?"

I said, "We took a little tumble, and pizza boy's Jeep got the worst end of the deal, but we have Callaway. Clark's unconscious, but Singer says it's likely just a concussion. We'll have to hump him out of here, but I'd rather get him back to the house than call in a medevac."

"That sucks for Clark, but I'm glad everybody else is all right. We saw the fire and tried to call several times, but no answer. We're on foot and moving your way. I'd say we're within a mile of your position now. If you can get Clark packaged up, we'll be there to help carry him out within an hour."

Callaway stood, turned up the mountainside, and took several strides away from the rest of us. Pistols came from holsters, and Hunter demanded, "Where do you think you're going?"

The sniper held up both hands, one of them still bloody. "Relax. If I was going to run, I would've done it while your old guy was pinned inside the burning vehicle. I'm looking for the doors to the Jeep. I noticed they were under the rear seat before we took the dive off the mountain. They'd likely make a decent litter if we can find them."

Hunter turned to me, and I gave a nod. He holstered his pistol and got to his feet. "I'll go with you just in case you get any ideas about turning into a rabbit."

Callaway said, "Rabbits don't last long out here. There are too many predators, and rabbits are tasty little morsels."

While Mongo and Disco continued their slow trek toward our position and the search for the missing Jeep doors continued, Singer knelt in the snow beside Clark and shone his light into each of Clark's eyes. The raging fire provided ample light for both Singer to see his patient clearly and the remainder of our team to find their way to our position. It wasn't exactly the star of Bethlehem, but it was definitely hard to miss.

Singer said, "I think he's coming around."

I spun just in time to see Clark's eyes flutter open.

Confusion ruled the moment he first shot his weary eyes left and right before finally turning his head in both directions in an effort to explain the scene to his brain. "What did you do, College Boy?"

"Oh, so now everything is my fault?"

His crooked grin replaced bewilderment. "You're in charge, after all, so even if you didn't do it, it's still your fault."

"Yeah, whatever, Sleeping Beauty. You're the one who drove us off a cliff."

"If I don't remember it, it didn't happen. How about briefing me up. It looks like it was quite a party."

The scene turned into story time with Singer as he replayed the events of the previous two hours.

"It's all coming back a little at a time for me, but where's the rest of our merry band of misfits?"

"They're on their way," I said.

"What about the sniper?"

"Believe it or not, he's the one who saved your life. He's out with Hunter looking for the doors from the Jeep so we can fashion a litter to carry your butt down this mountain."

"I don't think that's going to happen," Clark protested. "I've been carried off way too many mountains in my life. I'm walking off this one."

Singer gave him an arm, and Clark pulled himself to a sitting position. He squinted against the light of the fire. "Whew! This is a doozy of a headache."

Singer stood and grabbed Clark's belt in one hand and his arm in the other. "Let's get you on your feet and see if you can stand."

With considerable help from our sniper, Clark made it to his feet, but his knees were less than cooperative. After several minutes and a great deal of support from Singer, Clark walked in a relatively straight line without falling down.

Out of the blue, Clark asked, "Did you buy the helicopter?"

Singer laughed for the first time in hours. "I think he's going to be just fine."

Callaway and Hunter skidded back into our temporary encampment and held up only one Jeep door. "We were half successful."

Clark squinted, focusing on Doug Callaway. "Yep, it's all coming back. These guys said you saved my life."

Callaway shrugged. "Would you have let me burn up in the Jeep if the roles were reversed?"

Clark gave a slow shake of his head.

Callaway said, "Then no thanks are necessary, but we can square the tab if you'll pull my butt out of a fire when you get the chance."

"Consider it done," Clark said.

"Don't shoot!" came Mongo's resounding voice from the darkness. Seconds later, he and Disco took a knee to catch their breath. "That's some rough terrain. It's nice of Clark to join the party." Mongo motioned toward Callaway. "Is he the sniper?"

"He is," I said, "but he's a lot more than that. Without him, Clark would've probably died in *that* fire." I pointed toward the smoldering remains of the Jeep.

The big man seemed to mull over my story with a healthy dose of skepticism. "How do you feel, Clark?"

"I'm a little shaky, but I'll be okay."

"Like I said, there's nothing easy about the walk back to the house. You and I may have to play piggyback part of the way if you're not a hundred percent."

"I know an easier way down," Callaway said.

Every eye turned his way, and I said, "Let's hear it."

He motioned to the south—the exact opposite direction we made our way onto the mountain. "It'll add half a mile to the trip, but it's a pretty good trail, and that's not all. . . ."

We waited impatiently for him to finish.

He finally said, "My truck is parked about thirty minutes away."

Disco said, "Somebody needs to stay with this fire until it burns out. We don't want to be responsible for another wildfire in Yellowstone."

Mongo spoke up. "I'll stay here with Disco until it cooks itself into the ground. We've made the walk once in the dark. It won't be so bad when the sun comes up."

I didn't like the idea of leaving two teammates behind, but short of putting out the fire somehow, there were no other options. "Okay," I said. "We can blaze the trail for you and meet you at the trailhead in the morning."

Mongo pulled a roll of orange surveyor's tape from his pocket and tossed it to me. "Here. Blaze the trail with this. It's a little easier to see than machete scars in the bark."

I caught the tape. "Always the Boy Scout, huh, Mongo?"

He gave me a sharp, three-finger salute. "Always be prepared."

We followed Callaway to the south until we intercepted an animal trail through the timber. As we descended the mountain, the quantity of snow diminished, and the trail became easier to follow. I left pieces of orange tape hanging from trees every hundred yards and at every turn in the trail.

Clark's movement was slow but steady, and he planted his palms against his temples every few minutes.

I said, "Are you going to be all right, old man?"

"I hope so, but every step feels like a bass drum in my skull."

"It's not much farther," Callaway said. "My truck is just around the next bend."

We covered the remaining ground in twenty minutes, and I exhausted my supply of surveyor's tape just as the truck came into view.

"There it is, right where I left it. I'll be honest . . . I was afraid you guys might've found it and disabled it on your way up the mountain."

"If we *had* found it," I said, "it would be far less mechanically sound than you left it."

I put Clark in the back seat of the four-door Dodge pickup as Callaway climbed behind the wheel.

Hunter grabbed a fistful of Callaway's jacket and yanked him from the seat. "I don't think so, cowboy. You can ride shotgun, but I'm doing the driving."

"It's my truck," the sniper argued.

Hunter huffed. "No, it *was* your truck before you pointed a rifle at *our* house. Now it's *our* truck, and we'll let you know when —and if—we decide to give it back."

Callaway surrendered and climbed into the passenger side. When everyone was in and we were underway, the sniper motioned toward the rear floorboard. "There's water and rations in that bag if you're hungry or thirsty."

I pulled bottles from the bag and passed them around, carefully watching Callaway to make sure he was the first to drink. Protein bars and peanut butter made up the rations, but they were good enough to quiet our growling stomachs.

We bounced our way across the ever-flattening terrain until we reached a paved road leading east and west. Hunter spun the wheel and headed toward our rented house.

Sleep wasn't on the menu when we made it inside. It was time for 1600 milligrams of Motrin for Clark and the third degree for Callaway.

I started the inquisition with no time or tolerance for small talk. "Why do you think we're here looking for a mole on your team?"

"Because I've been doing what you're doing, except I've been at it for months. There's too much screwy stuff going on . . . We *accidentally* fail to make it home with a key piece of intel or hardware. Their former sniper died of a *supposed* heart attack in his sleep. It's a bunch of little things that don't mean much by themselves, but when you put them in a pile, they start to hum."

I scanned the faces of my team and saw the same question in each of their eyes. "Tell me about the previous sniper."

Callaway made a fist and straightened his wounded fingers several times. "You think I could get a handful of that Motrin and maybe some peroxide?"

Singer stood. "Come with me, and we'll get you cleaned up, but you've still got a lot of questions to answer."

They spent the next five minutes in the kitchen cleaning and bandaging Doug Callaway's hand while Clark, Hunter, and I huddled in the living room.

"Is he feeding us a line, or is this guy for real?" I whispered.

Clark glanced over his shoulder into the kitchen. "If he's lying, he's a master at it. I don't know what to think yet, but we should get Skipper to do some excavation into his past."

"Good plan," I said. "I'll get her on that."

I typed a text message into my phone.

Need deep background on one Douglas Michael Callaway, former Coast Guard sniper. ASAP!

On it, came her nearly instant reply.

Singer and Callaway returned to the living room, one of them bedecked with a bright white bandage on his right wrist and hand.

"Is that going to need stitches?" I asked.

"Not anymore," Callaway said. "Singer put in six of them already."

"You were about to tell us all about the sniper you replaced," Clark said.

The sniper uncapped a bottle of water and emptied it into his throat. "Yeah, about that. I've been with Brown's team for eighteen months. I'm sure you know Al Brown."

"We read his dossier," I said. "And if we were going to rule out any one of you as being the mole, Brown would be at the top of our list."

"Mine, too," he said. "He's a solid guy and a patriot to the bone."

"We're getting off track," I said. "Tell us about the other sniper."

Callaway cleared his throat. "I never met him, but he was a twelve-year Marine scout/sniper. Vince Tolley was his name. From all indications, he was a solid dude. He got out of the Corps on a medical after an IED took part of his left hand. The Marines were done with him, but he wasn't done with serving his country. At least that's what I heard."

I made shorthand notes as Callaway spoke.

"Anyway, I guess every team gets a sniper, but I don't know. I grew up in Idaho, so this part of the country is where I belong. They asked me if I wanted a team assignment up here, and I jumped at it. Now, I'm not so sure I made the best decision."

Another hour of questioning ensued until Callaway said, "I know I'm still the prime suspect, and I'll answer your questions until I'm hoarse, but I really need to hit the head."

"Go," I said. "It's down the hall on the right."

The four of us all took a knee and leaned in.

Singer whispered, "Is he really hitting the head, or is he running?"

"He's not running through that bathroom window," I said. "It's not big enough to shove a pencil through."

Singer shrugged. "Then I guess he's really using the head. Is he telling the truth?"

Clark glanced down the hall. "We'll know as soon as Skipper calls back, but we need to nail down the exact date he became the Montana team's sniper."

I said, "Great. Our plan is to keep asking questions to give Skipper time to work and get a good start date for him. Does everyone agree?"

Heads nodded, and Callaway returned from the latrine. "I hope I gave you enough time to come up with a plan to continue questioning me. If not, I can hang out in the head a little longer."

"No need for that," I said. "We had enough time, but thanks for the offer. We could play games all night, but we need to know exactly when you joined the team here in Montana."

"I came to the team in January of last year. They put me through my paces and made sure I could shoot and operate before they took me on a mission. My first real-world field operation was the second week of July. Since then, I've been on five assignments, not including this one."

Not including this one. Interesting choice of words, I thought.

"Of those five missions since the first one, how many weren't clean?" I asked.

Callaway ducked his chin. "Not clean? I'm not sure what that means."

Clark said, "How many of those missions had something about them that smelled like mole shit?"

"Oh," Callaway said. "Three. The first one was . . ."

We all leaned in, waiting for him to continue, but he didn't.

"What?" I said. "The first one was what?"

He frowned. "It's just that all of this is classified, and I don't know if you guys are . . ."

Clark took the floor. "Let me clarify your situation for you. We aren't investigators. We're assassins. And we have no intention of changing that on this mission. The mole is going back to D.C. in a box . . . or an envelope . . . and right now, we're thinking your remains will fit nicely in an extra-large UPS box. So, your choices are to talk or start trying on boxes. It's up to you."

Callaway took a long, deep breath. "My first mission was to stop the assassination of the Canadian prime minister. We did it, but the guy we killed turned out to be an office puke with the CRMP." The four of us sat in silence for a long moment, and the sniper said, "That's the Canadian Royal Mounted Police."

I said, "Yeah, we know what CRMP means. What we don't know is why you think some guy from payroll wouldn't necessarily be the threat."

"Because he cried like a baby when we caught him, and Toucan shot him in the neck during the interrogation."

"Toucan?" I asked.

"Yeah, Ted Snelgrove. We called him Toucan because of his nose."

"And what was Toucan's role on the team?"

"He was a general grunt, pretty good with a long gun, great with explosives, and not a bad medic. He's never afraid of a fight, and he's a little bit of a hothead sometimes."

"And why did he shoot your suspect?"

Callaway screwed up his face. "That's the thing. I don't know why he shot him. The guy was freaking out, but he wasn't a threat. We had him trussed up like a rodeo steer."

I raised an eyebrow. "Your man, Toucan, shot a suspect while he was tied up?"

"Yeah, that's what I'm telling you."

I didn't look away. "And Brown didn't have anything to say about it?"

"Oh, yeah. He beat the hell out of Toucan with his own pistol. I'm surprised he stuck around after that. Brown was pissed, but he didn't throw Toucan off the team."

Clark took over. "Let's move on. What else didn't pass the smell test?"

"This one is really messed up. We were security on a sea-going tug pulling a supply ship from the Aleutians to San Diego. Why they didn't put a team of SEALs on the boat, I don't know, but this one was another Toucan story. We stood four-hour watches, so we were on four and off eight, working as two-man details. It was like day thirteen or fourteen, and I was paired up with Cornbread—"

Singer held up a hand. "Wait a minute. Cornbread?"

Callaway chuckled. "Yeah, his real name is John Robert Dockery, but nobody called him by his name. In fact, he said only his mother and women he'd slept with called him John Robert because after a night with him, a one-word name just wasn't enough. I'll be honest. That freaked me out a little, but anyway, he's from somewhere in Georgia, I think, or maybe the Florida Panhandle, now that I think about it."

Clark reclaimed command of the scene. "Okay, we got it. The man's name is Cornbread. Go on with your story about the ship."

"So, we were on this sea-going tug, making five or six knots on a three-thousand-mile trip, and Cornbread got the screaming squirts. At the time, I thought it was from the slop they were feeding us, but none of the rest of us got sick, and Cornbread was fine by the end of the day. I said all of that to say Toucan volunteered to stand watch with me while Cornbread was splatter-painting the head. Toucan had just come off bow watch and said he'd rather be on the stern, if I didn't mind."

Clark snapped his fingers. "Pick up the pace a little, would you?"

"Sorry. Anyway, bow watch is windy and cold, so I didn't want Toucan sitting up there another four hours. I took the bow, and he took the stern. About an hour into the watch, I did my walk around from port amidships to starboard and back. When I glanced back, the crippled supply ship—or at least I thought it was the supply ship—was making smoke. The longer I watched, the more it became obvious that there was a ship astern of the supply ship and closing. Of course I hustled astern and pointed it out to Toucan, and he chewed me out like a boot camp recruit. I was still pretty new on the team, so I took it and returned to my post."

"Did you report it to Brown?" I asked.

"Absolutely! He told me he'd take care of it. I don't know what he said or did to Toucan, but that dude never said another cross word to me."

Clark checked his watch. "We're coming up on daylight, and I want to get my men off that mountain, so make this one quick."

Callaway said, "This one is the most detailed of the three, but here's the summary. We raided a den of Chinese operatives, and Toucan insisted on keeping the inventory book. When we surrendered the gear, everybody remembered nabbing two computers that somehow hadn't made it into the inventory log."

I said, "In all three instances, you claim Toucan is the problem. Did you know him before you joined the team?"

"No, I didn't know any of those guys until I got there last January."

My sat-phone vibrated, and I checked the screen. It was the ops center, so I stepped from the room and thumbed the button. "Tell me something good."

"It's not good or bad," Skipper said. "It's all pretty benign. Six years in the Coast Guard. Good clean record on a bunch of drug interdiction and human-trafficking missions. He's been to all the right schools, and his banking history looks exactly as it should. If he's the mole, he's hiding it well."

I called Clark and Hunter outside and briefed them on Skipper's intel.

Clark said, "I think he's clean. He's obviously got a beef with Toucan, but beefs are pretty common with type-A personalities. What do you think, Chase? You're the psych major."

"My gut tells me he's good. If he was the mole, he would've run while you were stuck in the Jeep. He knows these mountains better than the bears, and he could've vanished in the time we were fighting to get you out of the fire."

Hunter nodded. "I don't know. I tend to agree with you guys, but something just feels a little off. It'll come to me, but it's not enough for me to vote him off the island yet."

Clark turned for the door. "I'll babysit while you two talk to Singer."

Seconds later, Clark and Singer traded places, and we filled our sniper in on how we felt.

He listened intently, nodding the whole time. "I agree. I think he's clean, but I don't want you guys trading me for him."

"Not a chance," I said. "You're never leaving. You're the only hope the rest of us have on judgment day."

The three of us made our way back to the living room and gave Clark a nod.

He turned to Callaway. "Are you the mole, Doug?"

The sniper slowly shook his head. "I don't know for sure that there is a mole, but if there is, I can definitely tell you it ain't me."

"In that case, if he exists, will you help us find the mole?"

Callaway swallowed hard. "It doesn't feel right investigating my own team, but if there is a mole, he has to be stopped. I'll help you, but when all of this washes out, you've got to find me a home because this will destroy the team I'm on now."

Clark stuck out his right hand and then quickly withdrew, replacing it with his left.

Callaway stuck his non-bandaged hand into Clark's. "Welcome aboard. I'm Clark, he's Chase, and those two are Singer and Hunter."

Chapter 19
Now We're Huggers

The sun came up as it had done for eons, but this time it rose in the Montana Rockies on an exhausted team of tier-one operators who'd had no sleep for the previous twenty-four hours. The lack of sleep wasn't the only factor weighing us down. A mission of a scale nearing that of the Rocky Mountains themselves lay before us, a crippled piece of multi-million-dollar equipment sat helplessly only a few miles away at the local airport, and two of our now seven-strong team waited on the snow-covered slope of the mountain over which the day's sun had just taken its first breath.

Clark Johnson filled a coffee cup and popped two more Motrin into his mouth. "We've got to get Mongo and Disco. I'm too sore to bounce around out there again this morning, so I need a volunteer to go with Callaway."

I set my gaze on him and scowled. He got the message and backpedaled. "I'm sorry. What I meant was that Chase is going to assign a volunteer to go with Callaway to round out the rest of his men."

I gave Hunter the nod. "Callaway's truck is better suited for the job than our Suburban, so take it and him. Throw a couple shovels and rakes in the back just in case the fire's stubborn."

Hunter offered an abbreviated salute and stood. "Let's go, Callaway."

The sniper fell in step behind my partner. "There's no need to bring your shovels and rakes. I've got it covered, but I doubt we'll need them. There wasn't much in the way of flammable fuel around your Jeep."

"Oh, it wasn't ours," Hunter said. "We stole it from some pizza delivery guy."

Callaway checked Clark and me for any sign that Hunter was joking. He got none from either of us.

Clark took my arm as I turned to leave the kitchen. "Hey. Why Hunter?"

"Second-guessing my decisions, are you?"

He shook his head. "No, not at all. I just want to know what happened between your ears when you made the decision."

"That was an easy decision. I chose Hunter for two reasons. First, I know he'll shoot Callaway in the head if he puts any member of *my* team in jeopardy."

"You don't think Singer would do the same?"

"Oh, no, I'm confident he would. But the reason I didn't send Singer is a matter of psychology. I don't want our sniper getting too much information on Callaway this early. I want him skeptical, and I want him to watch him like a hawk. Singer will pick up on tiny cues that aren't exactly right from another sniper as long as he's not too close. Spending two hours in the cab of a truck might breed a little too much familiarity, leaving Singer to not pay attention as closely as I want him to over the next few days."

Clark gave me a wink. "You may have never worn a green uniform like the rest of us, but you know what makes a team work from your days in a baseball uniform. I've got more faith in you than you have in yourself, catcher. You've got nothing to prove to me except confidence."

I let his pep talk wallow around inside my skull for a few seconds before saying, "When freshmen catchers showed up, I watched them to see which ones were watching me. I was the starter because I did it right as far as Coach Woodley was concerned. The ones who thought they could bring their high school garbage onto the D-One field without learning from me rarely returned as sophomores."

I poured a cup of coffee as Clark mulled over my little speech. When I believed he had more than enough time to let it settle into his infantry brain, I said, "When Singer shoots, everybody on this team watches with absolute attention. When Hunter operates in the water, everybody starts to move like him. When you teach us how to end a fight, no one looks away. When Disco flies, I do everything I can to emulate his finesse. And Mongo, well, none of us can do what Mongo does, but when he picks up a Yugo, we all take bets on how far he can carry it."

"Speaking of Mongo, how's he handling the thing with Anya?"

I blew across my steaming-hot coffee and took a tentative sip. "On the outside, he's the same old tree trunk he's always been, but I think he's hurting."

"I thought so. Maybe you should pull him aside and spend a little shrink time tinkering around in his head."

I gave my best impersonation of Clark's crooked grin. "If I wasn't a psych major, I'd probably agree with you, but since I am, I'll give the giant what he needs. You handle me, and I'll handle my team."

He swallowed the last sip of his coffee and raised his mug. "You know, it's not easy stepping out of my role as an operator, but I'm glad I've got you to keep me straight."

I checked my watch. "I'm going to hit the sack for a couple of hours. If I'm not up by the time the rest of the guys get back, throw something at me. We've got a lot of work to do."

* * *

Sleep didn't come. Instead, it taunted me with moments of drifting near sleep with the jagged edges of reality pricking my peripheral vision. We'd taken on a temporary partner through inquisition and with the consent of every team member involved, but there was still something haunting me about letting Callaway inside the circle. In many ways, we were still hammering Disco into a shape that would fit in the puzzle that was our team . . . our family.

I wrestled with two distinctly different ideas concerning Doug Callaway, former Coast Guard sniper . . . whatever that meant. First, if he was the mole on the Montana team, he held the potential to be the highest threat to the safety of my team and the successful completion of our mission if he was on the loose. If he were the mole and we rattled his cage—and we obviously had with our midnight aggression on his mountainside position—he would perceive us as a clear-and-present threat to his freedom, and potentially, his life. Similarly, by bringing him onto our team, even if on the periphery, we could observe his behavior and truss him up the instant we saw something we didn't like.

If Callaway were not the mole, there's absolutely no chance I wanted him back in the loving arms of his team. First, he was too young and inexperienced to pretend my team didn't exist. He simply couldn't behave normally around his team, and Brown, the team leader, would pick up on the change immediately.

Every thought keeping me awake ended with the idea of Callaway's utility to my operation. He was a tool for me and my team. He gave us insight into the Montana team's psyche, operational style, capabilities, and perhaps most importantly, he gave us personality profiles of every member through casual conversation. If we were going to catch the mole, that's how we'd do it—by listening to subtle clues and accidental gaffes falling from Callaway's mouth.

Finally, something resembling sleep took me. Perhaps it was exhaustion or self-hypnosis, but my eyes closed, and darkness consumed me, but only for seconds. Instead of being allowed to sleep uninterrupted, I was yanked from slumber's embrace by the sound of two dinosaurs fighting—or perhaps mating—in the kitchen.

When I stumbled down the stairs, the sight in front of me was one of pure mayhem. A fountain of water rose from the kitchen sink where the faucet had been only a few hours before.

Standing in the shower of cascading water was our Jolly Green Giant with the faucet hanging from his enormous left hand. His eyes shot wildly between the geyser, the faucet in his hand, and me. With the innocence of a child, he said, "It was leaking, so I tried to tighten it."

I had only one choice, and that was to laugh. "Mongo, you could break a ball bearing with a glass hammer."

Seconds later, the spire of water subsided, and Callaway stood from beneath the sink. "There. I got it turned off, but there's no chance of repairing it. It'll have to be replaced. There's a hardware store about ten minutes away. I can have it fixed in half an hour if you don't want to get the owner involved."

I tossed Mongo a hand towel, and it looked like a washcloth in his hands. "I definitely don't want the owner involved. Let's get it fixed. Take Mr. Universe with you, and he'll pay for whatever you need to fix it."

The giant gave me a sorrowful look. "It's starting to look like I break everything I touch."

"That's not true, big man. It's just like Van Gogh said, 'Someone as beautiful as you isn't meant for a world like this.'"

Disappointment overtook him. "No, Chase, that's not how it goes, and it wasn't Van Gogh who said it. Don McClean said it *about* Van Gogh in the song 'Starry Starry Night.'"

I rolled my eyes. "How do you know this stuff?"

"Like I've told you before, I'm not just another pretty face."

"You'll always be a pretty face to me, Mongo. Now, go find a tent or something to dry off with, and get this sink fixed."

Callaway headed for the door, and Mongo mouthed, "Is he with us now?"

I checked over my shoulder and whispered, "Sort of, but keep an eye on him, and don't let him get away."

He gave me a wet thumbs-up and followed Callaway.

"Oh, one more thing before you go," I said. "Where's Clark?"

Mongo said, "He took Disco to look at a helicopter for some reason, but that's all I know."

* * *

By noon, we learned Callaway was a decent plumber, the kitchen floor had been mopped, and Clark was back from the airport.

Without preamble, I asked, "What did you think about the Four-Twelve?"

Clark offered an open palm toward Disco, so he fielded the question. "It flies like a Huey should. Everything is tight. The maintenance logs look good. There's no damage history, but I'm sure we'll change that, especially if you let Hunter fly it."

That earned Disco a jab with a fireplace poker.

Hunter said, "Sure, a guy wrecks one airplane, and the next thing he knows, he's branded a crash test dummy."

Disco shrugged. "If the shoe fits."

"The bottom line," Clark said, "is that the Board says they'll cover one million bucks, and the rest is up to us. So, I guess that means you've got some negotiations to work on."

I thumbed my phone and waited for Ratchet to pick up.

"Hey, Chase. I thought you might be calling. I met your guys out here this morning. Does that mean you want to meet Mrs. Templeton?"

"That's exactly what it means. Can you set that up for me?"

"Sure, I can. I'll give you a call back in a couple of minutes. When are you available?"

"I'd like to meet with her today if possible. Since our Caravan is down, I need something to fly, and we're sort of on a rare day off. We had a big night."

"All right. I'll call you right back. Oh, and tomato juice is good for that hangover."

"It wasn't that kind of night, but thanks for the tip."

I asked Disco, "What do you think it's worth?"

"Maybe a million six. It'd be a bargain south of that number, but I wouldn't think it would fetch more than one point seven five, even if it were on the market for a while."

Clark agreed. "I'd hit her at a million four and let her talk you up to one point five. I'll split it with you if you want a partner."

Disco said, "It would be a stretch on my finances, but I could borrow a couple hundred thousand if you want a third partner."

"How about this?" I said. "If I can put a deal together, both of you can consider it yours anytime you want it, but I'll eat everything north of a million."

Clark chuckled. "I won't try talking you out of that deal."

Disco held up both hands. "Me, neither."

I noticed Callaway listening in, so I gave him a look.

He asked, "Are you talking about the Four-Twelve the Templetons own at the airport?"

I nodded, but nothing more, and he got the picture.

Ratchet lived up to his promise. When I answered the phone, he said, "Mrs. Templeton will meet you at the FBO in thirty minutes. Bring your checkbook."

* * *

Grace Templeton wasn't the blue-haired widow-woman I'd expected. She stepped down from an Appaloosa mare in the airport parking lot in her boots, skin-tight jeans, and Western shirt. Before acknowledging me, she led the horse to a grassy area beside the building. The horse didn't seem interested in chomping on the still-dormant grass, but she stuck her head in a bucket of water beneath a downspout.

"You be a good girl, Ginger, and I'll be back in a few minutes."

The cowgirl clip-clopped across the parking lot and stuck her hand in mine. "You must be Mr. Fulton. For some reason, I pictured you being older."

Without any signs of makeup, she could've been a cover girl on any magazine on any newsstand anywhere in the world. I shook the offered hand. "As did I."

She blushed and toed the asphalt beneath her boot. "Yeah, Harold liked 'em a little younger, and they all loved him. That's probably what killed him. If it hadn't been the other women, it probably would've been me. There's only so much a Montana girl can take from one man—if you know what I mean."

I was left speechless and in search of anything to say, but she saved me. "You don't have to say anything. There's nothing to say that I ain't heard a thousand times. I'll be all right. I just need to turn some of Harold's toys into cash. We didn't have nearly the money he wanted everybody—even me—to believe. I ain't giving up the ranch. It's my own little corner of Heaven, but I'd sure like to get rid of that helicopter."

I held the door for her. "Come on inside where it's warm, and we'll see what we can do about taking it off your hands."

We sat in a pair of well-worn recliners in the pilot's lounge, and she started the conversation. "What kind of work are you in, Mr. Fulton? Ratchet said he wasn't sure."

"Please call me Chase, Mrs. Templeton, and I'm in the security consulting business."

"Come now, Chase. We both know that's what comes out of the eastern end of a westbound bull, but I'm going to let you get away with it. Just promise me you won't be using Harold's helicopter for anything illegal."

I couldn't stop grinning. "Yes, ma'am. I can certainly make you that promise. We're the good guys."

She inspected the lining of her felt hat. "That's what they all say, Chase. But we're not here to explore each other's résumés. I'm here to sell a helicopter, and you're here to buy one . . . unless you're just kicking tires."

"I don't have time for tire-kicking, ma'am. I want to buy your helicopter, and I've already paid Ratchet what he was owed for the engines and rotor blades."

She raised both eyebrows. "I guess you're not a tire-kicker after all. I'm not the kind of woman who beats around the bush. I've got about eighty thousand mouths to feed, from chickens to buffalo, and that doesn't leave time to dilly-dally. Do you have an offer for me, Chase?"

I hated negotiations that started that way. It is so much easier to negotiate when the seller is at least willing to define the playing field. "How much do you think it's worth, Mrs. Templeton?"

"Call me Grace, please. And I think it's worth somewhere north of a million dollars but south of a million three. Is that a big enough gap for you?"

"How did you reach that conclusion, if I may ask?"

"Of course you can ask. You just did. I came to that number based on the lowball offers the logging companies made and what Ratchet told me."

I nodded. "I think you missed the mark a little bit."

She frowned. "You're wasting my time and yours if you want it for less than a million dollars."

"I don't think you understand, Grace. It's worth more than you think, and I wouldn't be able to sleep if I took advantage of your situation."

"That's sweet of you, but by the looks of those bags under your eyes, sleep ain't something you get a lot of."

I instinctually rubbed my eyes. "We had a long night, and you're right. Sleep is a rare commodity in my world. I'm comfortable at a million four if you are."

She put her hat back on her head. "The rest of the world may need a contract two inches thick, but out here in Big Sky Country, a handshake means a lot more than ink on a paper some lawyer wrote. If you're sure about the million four, you've got a deal, and I've got to get back to work."

We stood and shook again.

I said, "As much as I love your idea of contract law, the FAA looks at things a little differently. I'll have a signed contract delivered to you this afternoon, and we'll close whenever you're ready."

"Close?" she said. "Does that mean you'll write me a check and I'll give you the keys?"

"Yes, ma'am. That's what it means."

"Come with me," she said, turning for the door.

I followed her back into the parking lot where Ginger still stood, patiently awaiting Grace Templeton's return.

The young widow opened a saddlebag and produced a manila folder and two sets of keys. "Here's a sales contract. We'll just fill in the blanks, and here's the keys. Ratchet has the other set. He's also got the maintenance logs. Harold always said those logs were more valuable than the helicopter itself."

"Harold was right, ma'am . . . except about thinking some other woman was better than the one he had."

She lowered her chin. "Women, Chase. Not woman. Women."

Using Ginger as a desk, we filled in the blanks and signed the bottom line. Jimmy, the lineman, witnessed the contract, and Penelope, the airport accountant, notarized it. I wrote a big check, we filled out the paperwork required by the FAA, and just like that, I was the proud new owner of a Bell 412 with brand new engines and blades.

I stuck out my hand for another shake, but Grace slapped it away. "Honey, you just wrote me the heaviest check I've ever seen, so that makes us huggers, not shakers."

Hugging was apparently one of Grace Templeton's greatest skills, and I felt like the check should've been a little heavier after the embrace.

I caught Jimmy before he headed off to pretend to be doing something important. "There's a couple of guys from Cessna who're coming to pick up my Caravan and ferry it back to Kansas. When they do, will you put my new helicopter in the hangar?"

"Sure, but you'll have to land it on the dolly. I can't move it on its skids."

"Come on," I said. "We'll do that now."

We fired up the chopper and hovered it to Ratchet's hangar, where its dolly rested, acting as a makeshift workbench for the mechanic. We cleaned it off, and I parked the 412 on the dolly as if I'd done it a million times.

Jimmy offered me a ride back across the airport on the tow, but I could've crawled faster than that thing ran.

Back at the house, Disco had everyone fed, and it was time to go to work.

Chapter 20
The Assassin Prays

"Find the pizza guy," I said. "We should buy him a new Jeep."

Singer piped up. "I'm on it. I kind of feel bad about that whole thing, so I agree."

The closest Jeep dealership was in Bozeman. Singer made a healthy deposit into an account with them and dialed up the pizza joint. "Hi, my name is Jimmy, and I'm looking for a delivery guy who works for you who drove a Jeep yesterday. Is he at work?"

"No, he didn't come in today, and we really needed him. He came up with some lame story about his Jeep getting stolen but not really. I didn't really listen, but if you think you can talk him into coming to work, I'll give you his number."

Singer took down the number and made the call.

Pizza boy said, "Man, this is all too out there for me. I don't know what's going on, but I don't like it."

"Don't worry," Singer said. "It's all taken care of. Just go up to Bozeman Jeep and pick out the one you want. Call me on this number if they have any questions at the dealership."

With all the housekeeping done, we reconvened in the living room, and I took the floor. "I know everyone is tired from a night without sleep, so although we're operational, the rest of the day is going to be light duty. If you don't already know, we now own a

Bell Four-Twelve. Clark, Disco, and I can fly it, and we'll teach anyone who wants to learn. Just like every other asset we have, the more people who can operate it, the more capable the team is."

The look on Callaway's face said his team didn't operate under the same standards. Having never been on another tactical team, I didn't know any other way to operate.

"Any questions on the chopper?" None came, so I continued. "I've made the decision—especially since we have a guest—that working the two operations simultaneously doesn't make any sense. We're stronger and more effective working together, so from this point forward, we're working one op at a time, and we'll start with Hannah June. Singer, I want you to get some sleep. I plan to stick you on the side of that mountain in a nest of your own. Pick your spotter, and we'll drop you in when you feel like you've had adequate rest to provide overwatch."

Singer nodded toward Callaway. "I want him."

I didn't expect him to make that choice, but I wasn't entirely surprised. No one makes a better spotter than another sniper.

Callaway's eyes darted around the room in obvious disorientation.

I said, "Let me guess. You'd like to know what the mission is, huh?"

"That might make all of this a little clearer for me."

I motioned toward the big screen television above the fireplace. "Roll that beautiful bean footage."

Singer connected the laptop to the television and started the show.

As the video played through our near collision and turned into a nausea-inducing melee, Clark's eyes turned to beach balls. "Who was flying? Nobody?"

Hunter raised a timid hand. "I would be the 'nobody' at the

controls, but stick with me. So far, there's no structural damage, but that's about to change."

The video rolled on, showing our definitive collision with the Yellowstone River and rattling the bones of my beautiful airplane . . . and everyone on board.

"That part was just for fun," I said. "Here comes the meaningful stuff."

The first time through the video, we watched in silence, then I had Singer pause and rewind to the start of the stable pass. "For Callaway's sake, here's the mission. There's a young woman likely being held against her will inside that compound. We're going to get her out."

He seemed to consider my position before asking, "What if she doesn't want to be taken out?"

"We'll ask her that after we get her out. Until then, we have only one goal, and that is to safely extract her without injury to her or casualty to our team, including you." He cocked his head as if unsure, but I cut him off before he could voice a protest. "You don't get a vote, Callaway. This is our mission, and it's what we're going to do. You're just along for the ride, right beside Singer."

"But what if—"

Clark started to take over, but I hushed both him and Callaway. "This is the mission, and there are no buts. Roll the tape again, and we'll brief the ingress."

Singer pressed play, and I talked us through the penetration of the perimeter. "Singer, you and Callaway will be on overwatch. No lead downrange unless it's to save our lives or Hannah June's life, got it?"

"We got it, boss."

I continued. "I suspect they're armed, at least to some degree, so we should expect some limited resistance. The rules of engagement are simple for this one. We get in, we find Hannah June, and we get out. No shooting except in defense against an unquestionable mortal threat. Break as many noses as you must, but don't launch any lead except to stay alive."

Heads nodded, and I downed a bottle of water before continuing. "Here comes the part I've been looking forward to. We will egress in two parties in two directions. Disco, you're only slightly taller than Hannah June, so guess who gets to wear the wig?"

Hunter winked at our chief pilot. "I've never been into older women, but I don't know . . . With some ponytails, you might be quite the looker."

Disco threw a couch pillow at him, but Hunter caught it and said, "I know how it is. You only pick on the boys you like, right?"

Clark cleared his throat. "All right, knock it off, knuckleheads. This is important. Go ahead, Chase."

"Hunter and I will exfil to the northwest with Hannah June. We'll blow the wall and head for this draw in the canyon, where we'll have staged one of the Suburbans. Mongo, Clark, and our girl Disco will make a show of running for the main gate. If they're unarmed, let them catch you and reveal Disco's little secret. That'll buy us enough time to get to the truck and reinforce the three of you."

Clark took a knee in front of the fireplace. "Hopefully, everything Chase just briefed will be unnecessary. If we can get in, grab the girl, and get out without waking anybody up, that's the best possible outcome. If, by some miracle, we pull that off, we'll all exfil through the main gate. Singer, you and Callaway will hike up and out. We'll pick you up on the ridgeline at first light."

I turned to Singer. "Bring up Hannah June's picture, and run through the iterations Skipper worked up."

He hit a few keys, bringing up a picture of an attractive young woman in her late twenties with shoulder-length blonde hair. "This is how she looked a few weeks before entering the compound." He clicked the mouse. "And this is how she might look today with a haircut and her natural hair color returning. I doubt they're giving away dye jobs behind those walls."

He ran through several more possibilities of how the former president's niece might look in the middle of the night through night vision. "She's five foot seven and weighed a hundred forty pounds ten weeks ago. I doubt she's gotten taller or shorter, but weight gain or loss is certainly possible."

"Any questions?" I asked.

Mongo said, "What's the contingency plan for casualties?"

"We're not expecting casualties, but if one of us goes down, somebody—preferably you—will carry him out. If it turns into a circus in there, we take absolute control. Nobody moves without our permission, and we search the house until we find Hannah June. If it all blows up, we centralize, disarm, and control, then find the girl and get out. Any more questions?"

Yawns and groans of tired minds and bodies answered my question. "Okay, that's it. Everybody hit the sack. Singer is our alarm clock. The rest of us are ready when he's ready. If you need something to help you sleep, I've got some meds."

No one asked for any help falling asleep, but Callaway didn't follow the rest of the team. He stood and held out his hands, palms-up. "Where am I supposed to go?"

"Follow Singer," I said. "For the time being, you two are joined at the hip, and there are two beds in his room. If you snore, don't fall asleep until after he does. I need him sharp tonight."

The room emptied except for Clark and me. "Nicely done, College Boy. I have more faith in you every day. Now, get some rest like you ordered your team to do. They're no good without you. I'll camp out here on the couch in case our guest of honor decides to make an exfil of his own."

Perhaps it was the confidence of knowing we had a definitive plan, and every member of the team had an assignment that brought merciful sleep for me that afternoon, but no matter what it was, I gave thanks to the God who hears the prayers of the assassin.

Callaway didn't run, and everybody, especially Clark, slept like the dead. Sometime after the sun sank into the Pacific, the front doorbell chimed, rousting me from sleep's padded cell. My watch said it was just past 7:30 p.m., so I listened for Clark to open the door and punch whoever had the audacity to wake him. But I never heard him move, so I crawled from my rack, pulled on a shirt, tucked my Glock into the back of my pants, and headed down the stairs.

I checked the sidelights flanking the front door but saw no one on the stoop or in the driveway. After drawing my pistol, I carefully opened the door, slicing the pie as I took in the environment in small wedges I could easily process, even in my post-sleep haze. No one was there, but headlights shone on the asphalt at the end of the long driveway.

On the top step lay six boxes, each about two inches thick and two feet square. I shoved my pistol back into my pants and lifted the boxes. When I placed them on the counter, I opened the top to reveal a beautiful supreme pizza with extra everything and crust like a down blanket. I read the handwriting inside the lid.

You guys are great, whoever you are. Thanks for the new Jeep!

It must've been the smell of the pizza that yanked Clark from dreamland—a task the doorbell couldn't do. "When did you order pizza?"

I shoved a piece into my mouth. "I didn't. It was a gift from some guy in a new Jeep."

Chapter 21
Saturday Night Fever

One by one, the remaining team members made their way down the stairs and dived into one or more of the gifted pizza boxes. Singer and Callaway were the last to show their faces.

I handed our sniper his first cup of the evening. "Good morning, sleepyhead. You must've crashed."

He checked his watch. "No, Callaway and I've been up for an hour or so. Since we've never worked together, we've been working some drills and streamlining our comms."

I checked across his shoulder. "What do you think about Callaway?"

Singer gave an abbreviated nod. "He'll be okay. He's not accustomed to shooting people yet, but that'll come. Apparently, the Coast Guard trains their snipers to take out boat engines from the deck of a helicopter. It sounds like fun to me."

"I don't want him on a gun," I said. "Just keep him on the spotting scope for tonight unless the world comes crumbling down."

"That's actually one of the things I want to talk with you and Clark about if you've got a minute."

I poured another cup and set it on the end table beside Callaway. "Welcome to the big leagues, junior."

He gave me a look, obviously uncertain how to reply. "It's just another day at the factory."

I snagged Clark, and Singer followed us to the study. Once inside, I pushed the door closed. "Here we are. What's on your mind?"

Singer examined the ceiling for a moment. "We've got a little problem. We used my Lapua as a jack handle last night, so there's no chance the barrel survived that stress. I have another barrel back in the armory, but not here. That leaves us with my Barrett fifty-cal and my three-oh-eight."

He paused to swallow a sip of coffee. "Anyway, I want both guns in my nest tonight, but that puts one of them on Callaway's shoulder. What do you think?"

I turned to Clark, but he only shrugged.

"You're the ringmaster of this circus, College Boy. Make a call."

I gave Singer's idea some thought. "What's the range from your nest to the compound?"

"Six hundred forty yards to the nearest wall, seven fifty to the main house, and nine twenty to the far wall."

"Whew, that's right at the limits of the three-oh-eight."

Singer said, "Yeah, it is, but they're my cartridges and my bullets, so I'm solid out to a thousand yards. They start dropping like a wounded Caravan after that."

I covered my heart with my palm. "Ouch. That stung a little."

"I'm just messing with you. Seriously, though, if I'm only taking one rifle, it'll be the three-oh-eight."

"In that case," I said, "put Callaway on the Barrett for materiel only. If we have to put anyone down—and I pray we won't—that'll be yours. And Callaway shoots only on your orders. I don't want him making any decisions up there."

"Got it," he said. "Let's go to work."

I put a hand on his arm. "Wait a second. Have you got anything, Clark?"

He shook his head. "I'm just the handler. This is your op. Run it the way you see fit."

Singer opened the door and headed into the hallway, and I turned to Clark, "I'd like your counsel."

His crooked grin showed up. "You're doing fine on your own, kid."

Back in the living room, a pile of empty pizza boxes littered the coffee table. "Well, you bunch of savages made short work of those. Anyone have anything to say before we strap up and go save the world again?" No one spoke up, so I gave the order. "Get these pizza boxes out of here so the bears will have something to play with, and let's mount up!"

Dressed entirely in black from head to toe, my team—plus one —looked like a swat team from a low-budget B-movie as we poured into the Suburbans. When we reached the West Yellowstone Airport, we looked like anything but Hollywood actors. Everyone had his game face on, and the joking came to an abrupt end.

"Disco, you're with me up front. Clark, you're on the door. Singer and Callaway, if we can put you on the ground, we will, but expect a fast-rope insertion. Mount up!"

The chopper came to life as if she'd been waiting twenty years to carry my troops into battle, and Disco turned into the colonel when he strapped into the left front seat.

We weren't light when I rolled on the throttle and pulled the old girl off the tarmac, but she gave no protest and climbed away to the northeast like a homesick angel.

The thirty-five-minute flight from West Yellowstone to Gardiner was uneventful as the new magic carpet and I got to know each other. I clearly had more faith in her than she had in me, which seemed appropriate. Making our first mission together in the dark, in the mountains, and under night-vision goggles was a terrible decision on my part, but I was making a pretty good career out of bad decisions that yielded good results, so changing the formula didn't make any sense to me.

Making the turn to the northwest over the Gardiner Airport, I started my scan for Singer's chosen spot. When it came into view, I pointed toward a sharp bend in the river. "See that spot where the river cuts back to the west?"

Disco leaned forward, following my fingertip with his glowing green eyes. "I got it."

"Singer's hidey-hole is directly above that bend about five hundred meters."

Disco took a long breath. "It's definitely steep in there. Can you keep us out of those trees and off the rocks for an insertion?"

"I don't know if I can do it, but I was sort of hoping you could."

"No chance," he said. "Not in the dark, in the mountains, in a new airplane. I might give it a try on a sunny zero-wind afternoon, but it's a death-wish maneuver under these conditions. Are you going to try it?"

I'm certain I made the decision in milliseconds, but for some reason, it felt like hours before I said, "No. We'll put them on the ridgeline. They'll have to hike in."

"Good call," he said as he peered out the window toward the ridge five hundred feet above our main rotor.

I pointed the nose up the canyon and started our climb. Disco flipped the switch to turn off the cockpit isolation in our headsets and briefed the snipers. "We can't put you in the nest, but we should be able to put you on the ground at the ridge. It doesn't look like we'll need the fast-rope."

"Roger," came Singer's response.

That's one of the things I loved most about working with him. When the mission was on, he was one of the most focused operators on the planet. If Disco had told him he'd have to hike twenty miles through blackberry briars in a swamp, his response would've been the same. I wondered if Callaway shared that mindset, but I doubted he'd be around long enough for me to find out.

As we climbed above the ridgeline, I made the long arcing turn to the south and glanced over my shoulder. "Sixty seconds. I don't plan to touch down."

Clark slid the door open to its stop and made room for the two snipers' gear and equipment to clear the opening. Singer and Callaway slung their rifles and packs and moved into the open doorway.

"Thirty seconds."

Before removing his headset, Singer said, "Thanks for the ride, Chase. We'll meet you back here at sunup."

I brought the chopper to a hover a few feet above the jagged terrain of the mountaintop.

Clark yelled, "Go! Go! Go!"

The two snipers stepped through the door, each with nearly a hundred pounds of gear strapped to their body, and hit the ground running.

Clark pulled the mic back to his lips. "Snipers away. Climb at will."

I pulled pitch and added enough left pedal to compensate for the increased torque and keep the machine from spinning beneath us. Clear of the ridge to the south, I lowered the nose and accelerated toward Gardiner Airport.

As the tension in my shoulders and arms relaxed from the hover work, the helicopter abruptly entered an un-commanded bank to the left. Shoving the cyclic to the right to arrest the roll rate, I expected the chopper to right itself and return on course, but no matter how much control input I made, we kept rolling left. The south wind blowing up the mountain slope was clearly stronger than the pair of jet turbines over my head. We had no choice but to ride the wave until it began its cascade down the lee-ward side and hope we had the energy to climb away.

In the calmest voice imaginable, Disco said, "Putting the nose in the wind might make things easier."

I crushed the right pedal and lowered the nose. And as usual, Disco was right. The main rotor clawed at the air until our altitude started building, and we slowly climbed through the ascending wind.

Back in control, I let out a sigh of relief.

Disco said, "Well, that was exciting."

"You know, you're welcome to get involved anytime I'm trying to kill us all."

He chuckled. "Ah, you weren't going to kill us. It would've all worked out, but we would've been descending at a pretty good rate when it calmed down."

I rolled my eyes. "Yeah, like I said . . . Get involved."

Gardiner Airport came into sight through my NODs, but I didn't call up the runway lights, opting instead to land under the goggles to draw as little attention as possible and save my night vi-sion. The landing was acceptable but not stellar, and I shut down the turbines on the small parking apron.

Clear of the chopper, Clark gave me a nudge with the butt of his rifle. "Find a little wind up there?"

"No, it found me."

"You did a nice job getting us out of there."

"I can't take all the credit. Disco threw in a little advice when things got hairy."

He elbowed our chief pilot. "Then thank God for Disco and ah . . . ah . . . ah . . . ah . . . stayin' alive."

"Get in the truck," I ordered. "You've got some real problems, and you need professional help. And a vocal coach."

With our snipers well on their way to digging in, the rest of the team loaded into the Suburban Skipper had staged for us at the remote airport. Off came our NODs as the headlights came on, and we hit the two-lane road through the canyon. We covered the fifteen miles in just over twenty minutes, putting us slightly ahead of schedule, so I turned to Hunter. "Get a comms check with Singer."

Seconds later, the sniper's voice filled my earpiece. "We're still moving in. It's slow-going up here. Everything that's not a tree is too slick to stand on, so we need another twenty minutes, at least."

Hunter said, "Roger. Advise operational."

"That gives us time to check satellite comms with the ops center." Just like E.T., Hunter phoned home. "Ops, Charlie-Two. Commo check, over."

Penny's West Texas drawl filled our ears. "Charlie-Two, Ops has you loud and clear. How me? Over."

Hunter said, "We'll be operational in one-zero minutes with open comms."

"Roger. Operational and open comms in ten."

I liked how Penny's voice sounded in my earpiece, but what I didn't like was the thought that she'd hear everything we said and did for the coming hour. She'd never been that close to an operation. The adrenaline, motion, and chaos of contact with an opposing force weren't things to which most civilians would ever be privy. I hoped she could handle it without freaking out. Thankfully, Skipper was there to prepare her for the excitement.

Clark backed the Suburban into a draw in a mountain crevasse and disabled the interior light. We waited as our snipers trekked to their perch from which they would watch and listen to every move we made as the hour hand swung ever closer to the witching hour.

We sat, silently playing out the coming night in our minds like professional athletes imagine their next game. Positive attitudes on the field made for high performance in the world of athletics, and on the real-world stage of tactical operations, anything less could send every operator home in a flag-draped casket.

"Charlie-Two, Charlie-Three Actual, and Charlie-Three-Bravo are operational, and we have eyes on you and the compound."

Something in Singer's voice didn't sound exactly right, but I couldn't put my finger on it. Perhaps he was winded from the slick hike into position, or maybe the mountains were messing with the radios. Either way, I didn't have time to psychoanalyze voice tones in the middle of the Montana night.

Hunter looked up, awaiting my command, so I gave it. "Let's roll. There's a girl on the wrong side of that wall, and we're going to remedy that. Light the strobes."

Doors flew open, and five operators hit the ground running with infrared strobes on each of our shoulders that emitted a pulse of light only visible through Singer's and Callaway's IR night vision. The technology not only made us easy to see, it also differentiated the good guys from the bad.

Our first hurdle was a ten-foot wall with two strands of barbed wire strung loosely at the top. Mongo picked up the pace and hit the obstacle at full stride. Our initial hope was that his mass times acceleration would equal enough force to prove Sir Isaac Newton's equation and tear down that wall, but the big man bounced off the structure like a rubber ball, so he changed tactics and spun with his back to the wall and his knees bent. His cupped hands made the perfect stirrup for Hunter. He sprang from the giant's palms, spreading a black moving blanket as he went. Defeating barbed wire requires a low-tech solution, and the blanket perfectly filled the role.

Hunter took up a position at the top of the wall, and I was next. Outweighing my partner by thirty pounds, I didn't envy Mongo's coming task. He didn't seem to notice and tossed me up the wall with little effort. Hunter and I spun around with our feet on the inside of the wall and our torsos toward our remaining teammates. Disco was the first over the wall. Mongo shoved him skyward, and Hunter and I eased him down the other side.

When he hit the ground, he reported, "Ground is soft. Keep coming."

No one responded, but Clark took a four-stride approach and stepped into Mongo's waiting hands. Knowing the ground to be welcoming on the inside, he bounded over the wall and landed in a perfect parachute landing fall and continuing onto his feet. He returned to the wall and grabbed my feet while Disco did the same for Hunter. With ourselves well anchored, Hunter and I lowered our hands and grasped Mongo's wrists. The goliath of a man climbed the wall using our grip as he came. We pulled with all our strength to heave Mongo's three hundred pounds over the top of the wall. His landing wasn't as graceful as Clark's, but he was quickly on his feet and pulling security while Hunter and I dismounted our perch.

For some reason, I looked skyward, perhaps thinking I might catch a glimpse of the satellite that would carry my next words through space and time. "Ops, Team is inside and continuing mission."

"Roger," was Penny's only reply.

Singer's baritone voice rolled through my earpiece. "Charlie-One, Charlie-Three Actual. If you approach the main house from the north, we'll be blind for the first seventy-five meters."

"Roger. We'll make our approach from the southwest," I said, still detecting something I didn't like in Singer's voice.

We moved in a wedge formation with our weapons at the low-ready position. The damp ground made it impossible to move silently, but we made no more noise than absolutely necessary. Hunter played scout and moved ahead of the rest of the team. He pressed himself against the southern exterior of the main house and peered through every window he approached, shining an IR light in each one that was invisible to the naked eye but glowed like the sun through our night-vision equipment.

He whispered, "It looks like the first floor is all common space. Sleeping quarters must be upstairs. I've got one stairwell at the west end and one along the northern wall at the front. No motion on the first floor."

I said, "Roger, we're moving in."

Continuing our wedge formation, we approached the front porch of the structure. Clark cautiously climbed the icy stone steps and tested the planks of the decking. Nothing creaked, so he continued across the porch and knelt at the door.

I whispered, "Ops, we're making entry through the front."

"Roger."

Clark pulled his pick kit from his cargo pants and paused just before sliding the tensioner into the lock. His frozen position made me suspect he heard movement beyond the door, but I was soon proven wrong. Seconds later, he reached up and gave the knob a twist. It turned easily in his hand, and he pocketed the picks.

We moved one by one across the same planks Clark tried, and we entered the front of the structure.

"We're in."

"Roger."

Moving in teams of two, Disco and Clark took the north wall while Mongo and Hunter took the south. I moved silently through the center of the vast open space of the first floor. A makeshift chapel, complete with a pulpit and baptismal, consumed most of the space, and a large, industrial-style kitchen made up the western third. I motioned for Hunter and Mongo to take the back stairs, and they followed my hand signals in silent strides up the wooden treads. Mongo's bulk rarely allowed for silent movement on stairs, but I never heard a sound as they ascended.

With the first floor clear, I moved into position with Clark and Disco. My handler took point, and I slipped between him and Disco. The pilot's lack of tactical experience placed him in the rear, well clear of the fight, should one break out.

Reaching the top of the stairs, I gave two clicks with my tongue to alert Hunter and Mongo we'd arrived. Hunter returned the sign.

The front portion of the second floor was an open-bay barracks-style arrangement with thirty to forty bunks. We moved through the environment littered with snores and sighs. About half of the beds were occupied, but only by men. If Hannah June Meriwether was in the house, she wasn't in that room.

We moved from the sleeping quarters across the common area in the center of the second floor and discovered a large communal shower with a dozen sinks and at least as many stalls.

At the western end of the structure, we found a carbon copy of the men's bay filled with non-snoring sleeping figures, but the barracks of slumbering women is not what nearly stopped my heart.

Mongo and Hunter stood motionless across the room with their backs pressed tightly against the north wall, and the ghostly form of a nightgown-clad teenage girl carrying a candle moved silently through the room.

Chapter 22

Wrong Place, Wrong Time

The candle-bearing girl continued her movement through the bay and directly toward Clark, Disco, and me. She was clearly making her way to the opening through which we'd come only seconds before. A late-night bathroom call was about to end in a moment the girl would never forget.

Clark motioned for us to retreat, so I reached for the wall behind me to retrace my steps back into the common area. Disco's first move was with his feet instead of feeling for the opening. His first step was clumsy and sounded like an explosion inside my head. I froze as the girl raised her candle in our direction and said, "Who's there?"

Light discipline is a skill most people will never develop. Holding a burning candle in front of one's face in hopes of seeing across a room is ludicrous, but that's precisely what she did.

I reached out and took Disco's wrist in my palm and pressed his hand to the door casing. He continued with cautious strides through the opening until all three of us were clear of the bay and tucked neatly into an alcove barely large enough for us. We were seconds away from being discovered, but Clark and I had an unspoken plan from our days of operating. The feeling was like an old familiar chair—comfortable and predictable.

As the girl continued toward the door, we watched her every stride and anticipated each other's coming movement. The instant she stepped through the opening, the candle's light rewarded her eyes with the terrifying sight of three men in full tactical gear, night-vision goggles, and rifles.

In moments like that, a sane human has one of three reactions: fight, flight, or freeze. I had my doubts about the sanity of the people inside the compound, so predicting the girl's reaction was impossible. Thankfully, though, her subconscious mind chose flight, and flight is something we were well-prepared to deal with.

Before a person screams, the most primitive part of our mind, the hippocampus, forces our diaphragm to contract, filling our lungs with air. All of that neuromuscular activity takes about a third of a second. That was more than enough time for an old pair of commandos to take control of the situation.

We leapt into action. Clark covered her mouth with his right hand and cupped his left around the back of her head, effectively stifling the coming scream. I knelt before her and caught the candle falling from her hand. The only thing worse than the girl screaming and waking everyone in the building would be for us to start a fire. We would not let the night turn into another Waco.

Controlling her head, Clark pulled her body against his, and I sank the syringe I'd pulled from my pocket into her thigh. Her adrenaline likely prevented her from feeling the needle, and I was able to empty the tranquilizer into one of the largest muscles in her body without making a sound. The drug was far from instantaneous. It would take several seconds for it to work its magic, especially with gallons of adrenaline flowing through her.

Clark pressed his lips to within centimeters of her ear and whispered, "If you make a sound, you'll be dead before you hear your own voice. Understand?"

She nodded, but defiance rose inside her, and she lifted a foot to kick the wooden floor, trying wake her sleeping cohorts and turn my operation into a train wreck. I caught her ankle in my palm and shoved her heel into her other ankle, making it impossible for her to kick with either foot.

I felt the tranquilizer begin its sinister work when the muscles of her legs softened, and the knee of the only leg still planted on the ground buckled. I caught her in my arms and hefted her noodled form against my chest. Walking silently with an extra hundred pounds isn't easy, but I had no other choice.

I crossed the floor and made my way back into the men's bay. Believing I'd gone as far as I could without waking the snoring throng, I laid the girl on one of the unoccupied lower bunks and pulled the cover across her body.

As I stood up and turned for the doorway, I was pleased to see Clark and Disco covering the exit. With the disaster averted, we moved with practiced stealth back to the women's bay. The five of us crept through the bay, checking every face against the photographs we'd studied. Of the thirty women in the bay, one of them had to be Hannah June Meriwether, and we were determined to find her.

Our search continued for eight minutes, with each of us double-checking the bunks the others had already checked. There were women of every imaginable description, from petite homecoming queens to obese grandmothers who probably made better waffles than even Disco, but no matter how hard we looked, there was no Hannah June.

I gave the cutting motion across my throat, signaling I was calling off the search. The team formed a single-file line behind me, and we moved to the forward set of stairs. We moved in relative silence until we were through the front door and back on the lawn.

I said, "We're clear of the house. No joy on the objective. We're moving for the front gate."

"Roger," came Singer's reply.

Penny whispered, "Did you kill that girl?"

Clark said, "No, we just rocked her to sleep and put her back in bed . . . Just not her bed."

We formed up in a wedge for our egress, and Hunter pulled rear security. No one came from the house as we moved toward the gate, and I held up a fist as we approached the only bottleneck on our exfiltration route.

"Charlie-Three Actual, are there any sentries on the gate or vehicles approaching?"

"Negative, Charlie-One. The coast is clear."

I definitely heard it that time. Something was wrong with Singer, and the second we were clear of the compound, I had to know what it was. Lowering my fist, I moved forward toward the gate. When I heard the tell-tale click of a motion-activated switch, my heart thudded to a stop. Before the team could take cover, we were struck with a beaming floodlight mounted high above the gate. In the same instant that the five of us dove for the shadows, the light exploded, sending shards of glass in every direction. A second later, the report of Singer's 308 rang through the night air, proving the theory that a target is dead, long before he ever hears the sniper's shot.

Across the gate we went and hit the asphalt at a sprint. Running our own cut-down version of the Mogadishu Mile, we slid onto the seats of the Suburban three minutes after climbing the gate.

I caught my breath and poured a bottle of water down my throat, but the instant I could talk without gasping, I abandoned the tactical call signs. "Hey, Singer, are you all right?"

"I will be," he said. "But I won't make it back to the ridgeline. Callaway and I got tangled up setting up our nest, and I think I may have broken my ankle."

I clamped my eyelids closed and groaned. I wanted to scream. First, our objective wasn't inside the compound, and now our sniper had a broken ankle. Forcing my brain to stay inside my skull, I tried to sound calm and under control, but what I felt boiling between my ears was far removed from both calm and controlled. "Get yourself into a Swiss seat and teach that Coastie to tie his own. I'll put a rope in your lap in twenty-five minutes."

Clark crushed the accelerator, and the rented Suburban fishtailed before finally finding purchase on the asphalt. The drive that had taken twenty minutes from the airport took less than ten getting back.

The Green Beret behind the wheel slid the Suburban to a stop six feet from our chopper, and I gave the assignments. "Clark, you're on the door again. Disco, you're up front with me. Mongo and Hunter, I want the two of you back on that compound, but keep your comms open. Watch for anything or anybody coming or going. I'm going to fly our snipers off that mountain and put them in the field a mile east of the compound. When you see us coming, get down there, put some light on the ground, and talk us down. Got it?"

The turbines were spooled up, and the three of us were airborne before Mongo and Hunter made it back to the highway in the Suburban. Clark rigged a rope with a pair of IR chemlights on the loops containing the carabiners. As we approached the sniper's nest, frigid air filled the cabin of the chopper when Clark slid open the door.

"The rope is out, but the wind is too strong. We'll never be able to put it in their hands."

Disco said, "Haul it back in, and hang a sandbag on the end of the rope."

Clark hauled the heavy rope back aboard, hand over hand, and scoured the cabin in search of anything resembling a sandbag.

"How about a seat?" he asked. "I'm a little short on sandbags back here."

"Anything heavy will do," Disco said.

Clark pulled the pins from the rear seat and tied the rope to its frame. Out the door it went, and when it came to rest, the rope was as straight as an arrow and hanging directly beneath the chopper.

I eased up the slope, approaching Singer and Callaway with every ounce of skill I could force from my hands and feet. The wind was torturous and ever-changing. Holding the helicopter in a hover was like trying to stand on a basketball with one foot . . . while drunk.

Disco asked, "How many times have you done this?"

Still concentrating on the task at hand, I said, "Counting this time, it'll be one."

I felt his hands and feet join mine on the pedals and cyclic.

He confidently said, "I have the controls. You monitor our torque, and Clark, you talk me into the nest."

"You have the controls," I said with more relief than my tone implied.

The wind from the rotor wash roared through Clark's microphone as he hung the upper half of his body out the door with the rope in one hand and both eyes scanning everything in sight. "Up thirty," he yelled, and Disco gently increased our altitude precisely thirty feet. "Left fifty!"

Just as he'd convinced the helicopter to obey his command to climb, Disco slipped us sideways, and Clark called the countdown.

"Thirty . . . Twenty . . . Ten . . . Easy . . . Easy . . . Hold! . . . Ahead fifteen."

Disco lowered the nose almost imperceptibly, and the heavy machine inched toward the mountainside. His command of the chopper was like nothing I'd ever seen.

Suddenly, the nose plummeted, and we closed on the granite face of the mountain like a charging bull. I raised my arms against the coming collision, but Disco saved it by some miracle. We were climbing and retreating. When I focused back on the instruments, the torque needle climbed into the red.

I said, "Over torque! Over torque!"

"It doesn't matter," Disco said. "I have to stay out of the down-draft."

As we retreated, the needle left the red and returned to the much-friendlier green arc.

Disco pulled his hand from the collective and wiped the sweat from his face. "Okay, Clark, let's try it again."

"Up ten."

Disco and the helicopter obeyed.

Clark said, "Ahead twenty."

Training my eyes on the treetops, desperately searching for any sign of another downdraft, I forced my eyelids to resist the over-whelming urge to blink.

"Easy . . . Ahead five . . . Easy . . . Hold!"

Disco froze the controls, and the chopper felt like it was sitting on the ground. Hovering only feet from a sheer mountain face at high altitude, in the dark, under NVGs, our chief pilot made it look like an afternoon in a recliner.

Singer said, "We're on. Callaway is on top."

Disco replied, "Expect up and back. When we turn away from the mountain, get both hands out to stabilize yourselves, or you'll spin like a top."

"I got you, Disco. I've done this before, but never in the middle of the night . . . with a broken ankle."

Up and back we went until Disco turned for the field, and the lights of the Suburban hit the meadow. We came to a hover fifty feet in front of the truck and slowly descended.

Hunter made the calls. "Thirty . . . Twenty . . . Ten."

Disco skillfully urged the collective a millimeter higher, and Singer's good foot kissed the ground like a butterfly. Hunter unclipped the sniper and threw him over his shoulder. By the time Callaway was on the ground and unhooked, Singer was in the back seat of the Suburban and already strapped in.

"Get that rope in," Disco ordered.

Clark hauled with all his might until the makeshift sandbag seat landed on the deck. Spent, he slid the door closed. "Gear is inside."

It was time for Disco to show me what our new flying machine was capable of doing. We hit 120 knots and never got above fifty feet off the deck. We beat Hunter to the airport, but only by two minutes.

Two minutes after that, the whole team was aboard, and the nose of the Bell 412 was pointed directly at the emergency room in Bozeman some forty miles away.

Chapter 23
Ballistics 101

Disco was on the controls, and I was on my knees in the helicopter cabin, where my friend, spiritual advisor, and team sniper lay with the toe of his boot pointing in the wrong direction. Doug Callaway, our captured—or borrowed—sniper from the mole-infested Montana team, knelt with one knee on each side of what used to be Singer's ankle.

The Coastie withdrew a pair of medical shears from our trauma bag and sliced into the leather and laces of Singer's boot. With the worthless footwear tossed aside, Callaway said, "This is going to hurt, Jimmy. Tell me when you're ready."

When most men would be flailing like a fish and cursing with every breath, Jimmy "Singer" Grossmann took a long, full breath, pulled the collar of his jacket between his teeth, and nodded like a rodeo cowboy ready to explode from chute number two aboard a two-thousand-pound Brahma bull.

Callaway threaded one hand around Singer's heel and the other over the top of the swollen, discolored foot, and leaned back. The sound of the bones grinding inside the demolished former weight-bearing joint was louder than the turbines and rotor screaming above my head. Singer let go an animalistic groan from somewhere deep inside his soul, and I watched his eyes roll back in his head.

He fought off the demons dragging him into unconsciousness, swallowed hard, and released the cloth from between his teeth. By the time our sniper caught his breath, Callaway had the splint in place and wrapped tightly with the green, elastic tape from the med bag.

With the broken bone—or bones—set and splinted, Callaway tossed me a vial and syringe. I drew up enough morphine to make the choir director see the angels dancing around his head, and I slipped the needle into his upper arm. The warm narcotic flowed through his body and replaced at least a portion of his pain. The relief shone in his eyes, and he exhaled through pursed lips and chipmunk cheeks like Louis Armstrong playing the trumpet on Bourbon Street.

The tunnel-vision focus an operator experiences when a mission falls apart is one of the deadliest conditions any tactical commander can experience. It happened to me. The only thing I saw, heard, or acknowledged in my world was lying—now intoxicated—beside me with a surgery, cast, and months of recuperation in his future.

Penny's voice yanked me from my tunnel. "Uh, Chase . . . I mean, Charlie-One. Is everything okay?"

Another cardinal rule had suffered a terrible fate by my hand. I failed to keep the ops center apprised of what was going on. Completely blind, with only ears to experience the action, I imagined Penny and Skipper on the edge of their seats.

"No, everything is not okay. We're on our way to the hospital in Bozeman. Singer broke his ankle on the side of the mountain, and Hannah June was not inside that house."

Penny surprised me with her operational reply. "Roger, Charlie-One. We're on the phone with Bozeman Medical Center now. The helipad will be lit and gurney waiting. Run it on your Secret Service cred-pack. Over."

I'd expected a thousand questions and an outpouring of concern, but Skipper had obviously prepared Penny for the scenario. I found myself wanting to turn the conversation into a moment of affection, but her professionalism reinforced mine. "Roger. Close the open-channel comms. I'll report when we know more. Charlie-One, out."

The electronic click in my earpiece was the only audible indication that I was now disconnected from the world outside the helicopter.

"Hey, Disco. Did you copy Penny's transmission?"

"Affirmative, Chase. We'll be on the helipad in four minutes."

Disco missed his estimate, but not by much. Five minutes later, the rotors were whining to a stop as a pair of orderlies tried to pull our sniper from the chopper. Mongo didn't approve. He elbowed them aside and hoisted Singer from the chopper, depositing him on the gurney as gently as a proud new poppa lays his baby in the crib.

Hunter and Clark flanked the rolling gurney like a rock star's bodyguards as the orderlies rolled Singer through the sliding automatic doors of the ER. I trailed only a few paces behind with my cred-pack. An admitting nurse stepped into our path and held up a hand. She started to say something like, "You can't go back there," but Hunter encouraged her to step aside. I stuck my Secret Service badge in front of her trifocals and kept walking.

The practice of medicine, especially emergency medicine, appeared fraught with inefficiency and unnecessary paperwork. It took longer to answer the nurse's questions than to wheel Singer into surgery.

An armed tactical team clad in all black is hard to ignore, especially inside the sterile confines of a hospital, so I said, "I'll stay with Singer while you guys guard the helicopter."

"Guard the helicopter? Is that the best you could come up with, College Boy? You could've just said, 'Wait outside so Action News at Eleven doesn't get footage of us raiding the Bozeman ER.'"

I gave Clark a shove. "Okay, then, do that. I'll let you know when he's out of surgery."

Pulling off my jacket, overshirt, and hat, I shoved the pile of laundry toward Hunter. He caught it and reached for my sidearm. When I was disarmed and half undressed, I looked more like a local militia leader than a G-man commando, and in the wilds of Montana, that's a pretty good look.

A surgeon wearing freshly laundered green scrubs approached and sat beside me. "I assume you're Special Agent Fulton. Nobody else in here looks the part."

I stuck my hand in his. "Call me Chase."

"Okay, Chase. Your agent is going to be fine. There are two bones in the lower leg—the tibia, that's your shin bone, and the fibula, which is the smaller of the two and more prone to fracture. At the end of the fibula is the lateral malleolus. That meets the talus to make up the ankle. Your agent fractured both his talus and his fibula, just above the lateral malleolus. The breaks were clean— not at all like I would expect to see from a fall. The injuries looked more like the result of something quite heavy being dropped onto the side of the ankle while the foot was firmly planted on a hard surface. The sports medicine guys see this kind of injury in the legs and ankles of football linemen. Anyway, we were able to repair Agent Grossmann's injuries, but I'm afraid he won't be doing any fieldwork for a while. You'll have to assign him a desk job for three months or so. Do you have any questions?"

"When can I see him?"

The surgeon checked his watch. "They'll be waking him up any minute, and he'll be in recovery for a couple of hours. Come on back. I'll show you where he'll be."

I followed the doctor through a series of double doors and a labyrinth of corridors until we came to a room labeled "Surgical Recovery." The surgeon strolled into the room as if he were the king of the court . . . and perhaps he was.

"There he is," the surgeon said, laying his hand on Singer's arm. "How are you feeling, Agent Grossmann?"

Singer shot me an anesthetic-induced, glassy-eyed gaze, and I gave him a knowing "play the game" nod. The sniper gazed up at the man who'd just put his ankle back together. "I feel great. I'm ready to go back to work."

The doctor chuckled and explained the technical surgery to Singer in terms no layman could possibly understand, and I saw it coming: my sniper was about to toss out a zinger.

"Sure, doc. That sounds just like the formula for calculating the ballistic coefficient for small arms, where the ballistic coefficient is used in point mass trajectory from the Siacci method – of course, that's less than twenty degrees—and is equal to the mass of the projectile divided by the square of the measured diameter of the bullet times the coefficient of form. And, of course, the coefficient of form can be derived by six different methods, but as everyone knows, there's a seventh method that's more complex but ultimately far more accurate. Depending on the trajectory model used, each of the six—or seven—methods are applied differently. The G model and Beugless/Coxe model are, of course, the gold standard, except at high altitude."

It was the doctor's turn to glaze over. "What's he talking about?"

I shot a thumb toward my sniper and one of my favorite people on the planet. "He wants to know if you fixed his foot, doc."

"Yes, I fixed your foot, but you're going to be on crutches for a few weeks. We'll send in the physical therapist to teach you how to use them before we release you tomorrow afternoon."

Singer looked up at me, clearly expecting me to release a zinger of my own, so I didn't let him down. "Doc, this man knows more about crutches than he knows about ballistics. Would you like for him to explain them to you?"

"No, that won't be necessary."

I threw an arm around the surgeon's shoulders. "Good. Now you can sign his discharge paperwork, and we'll be out of your hair."

"I'm afraid he'll have to remain in the hospital . . ."

I gave him a squeeze. "In that case, he's leaving against medical advice. If we feel he needs more quality time with you, we'll bring him back. Thanks for your help, doc. Uncle Sam will foot the bill for this one, and I'm sure it goes without saying that seven armed commandos were never here tonight."

We loaded our cast-clad sniper back on board the chopper and touched down at the West Yellowstone Airport less than an hour after a drowsy physical therapy tech handed Singer his shiny new crutches.

Mongo carried Singer across the threshold as if a clergyman had just pronounced them man and . . . whatever . . . and we settled into the living room for the after-action review.

I took the floor. "All in all, the night was a hundred-car banana train wreck in a swamp. Everything went wrong, and we're going to figure out why. Failure point number one was bad intel, and there's nothing we can do about that. The Board fed us what they thought they knew, and they were wrong. It happens, but no one had any doubt that Hannah June Meriwether was inside that compound. We should've been told she was *believed* to be inside the compound instead of being told she *was* inside the compound. I'll eat that one. I should've asked more questions."

I paused to get some water down my throat. "Thing number two is that we suffered a casualty on an op where nobody should've gotten so much as a broken fingernail. Now we're down a man. Everybody is crucial, but our sniper, for God's sake . . . No one is more crucial than him. Tell us what happened up there."

Singer eyed his brilliant white cast. "It was just an accident, Chase. Everything was frozen, and the nest I chose wasn't big enough for two of us. When I spotted it, I was only looking for a one-man hole. When you put two men in one little nest, they're going to get tangled up. That's what happened, and I came out of it on the losing end. It's as simple as that."

"I don't like it," I said. "But what's done is done. Nice shot on the light, by the way. That had potential to get real ugly real quick. Good thinking and good shooting."

Singer nodded.

I continued the review. "All of you, except Callaway, know me well enough to know I always claim the blame, and tonight is no exception. I put us in a nasty position on top of that ridge and al-most got us all killed. I've spent the entirety of my flying life in the Southeast, where we don't have mountains that produce wind like we encountered up there tonight. Disco got us out of the coffin I tried to throw us into, so we owe him a case of whatever he drinks."

Disco shook his head. "You didn't have us heading for a coffin, Chase. It was just a new learning experience for you. I was glad to help."

"Now, let's talk about the helicopter. I think we saw tonight how it dramatically increases our capabilities. Getting Singer and Callaway off that mountain would've involved a lot of people we don't want meddling in our business if we hadn't had the chop-per. I think it was worth every penny. Does anyone have anything more to say about the chopper?"

"It needs a winch," Singer said. "Flying around dangling from a rope isn't nearly as much fun as it sounds."

A few chuckles rose, and I turned to Disco.

He answered before I could ask. "I'll take care of that."

I swallowed the remainder of my water. "Okay, so we're back to square one on Hannah June, and we're down a crucial man."

Singer interrupted. "Only half of that is true, Chase. We are definitely back to square one on Hannah, but we've still got a perfectly good sniper, even if he was in the Coast Guard."

Every eye in the room fell on Callaway, and he suddenly looked like the cat who ate the canary.

"So, what about it?" I asked. "Are you up for playing substitute shooter while Singer is on the mend?"

He licked his lips. "Sure I am, but you're wrong about Hannah June."

Chapter 24

I Should've Listened

Callaway suddenly had everyone's attention.

"What are you talking about?" I demanded.

He scanned the room as if in fear for his life. "I tried to tell you before, but you told me to shut up . . . twice. I'm still an outsider, so I didn't push the issue. I assumed you had intel I didn't have."

I felt my blood starting to boil. "Now is not the time to beat around the bush, Callaway. Spit it out."

He planted himself on the arm of the couch. "I told you I grew up in Idaho, so this part of the world is my home. Locals know things outsiders don't, especially about the fringe groups like the cultists."

I growled. "That's enough background. Give us the goods."

"When you first join the cult, they don't take you into the compound for a few months. There's an indoctrination phase where they brainwash you, and they can't do that in the general population. That part isn't here. It's up in the Bitterroot Mountains, about seventy miles west of Butte, near a little settlement called Sula."

Clark was suddenly on his feet, and I didn't intervene. The lesson Callaway was about to learn would be far harder to forget if it came from Special Forces Master Sergeant Clark Johnson instead of number twenty-one, the starting catcher for the Georgia Bull-dogs.

"Listen to me, boy . . . and listen good. I don't know how shit worked in the Coast Guard, but you're not in the shallow-water Navy anymore. You're neck-deep in combat arms. Some jackass named Sun Tzu said never interrupt your enemy when he's making a mistake, but we're not enemies."

Mongo held up a finger. "Uh, Clark, Sun Tzu didn't actually—"

"Shut up, Mongo. I'm making a point."

The giant crawled back into his cave, and Clark crawled back down Callaway's throat. "If you've got inside information about a mission, you don't sit on it. You get that intel on the table, no matter who tells you to shut up. Do you understand me?"

I thought I detected a moment of hesitation in Callaway, as if he might've been on the verge of getting in Clark's face. That wouldn't end well, but it would solidify Clark's point.

Instead of standing up, he said, "So, are you in charge, or is Chase?"

Clark drove a finger toward me. "I'm in charge of him, and everybody in this room is in charge of you until you prove yourself under fire. And don't you forget it."

The fire in the sniper's eyes dwindled, and he bit his tongue. "Yes, sir."

Clark waved a hand toward me. "Continue."

"All right . . . Tell us about the compound in Sula, and don't leave out anything."

Callaway said, "First, you need to know I've never seen it. I've only heard about it, but I heard about it from people I trust. I know the Bitterroot Mountains like the back of my hand. I killed everything from coyotes to elk and everything in between while I was a kid in those mountains. They say the compound is stuck back in a box canyon, and there's only one way in and out. It's secluded, private, and easy to defend."

"Can you find it?" I asked.

He nodded. "Yes. Get me onto that NGA mapping program you've got, and I'll show you where it is."

I opened the laptop and signed on before sliding it toward him. A few seconds later, he plugged the cable into the television, and an aerial photo of Sula, Montana, filled the screen. He moved the cursor until it pointed to a box canyon that was just as he described. "There it is, right there. One way in, and one way out."

"Zoom in, and let's see what kind of detail the NGA satellites captured."

He zoomed into the canyon, and the square corners of a man-made structure shone like a flashing light among the natural arcs and curves of the canyon walls.

I sighed. "Nature abhors a vacuum and straight lines. It looks like we've got a new objective, boys."

I closed the laptop. "Thanks, Callaway. Get some sleep, everybody. Clark and I are going to work up a battle plan for assaulting that compound, and we're going to make them regret pinning their backs to the wall."

Callaway didn't stand. "I'll stay and help with the plan if you want. I'm not sleepy."

"Go to bed, Coastie. You're the closest thing we've got to a sniper, and we'll need your eyes and trigger finger well rested."

Clark, Skipper, and I spent the next two hours gathering, dissecting, and analyzing every piece of intel we could piece together on the indoctrination compound. By the time the sun came up, we had a solid plan, but it relied heavily on Callaway's ability to hit what he aimed at. It was time to baptize our new sniper with fire.

I hit the sack with details of the plan banging around in my head and doubts about Doug Callaway slowly fading. The intel he provided may have saved our mission . . . and the former president's niece.

* * *

When I finally crawled out of the rack around noon, I found Singer holding court on the back deck with his student nestled behind the Barrett fifty-cal. His casted foot lay on a black plastic garbage bag, and one of his crutches was pressed against his cheek and shoulder in a perfect firing position. I watched as he taught and Callaway listened, but I didn't open the door. Whatever was happening on the deck was designed to improve our new sniper's skill and set Singer's mind at ease for leaving us down a man.

"I made some soup. It's on the stove if you want some."
I turned to see Disco practicing drawing and target acquisition in front of the full-length hallway mirror. "This place must've turned into some sort of shooting school while I was asleep."

Disco said, "I heard Singer preaching to the new kid a couple of hours ago. It was a master class on making the transition from shooting boat engines to human bodies. I'm glad my job is easy. Anybody can fly, but that stuff they're doing out there isn't for the faint of heart."

I filled a bowl with Disco's soup and spooned my first bite into my mouth. "This is amazing. From now on, you're definitely the dedicated cook when we're on the road. You'd make Maebelle proud, but don't let Clark see you wasting all that motion on your draw."

He stared down at his pistol resting on his right hip. "I thought I was getting better."

I placed the soup bowl on the counter and stepped behind him. "You're doing fine for a civilian, but we're not playing gunfighter . . . we're living it. Every wasted millisecond gives the other guy more time to kill us." I pointed toward his feet. "Point your toes at the target. Your motion is always going to follow your toes, so we always start with that foundation."

He adjusted his stance.

"Good. Now, slowly grip the pistol, and stop."

He did as I instructed.

"Now, release the retention, and start out of the holster nice and slow."

He followed the instructions and watched the slide of the pistol emerge from the holster.

"Don't look at the gun," I said. "You know where it is. Look at the target. Your feet and eyes stay on the target. Now, slowly complete the draw, and without looking, tell me when you think the muzzle is clear of the holster."

He slid the pistol two inches above the front lip of his holster. "Okay, there."

"Don't look," I said. "Just feel and remember where I put your arm." I moved his arm and the pistol down until it was almost touching the holster. "Right there. Whatever you feel right there, keep that in your head, and practice it a thousand times. You're clear of the holster. That's a critical position in the draw. As soon as that muzzle is out of the holster, you have to start rotating that barrel toward the target. Have you ever watched a gunfight in an old Western movie?"

"Sure I have."

"Remember how the gunfighters would fire from the hip as soon as their revolvers came out of the leather?"

"Yeah, they always did that, but I never thought about it."

"That's not just Hollywood and Spaghetti Western garbage. In a real fight, you have to be able to pull the trigger and put lead on a target faster than the other guy or you'll be the one on his back, bleeding out in the middle of the street at high noon."

"So, are you saying I should shoot from here?"

"No, not unless you have to. For the sake of innocents behind your bad guy, it's always better to get a good sight picture before you pull the trigger. But if it comes down to you or the bad guy, always make him pay for starting a gunfight with the wrong hombre."

I stepped back, and he went through the stance and draw several more times while I watched. "Much better. Keep practicing while I practice getting more of that soup down my throat. Do you want a bowl?"

He shook me off. "No, I'm not a fan of soup, but I thought you guys would like it."

I refilled my bowl. "You were right."

Back-deck sniper class ended, and Singer hobbled in behind Callaway at the same time Clark descended the stairs. Soon, the living room was once again our conference room.

I opened with, "How's the foot?"

Singer waggled it in the air. "It itches, and I hate the cast already, but I'll survive."

"How was class, New Guy?"

Callaway pointed with his chin toward Singer. "I'd say he's a pretty good teacher."

"You'd be right about that," I said. "We have some decisions to make. I want to hit the Bitterroot Mountain compound tonight before word gets out that we were sneaking around inside the local encampment last night."

Disco looked up. "That reminds me. Why did you put the girl in the men's bay last night?"

"I'm glad you asked. It was an on-the-spot psych call. The girl was going to wake up this morning with a fantastic tale about commandos dressed in black in the middle of the night. If I'd put her back in her bed, her story might've been easy to believe, but since she woke up in the men's bay, she had some explaining to do. It's likely she broke into the story about running into us on her late-night trip to the bathroom, but since she was discovered in the men's bay, I gambled that the leadership would think her story about commandos was made up to cover her unpermitted middle-of-the-night dalliance. That's all it was—a little misdirection."

Our chief pilot grinned, and since he wasn't wearing a hat to tip, he offered a brief nod of respect.

"So, back to tonight's raid," I said. "We're going in blind, with no idea how many people we'll encounter or how well armed they'll be. I believe security will be a lot tighter because they have to worry about new parishioners jumping ship and running home to Mommy. That's likely part of the reason they picked that location. If anybody runs, there's only one possible direction."

Singer grabbed a handful of Callaway's shirt. "Did you hear that? It's a shooter's alley. Wherever you set up, your fan of fire is going to be narrow, so don't miss."

"Got it," Callaway said.

I continued. "It won't be a walk in the park like last night. We'll have to put down at least a couple of guards to get in."

Callaway narrowed his eyes. "I don't know how I feel about shooting gate guards, just to get inside, so we can *maybe* rescue somebody who *may* not want to be rescued."

"Relax," I said. "We're not shooting any guards unless they start it. We've got plenty of tranquilizer, and any one of us can get the drop on an untrained cultist gate guard. We'll either get behind them covertly and wrap them up, or we'll just walk up to the front gate and knock. Either way, they don't stand a chance. The only issue is getting inside before the guards notify the interior."

A look came over Callaway's face, and I saw his wheels turning. "What is it, sniper?"

"Two things. First, how are we going to get there in time for a night op? The helicopter doesn't have the fuel to make it up there and back with all of us on board. Plus, it's a long drive up there in the Suburban, and there's no good route."

"We've got that covered. Don't worry about it. What's your second concern?"

"It's not really a concern. It's really more of an option. I was studying the aerials earlier, and it looks like we could get above the compound and rappel onto the roof. It's rugged terrain, but it gives us one more avenue of ingress."

I pointed at him. "See? That's the kind of stuff that's worth interrupting a briefing. We'll take a look at that option, but getting out is another story. We only have one road out of there, and there will be resistance. The only question is, how much and how hard?"

Chapter 25
Wild Men with Shovels and Axes

My phone vibrated right on cue. "Good afternoon. How's my favorite analyst?"

Penny said, "I'm not an analyst yet. I'm just an analyst in training. But I've got some good news for you."

"Let's hear it. I'm a huge fan of good news."

"Our friends over at the Department of Interior just happen to have a couple of Forest Service vehicles lying around they don't need up in Missoula, and they said we're welcome to the trucks as long as they don't come home full of bullet holes. They also said the smoke jumpers up there have about a hundred barrels of jet fuel that aren't under lock and key. They'll never miss five or six of them."

"That is good news. Do you think you could talk them out of some mountaineering gear? We could use some rope, carabiners, and pitons. You know, your run-of-the-mill Ranger Rick stuff."

"I'll see what I can do . . . Wait. It looks like Skipper's already on it. What else do you need?"

"If Skipper scores the gear, that should do it."

"I just got the thumbs up. The gear will be in the trucks."

"Great. Did Skipper get everything lined up in Boise?"

"She's nodding her head yes, so apparently, she did. Are we on open comms again tonight?"

"Always," I said. "That's the only way Skipper can anticipate what we'll need on the fly."

"Okay, but it's nerve-racking to hear all of that."

"If you think last night was a show, you're going to get an earful tonight. You ain't heard nothing yet, baby."

"Whatever. Just don't get hurt. We've already got enough of you on injured reserve."

"We'll be fine," I said. "What could possibly go wrong? We're assaulting an encampment of cultists with a sniper on overwatch who we've never seen shoot. We're doing it all using borrowed U.S. Forest Service vehicles and stolen jet fuel from a bunch of smoke jumpers who are wild men with axes and shovels. It's practically the perfect operation. Who could ask for anything more?"

"Real funny, Chase. Those are real people with real lives you're talking about. I mean it. Be careful."

"We're not real people, my dear. We're the people the real people call when they run out of options. We'll be fine, and I'll be home in a few days. Don't worry."

She huffed. "Yeah, right. That's like telling the wind not to blow. Just be careful."

I hung up and shared the good news with the team. "All the boxes are checked, and the passports are stamped. It's time to go to work, but before we do, Disco made a pot of soup, and it's fantastic. I recommend getting as much of it down your gullet as possible. It's going to be a long, hungry night if you don't have a belly full of calories."

My team was good at a great many things, but eating had to be near the top of the list. The soup vanished in no time, but Callaway steered well clear of the kitchen, opting instead for a stack of protein bars.

"You got something against soup?" I asked.

He shook his head. "No, I love soup, but I've got a weird allergy to green peppers, and I noticed the soup had a lot of green floaters."

I shrugged. "It's your loss, but that just leaves more for us, so I'm not complaining."

I watched the dishes pile up in the kitchen sink, and I gave the order. "Let's load up."

Everyone stood . . . except Singer.

I motioned for him to get up. "You're not getting out of a mission just because you broke a foot. You're going with us. We might find ourselves in a butt-kicking contest, and that cast will come in handy."

He hopped to his one good foot and pulled his crutches from the end of the couch. "Do you have any hundred-mile-per-hour tape?"

"I've got a roll in my pack. Why?"

"I need to borrow it, if you don't mind."

I pulled the roll of green duct tape from my pack and tossed it toward him.

He caught it with one hand. "Thanks. I'll put it back when I'm done." He crutched his way down the steps and into the waiting Suburban with the rest of us.

The short ride to the airport was silent as each of us concentrated on the coming night's festivities.

When we parked outside the hangar, I gave the assignments. "Disco, you're on the helo with Hunter. Everybody else is with me and Clark on the Citation."

Jimmy was nowhere in sight, so I assumed the role as tug operator. Fifteen minutes later, the 412 was on the ramp, perched high on its cart, and the Citation was glistening in the afternoon sun.

Callaway looked up at the jet. "You've got to be kidding me. That's yours?"

"What? Doesn't your team have a jet?"

He laughed. "My current team does."

Disco and Hunter took off first in the helo and headed northwest while the rest of us loaded up into the Citation.

Clark took the captain's seat before I could get to the cockpit, and he grinned when I finally folded myself through the door and onto the seat beside him. "It looks like you've got the radios, College Boy. I'll take care of the hard part. Besides, after your performance on top of that mountain last night, I'm not sure I want to be your passenger."

"Just fly the airplane," I said. "I know it's tough for you to do more than one thing at a time, knuckle-dragger."

The two-hundred-mile flight from West Yellowstone to Missoula took thirty-six minutes, and it took us over some of the most beautiful scenery on the planet.

"I might want to retire up here someday," I said.

Clark laughed. "I don't think so. You'd never make it through the first winter. You'd freeze to death."

"Okay, so maybe I'll have a summer house up this way."

As we began our descent into Missoula, my stomach gave a rumble I hadn't expected.

Clark asked, "Are you okay?"

"I think so. I've never been airsick, but that didn't sound right."

"Ah, it's just nerves. It'll be fine once the bullets start flying."

"Let's hope it doesn't come to that."

Clark's landing was textbook, as always, and we taxied to the smoke-jumper ramp, where a pair of four-wheel-drive Forest Service work trucks waited near the fence, each with two drums of jet fuel in the back.

"I guess it's good to have friends in high places," I said.

"Yep. Things are coming together a little too easily to suit me. I've got to be honest. It makes me nervous."

"What is it they say about even the blind hog finding an occasional acorn?"

He scratched his head. "I thought it was . . . you can put lipstick on an acorn, but it's still a blind hog in the mud."

"Yes, of course that's it. You're an idiot."

He grinned. "Yeah, but I'm a pretty idiot."

We secured the airplane and met Singer, Callaway, and Mongo at the bottom of the stairs.

I motioned toward the battered pickup trucks. "Our chariots await."

Callaway stood with a look of bewilderment on his face. "You guys are insane. You buy helicopters on a whim, you fly around in a Gulfstream, and you steal jet fuel from the Forestry Service in beat-up trucks."

"That's not true!" I said. "It's a Citation, not a Gulfstream. Now, get in the truck."

Clark and I took the lesser damaged of the two trucks and left Singer, Mongo, and the new guy in the really ugly ride.

We hit Highway 93 south toward the Bitterroot Mountains. Forty-five minutes into the trip, I said, "Pull off the road up here. My stomach isn't enjoying the ride."

"First you were airsick, and now you're carsick? What's going on with you?"

"I don't know, but I don't like it."

Clark signaled and pulled off the side of the highway. I kicked open my door, and a stomachful of Disco's soup hit the ground before my feet did. I wiped my mouth and pulled a water bottle from my pack.

"Are you okay?" Clark said. "This isn't like you."

"I'll be fine now that I've got that out of my system. Let's go."

We pulled back on the road and continued our trek.

Clark eyed me with concern. "Did you eat something I didn't?"

"Not that I know of. All I've eaten is the soup and five or six bottles of water."

He frowned. "That can't be it because that's all I've had as well, and I feel fine."

"Who knows? Maybe I developed an allergy to green peppers like Callaway."

"What are you talking about? He's not allergic to peppers. He didn't pick them off the pizza."

"Are you sure?"

"Yeah, I'm sure. I threw away the paper plates when everyone was finished, and there were no leftover peppers anywhere."

I laid my head back against the seat and let my eyes close as I replayed the conversation over and over again.

Finally, Clark punched my leg. "Snap out of it. We've got an op to run."

"Yeah, yeah. I'm fine. I was just thinking."

"Just think about the op."

"Speaking of the op . . . We need to put eyes on the entrance to that compound before we lose daylight."

"As always, I'm way ahead of you. Our turnoff is right up here."

Clark made the turn, and then another, until we found ourselves on a mud and gravel road leading into a forest right out of Fern Gully. He said, "According to the aerial shots, it opens up back here."

We drove for another mile, and Clark's prediction came true. The standing timber parted to reveal a steep-sided, narrow canyon. We rolled to a stop and stepped from the vehicles.

I said, "Callaway, is this what you expected it to look like?"

He studied the terrain. "Exactly."

"Good. Now we've got a picture of our egress route, but how far is it back to the compound from here?"

"Just over a mile," came Singer's voice from the back seat of the second truck.

We moved closer to him. "I should've known you'd have it memorized. How many turns in the canyon are there in that mile?"

He closed one eye and stared toward the roof of the truck. "Four. The first one is a forty-five to the left. The next two are back-to-back cuts to the right for about seventy-five or eighty degrees, and then a hard ninety back to the left. The compound rests five hundred yards from the last bend."

I studied my mental picture of the canyon. "Set off three IR beacons in this clearing. This will be our rally point and valet parking for the chopper."

Clark and Callaway set up the beacons, and we made our way back to the highway.

Ninety minutes after leaving Missoula, we pulled into the Bitterroot Ranger Station to find our shiny new Bell 412 sitting on the helo pad beside the fire tower. Clark pulled the truck alongside the chopper, and Mongo followed close behind. Hunter and Disco made short work of pumping the jet fuel from the barrels and into the thirsty tanks of the helo.

A burly ranger stepped from the station and approached. "How's it going, guys?"

I spun on a heel. "Everything's fine. Thanks for letting us use your backyard as a refuel point."

"No problem. We do it all the time. I've tried to get them to put a tank in the ground, but they never listen. I'm just a lowly little park ranger."

"I know the feeling," I said. "They never listen to me, either. Are you sure it's okay for us to leave the empty barrels with you?"

He looked excited. "Absolutely! I've got a dozen projects that I can use them on. In fact, if you come up with anymore, I'd love to have as many as you can bring."

"I'll see what I can do," I said. "Thanks again. We'll be out of your hair an hour or so after dark."

He motioned toward the ranger station. "You're not bothering me. You guys are welcome to come inside and wait for dark. We've got a good woodstove and a clean bathroom."

"I think we'll take you up on that. Thanks."

When the refueling was done and the barrels were stacked behind the station, we moved our party inside.

I lagged behind and caught Callaway by the arm. "Hang on a minute before you go in. Didn't you tell me you were allergic to green peppers?"

He stared at the ground, apparently embarrassed to have been caught in a lie—even a harmless one like a fake allergy. "Yeah, I did say that, but it wasn't true. I just didn't want to hurt Disco's feelings. I tried a bite of his soup, and to be honest, I didn't care for it. I'm kind of a picky eater."

I squeezed his wrist. "No lies on the team. None. Ever. Not even to save somebody's feelings. If we let each other get away with little white lies, how will we know when they turn into big dark ones?"

He nodded. "I got it. I'm sorry. It won't happen again. It's always a little shaky when you're the new guy on the team."

I let go of his wrist and patted him on the back. "Just make sure that if it comes out of your mouth, it's the truth. We're glad to have you. With Singer grounded, we'd be in a mess without someone to fill his shoes."

"Or just his shoe," he said.

"You're going to fit in just fine, Callaway. Get inside where it's warm."

We drank Forest Service coffee that tasted like boiled shoe leather, and then we raided the vending machine for two hours. I hurled what little soup remained in my stomach and opted for a bag of potato chips, thinking the salt might settle my stomach. Ten minutes later, it was working.

I said, "Unless you guys are scared, let's clock in and go to work. It's time to do what we do best."

Chapter 26
That's Not What I Expected

Disco and I put the helicopter in the clearing with the help of the infrared beacons, and the rest of the team pulled up in the trucks within minutes of us shutting down the turbines.

With everyone huddled up, I said, "Let's open up the comms and get everybody on the same sheet of music." I rigged my satellite transmitter for open channel comms. "Ops Center, Charlie-One. Commo check. Over."

"Charlie-One, Ops Center has you loud and clear. How me?"

"I have you the same," I said. "Stand by for the countdown."

Clark initiated the checks with his handler call sign. "Charlie-Hotel."

Hunter said, "Charlie-Two."

Mongo said, "Charlie-Four."

Disco sounded off. "Charlie-Five."

Everyone turned to Callaway, and he held up his palms.

I said, "The sniper is always three."

He gave a thumbs up. "Charlie-Three."

Skipper reported, "All Charlie elements are loud and clear."

I issued the operations order. "Here's how it's going down. We'll drive the vehicles halfway to the gate and stage them there. After that, we'll proceed on foot as split elements. There's too much chance of getting mowed down if we move as one unit and encounter an ambush, so I want Callaway, Mongo, and Hunter in the first vehicle on the right wing. Clark, Disco, and I will follow and take left wing. At the last bend, I want Callaway as high as he can get without being seen from the compound. We'll all move to that point, so we'll know his overwatch position before we climb the walls. Does everybody understand?"

Heads nodded, so I continued.

"After we get overwatch in position, the rest of us will pull back about three hundred yards and play spider monkey. We'll get as high as we can and flank the compound. We'll rappel in from the back with as much stealth as we can manage. If we get spotted, the rules are a little different tonight. If they're armed, don't give them time to start a gunfight. End it with your weapons suppressed. I don't want to hear gunfire echoing through the canyon. If we hear anything unsuppressed, it'll either be Callaway or the bad guys. Got it?"

"Yeah, suppressors only," Disco said. "We got it."

I said, "Callaway, I don't want you shooting without the command from one of us inside the compound. When we find the girl, we're bringing her out the front. There will be a confrontation at the gate—there's no question about that. But if at all possible, we want to do all of our work up to that point undetected. Any questions?"

None came, so I looked to Mongo. "Let's get you in the chopper. As soon as we report clear with the girl, I want those rotors spinning so we can be airborne the second we reach the clearing. We'll be moving as fast as we can on the way out, but we may have an uncooperative girl on our hands. If we have to, I'll put her to sleep, but she'll hopefully be willing and anxious to run."

Mongo took it upon himself to "help" Singer into the left front seat of the chopper.

Singer said, "Thanks for the ride, you big buffalo. Now, get me a rifle and enough ammo to cover you if you've got bogies on your six on the way out."

Mongo dutifully obliged and loaded a rifle, a pistol, and enough ammo to start—and hopefully end—a war into the cockpit with our crippled sniper.

I twisted a finger in the air. "Lock and load. Let's go get that girl out of there."

We piled into the trucks per my plan and headed into the canyon. After we passed the first two turns, I ordered, "Goggles on. Lights off."

We went dark and slowed our pace. Stopping just short of the third turn, we parked the vehicles with their headlights pointed toward freedom. On foot, we made our way, in two elements, deeper into the canyon. The massive walls towered above us like skyscrapers in Manhattan, and the canyon floor narrowed with every step.

"Okay," I said. "Dead silence now. We escort Callaway to his nest and back away."

Wordlessly, we proceeded until the final bend in the rock walls formed an alley directly to the front gate of the small compound. As the rest of the team helped Callaway plot a course up the rock wall, I studied the entrance to the compound. A pair of squatty guard towers flanked the hinged gate that appeared to be no more than six feet tall. Getting out was going to be a breeze, but the pair of shadows in the guard towers didn't look like weekend warriors. Their posture, movement, and even the motion of their heads as they scanned the area painted them as well-trained sentries.

I felt my stomach spasm, and I choked back the coffee and potato chips that clearly wanted out. As quietly as possible, I made my retreat between the third and fourth bends and took a knee.

There was nothing I could do to keep the contents of my stomach from landing on the ground in front of me.

The sound of my team retreating toward my position wafted through the canyon.

Clark whispered, "Charlie-One, are you okay?"

"I'm fine now," I whispered back. "I've just got some kind of stomach bug."

"I'm glad to hear it's not motion sickness. I was starting to think you were going soft on me."

"Never," I said as I climbed back to my feet and wiped my face.

Believing we were out of earshot of the compound, our whispers became muted tones.

I said, "I think I spotted a decent course up the wall about a hundred feet back. Let's go climbing."

The trail I spotted turned out to be nothing more than a shadow running diagonally across the smooth stone face. The portions of the walls that weren't solid rock held tiny patches of dirt and snow with evergreen shrubs protruding from the crags. I started up the wall, using the sparsely spaced evergreens as handholds as I went, but the higher I climbed, the fewer places I found to put my feet.

Before I could say it, Mongo came through my earpiece. "This isn't going to work. There's no way up these walls. We need a plan B."

"Same here," I said. "It's no use. We're going in through the front. Remember, we're not starting the gunfight, but if *they* do, we have to make them pay. We're sitting ducks in this terrain if they open fire."

Moving as close to the walls as possible, the five of us made slow, steady progress toward the gate. As we rounded the final bend with Callaway perched twenty feet overhead, Clark whispered, "Remember, Disco. Two to the chest, and one in the T-box."

As our snail's pace continued, the unmistakable sound of guts rumbling poured into my earpiece. I wasn't the only one with the stomach bug. I was just patient zero. Both elements made it to the front wall of the compound without detection from the guards, but getting over the gate and subduing both guards simultaneously was a pipe dream.

I whispered, "Hold," and both elements froze. "Charlie-Three, on my command, unlock the gate for us, and then put some neck-high shots on both guard towers. If you can pin them down, we'll do the rest."

Callaway said, "Roger."

We inched closer to the gate until our backs were against the wall and the pair of guards were directly over our heads.

I eyed my team, and everyone gave a nod. "Hit it, Three!"

The locked closure on the gate exploded in a shower of sparks and flying debris. Mongo stepped from the wall and sent a thundering kick to the swinging gate. Its hinges moaned and creaked, but the heavy barricade swung inward six feet.

What happened next is impossible to describe in real time. A lifetime of fighting unfolded in a fury of unimaginable noise and devastation. It lasted only seconds, but in those few fleeting sweeps of the second hand, a hail of automatic-weapons fire rained down on us from the guard towers. Sounds of lead striking stone and timber echoed through the canyon. An animalistic voice I didn't recognize cried out and fell to the ground in a mighty thud. My stomach churned, and my ears thundered with the sound of gunfire from every direction. We returned fire with discipline and determination. Sending lead flying in every direction would only turn the already bad situation into a mass casualty event, and that was the last thing any of us wanted or needed.

I yelled into my mic, "Callaway! Put some lead on these guys!" Despite my beseeching, his rifle remained silent five hundred yards away. I could only imagine that the voice I couldn't identify had been his, and the thud had been the ungodly sound of his body striking the canyon floor. We were in the fight of our lives with no overwatch and no visible means of escape.

In a moment of rare calmness and clarity, I took in the scene unfolding around us. We were pinned down by an enemy with a superior position and a seemingly endless supply of ammunition. Suddenly, the picture came into focus and I yelled, "Crossfire!"

Mongo's enormous form raised his rifle and trained it on the sentinel above my head, and the three of us on my side poured lead into the guard tower on the opposite side.

After spilling pound after pound of spent shell casing on the canyon floor, the gunfire from above fell silent. I moved to the wall's edge where it met the swinging gate, and I quick-peeked inside. The guard from Mongo and Hunter's side was lying half out of the tower, blood pouring from his wounds.

Mongo leaned in. "Both bogies down." Then he took a knee and emptied his stomach onto the bloody earth at his feet.

There couldn't have been a worse time for my team to be falling apart.

I ordered, "Sound off. One's up."

Clark said, "Hotel's up."

Mongo raised a hand. "Four's up."

Disco's heart must've been pounding in his throat. He let out a meager, "Five's up."

I adjusted my throat mic. "Two and Three, report."

Only silence returned.

I had no doubt Callaway was dead from the second after his muzzle flash gave away his position, but Hunter's silence terrified me.

"Where's Hunter?" I said.

A new kind of sickness overtook me when Mongo said, "He's down, Chase."

My NVGs took a hit during the fighting, so I was left blind in the inky black of the deadly end of the box canyon. Any possibility we had of remaining stealthy was gone with the wind, so I squeezed the pressure plate on the forearm of my rifle, sending a beam of brilliant white light across the ground. When the light fell on my partner, he was dragging himself backward with a tourniquet in his teeth and his rifle dangling impotently across his chest. Like mine, his night-vision devices were torn from his head, and a trail of blood darkened the ground in his wake.

I slung my rifle beneath my arm and ran to his side. His leg, just above the knee, was pouring blood, so I yanked the tourniquet from his teeth and wound it around his thigh. I twisted the tensioning handle until pouring blood became a trickle. Pulling the Velcro strap across the handle, I laid his hand on top of the tourniquet and hit his right thigh with a syringe of morphine.

I raised the light to his chest and looked into his weary eyes. "You are not going to die tonight. Keep that tourniquet tight, and keep your eyes open." I grabbed his collar and dragged him to the intersection of the compound wall and the sheer rock face. "You hold this position. We'll be back for you."

I pulled two spare rifle magazines from my pouch and threw them between his legs. "Hold this position!"

Every part of me wanted to throw him over my shoulder and run for the chopper, but the mission demanded more of me and what remained of my team. In the most painful decision of my life, I turned away from my critically wounded partner and moved back into position with the three operators I had left.

Refocusing my attention and determination, I said, "Hunter's down but alive and stable for now. We're continuing mission."

Mongo took point and led us through the gate. Clark snapped pictures of the faces of the fallen sentries and quickly sent them to the ops center for identification—if we lived through the remainder of the night.

If more sentries had eyes on us from inside the structure, the courtyard of the compound was thirty feet of killing fields. The lights that were visible through the windows when Callaway blew the gate were now extinguished, and the structure was entirely blacked out.

I tapped Mongo's arm. "I've got the lead. Take rear guard."

The big man hesitated for part of a second before falling back and putting his massive frame at the rear of our formation. We couldn't shoot around him if the fighting kicked off again, so putting him behind us was our only hope of winning the next gunfight.

Skipper's voice filled my ringing ear. "Charlie-One, Ops Center. Intel."

She picked the worst possible time to feed me intel, but whatever it was qualified as critical to her, so, trusting her gut, I said, "Send the intel."

"A pair of Montana livestock agents discovered Alvin Brown, the Montana team leader, in a barn on his property. They're en route to the ER and suspect a massive drug overdose."

I fought to piece the information together in my head, but nothing seemed to fit. Instead of asking a question to clarify the situation, I said, "What the hell is a livestock agent?"

Before she could answer, a rifle round that was fired from the roof of the compound struck the ground only inches from my boot, sending us sprinting toward the front of the structure to put some roofline between us and the new gunman.

I squeezed my mic against my throat. "Whoever's behind that gun isn't a soldier like the gate guards. They wouldn't have missed."

"Agreed," Clark said. "But he's still got a gun and the high ground." Almost before he got the words out of his mouth, his stomach revolted against Disco's soup and fell victim to the same virus as Mongo and me.

With my determination still intact, even though my team was falling apart, I rewrote the rules of engagement. "Find the girl, and kill anybody who gets in your way."

Chapter 27
Practice Makes Perfect

Clark led the charge up the stairs leading to the front porch of the structure. His demeanor under fire was like a monk in prayer. The sky could be burning over his head, and Clark Johnson would continue movement to the objective as if on a Sunday-afternoon stroll.

We needed the cover of the roofline to rob the elevated gunner of his advantage. Movement to cover was our immediate mission, and there was likely no one better than Clark to put what remained of my team in a safer position.

If we could make the porch, it would be impossible for the rooftop gunner to get an accurate shot on us. He could pepper rounds through the roof in hopes of hitting one of us, but our chances of surviving such a desperate maneuver were high, and I was willing to risk it.

As Clark's boot hit the top step, he suddenly froze and threw up a fist, stopping all of us in our tracks. "It's a tripwire."

I grabbed Disco's collar. "Step over the wire, and put your back against the front wall. Kill anybody who steps into the courtyard behind us."

Without a word, he followed the order and took up a cover position with his rifle at high ready. Mongo instinctually sidestepped the stairs, took a knee, and scanned the front edge of the roof for the shooter, while I knelt to investigate the tripwire pulled taut against Clark's boot.

I followed the wire first to its end on the right side and found its anchor point. Whatever threat the wire held, it was at the other end. Still without NVGs, I slid my fingers the length of the wire to its terminus at the left side of the steps. That's where I found a 14-ounce gift from God: an M67 fragmentation grenade with Clark's tripwire threaded through the pin.

I slipped my wire cutters from my kit and clipped the thin wire. Next, I worked the grenade from its position between two flat stones and palmed the device like my old familiar friend, the baseball. "Draw some fire, Mongo."

The big man ripped a pair of stones from the steps and sailed them into the courtyard like Frisbees. His decoy worked, and the rooftop gunner put four rounds in the dirt around the sliding rocks. While his attention was focused on Mongo's harmless rocks, I pulled the pin and let the lever swing away and spring free of the main body of the grenade. The M67 fuse is timed for a four- to five-second delay before killing everybody within fifteen feet. If the grenade rolled off the roof before detonating, the four of us would be well within that kill radius.

With the lever flying through the air, I silently counted "One . . . two . . . three," and tossed the weapon onto the roof. The four of us dived for the deck, anxiously awaiting the explosion.

The body of the grenade hit the metal roof with an audible thud and immediately began rolling for the edge. Running footsteps thundered overhead as our gunman threw himself from the rooftop in a desperate attempt to survive the coming blast.

The explosion came the same instant the gunman hit the ground ten feet in front of the steps. If we'd not been deafened by the grenade's roar, the sickening sound of legs breaking beneath the gunman would've filled our ears. The man riled in agony with his AK-47 lying harmlessly in the dirt a few feet away.

Mongo reached him in two enormous strides and grabbed the man's left boot. He dragged the gunman across the ground and deposited him on the stone stairs, then put his face inches from his. "Does it hurt?"

The man growled as the pain of the broken legs consumed him.

"I guess it does," Mongo said. "But I can make it stop. Would you like that?"

The incoherent former gunman twisted and howled like a wounded animal, and Mongo delivered an open-handed slap across his tortured face. "Tell me how many more there are inside."

The man spat, sending blood and spittle spraying into the giant's face. Mongo calmly wiped it away with his sleeve and lifted the man from the steps. He tossed him like a rag doll against a stone column supporting the roof of the building, and the horrific sound of more bones succumbing to stress echoed through the night air. The man's limp body fell to the floor of the porch, and Mongo rolled him over as Clark took another picture and sent it bouncing off satellites miles overhead.

My team was, once again, on its feet and headed for the door. I landed a heel kick beside the knob, and the heavy wooden barricade rattled but didn't surrender. A flurry of 5.56mm rounds and one more powerful kick did the trick. The door swung inward and crashed against its stop.

I stepped aside as Clark tossed a pair of flash grenades through the opening. Seconds later, the ear-piercing crack of the explosives, coupled with the flash of white light, left everyone inside stunned and incapable of putting up a fight.

Clark was first through the door, and he cut to the left, his weapon-mounted light flooding the room with a blinding glare. I stepped through the opening half a second behind him and turned sharply to the right. Mongo filled the doorway and roared through the space like a bull on the streets of Pamplona. Disco held his position and continued covering the courtyard.

The interior space was a vast, open area with small doors lining the walls. Several women dressed in simple, oversized dresses lay scattered about the space. Most were holding their ears after the flash-bang, but a few shielded their eyes against the assault of our lights and peered desperately through squinted eyelids. I quickly wrote them off as noncombatants and started kicking doors. Mongo and Clark followed suit.

As the first door splintered beneath my boot heel, I shoved the muzzle of my M4 through the jagged opening to find a pair of bunk beds, a chamber pot, and two women chained to the metal posts of the beds. They were dressed identically to the women in the center of the building, but there was one dramatic difference: the shocked expressions of the women on the floor behind me were the result of the flash-bangs Clark delivered, but the women chained to the beds wore the blank expressions of drug addicts staring into nothing, oblivious to the world around them.

I examined the faces of the captive women, hoping to find Hannah June behind their glazed eyes, but neither woman resembled the former president's niece.

They were safer locked to their beds than roaming freely through the space, so I left them the way I found them and moved to the next door. My kick and search revealed identical results as door number one. I checked over my shoulder to find Mongo and Clark discovering the same women in the same condition in every room they searched.

"Keep searching," I ordered. "Hannah has to be behind one of these doors."

The instant my boot contacted the next door, my earpiece came alive with Skipper's voice. "Charlie-One, Ops Center. Intel."

"Go with intel," I said as I continued my work. To my surprise, the room I'd just entered was empty.

Skipper said, "I have IDs on your three shooters."

"Send it!"

"The two at the gate were Ted 'Toucan' Snelgrove and John Robert 'Cornbread' Dockery."

I took a knee inside the empty room. "What? Are you sure?"

"One hundred percent. But that's not all. The third man is Aaron Copeland. Chase, that's almost the entire Montana team. The whole thing is a setup. You've got to get out of there."

My eyes fell to the floor in disbelief as my light played across the wooden planking of the room. I replayed every moment of the mission through my head until my eye caught a glimpse of a yellow and green striped cord running up the back wall of the room.

I dived through the small door and back into the open space in the center of the building. I yelled, "Det cord!" But I was an instant too late. Just as Clark drove his foot through another door, the world turned into fiery chaos. The explosive cord cut the building in half, and debris rained down on us from every direction. I thought I saw Clark's body flying through the air just before everything in my world faded to black.

When I came to, nothing around me made sense. I forced myself to analyze one piece of the puzzle at a time, allowing my mind to put together the mosaic of the scene in front of me. My ears rang as if I were trapped inside a church bell, and my sight faded through degrees of blur as I scanned the room. Clark's left leg was visibly protruding from a pile of wood and plaster near the edge of my vision, and a heap of material I couldn't identify moved like a giant turtle near the back of the room. It had to be Mongo, but I couldn't see his face.

As my eyesight continued to clear, a two-headed form moving through the center of the room slowly came into focus. One of the heads wore shoulder-length hair and dragged her feet through the scattered debris. The second face was all too familiar. Doug Callaway, our second-string sniper, pushed his way through the detritus with a pistol pressed to the side of Hannah June Meriwether's head.

I willed my arms to draw my pistol, but I was trapped beneath hundreds of pounds of material that had been a structure only minutes before. No matter how hard I tried, I couldn't make my arms respond to my mind's commands to shoot Callaway.

Clark's boot was motionless, and the heap that was Mongo rose and fell like a wounded animal dragging itself from the road. We were powerless to stop Callaway from getting away with Hannah June.

Fury laced with rage overtook me, and my heart pounded like thunder inside my chest. Callaway had to be stopped, but none of us could do it.

I bored holes through the traitorous sniper with my eyes, begging for the power to move, but it wouldn't come. Instead, from the front of the demolished structure, a force I'd underestimated stepped through the dust-filled air and leveled his pistol in practiced, mechanical precision.

I didn't hear the weapon fire, but the scene played out in slow motion before my eyes. The 9mm round left Disco's muzzle and entered Callaway's skull in the perfectly placed T-box shot. As his central nervous system collapsed in an instant, the back of Callaway's head exploded as the hollow-point round made its exit and his knees turned to mush.

Hannah June Meriwether was left standing in the center of a dystopian hell. Disco holstered his pistol and caught the woman before she collapsed. I watched him disappear through the area that had been a front door moments before. Getting the girl to safety had been our priority, and our chief pilot turned commando accomplished the mission while the rest of us lay in stunned semiconsciousness. I was proud of him for having the grit to complete the mission in spite of everything else, but my pride doubled when he waded back through the minefield of the demolished structure with the shadowy form of a man hobbling on one crutch in his wake. Behind Singer, the forest ranger stood with an enormous floodlight, its beam cutting through the darkness like that of a lighthouse. I managed to croak out a cry for help, and Singer's light hit my face.

My next memory was of lying in the bed of the dilapidated Forest Service pickup with Mongo lying beside me and mumbling something about a Russian girl who could go to Hell.

Clark limped up to the truck and laid a filthy, bloody hand across my chest. "Say, have either of you seen a Danner boot, size ten? I seem to have lost one."

Chapter 28
I Can't Fly

I had no way to know the extent of my injuries, but nothing hurt. That was rarely a good sign. The body has a way of letting the brain know what's broken and battered unless the damage is more than the brain can manage. Then, it tends to look the other way and let the brain believe everything is hunky-dory.

Although Hannah June was safe, our mission was far from over. Our plan had been for Clark and me to fly her to Boise Airport in the Bell 412 while the rest of the team led any pursuers on a wild goose chase with the borrowed Forest Service vehicles. Waiting at Boise would be a team of Secret Service agents—real ones—and an emergency medicine contingent.

There would be no wild goose chase, but the most important element of our egress plan remained. I looked up at my handler, and he met my gaze.

"What is it, College Boy? Did you stub your toe or something?"

I think I smiled, but I couldn't tell for certain. "I can't fly."

He let out a pain-filled chuckle. "Don't be so hard on yourself, kid. You'll never be as good as me, but you're a decent pilot."

"No," I groaned. "I can't fly Hannah to Boise."

Clark settled onto the tailgate and slapped the side of the truck. We started moving, slowly at first, then picking up speed as the tires bounced across the canyon floor. I counted turns until I heard the rotors of our chopper spinning and the turbines whistling their sweet, monotone song.

Clark slid from the tailgate and let out a guttural cry when his feet hit the ground. He turned and vomited as if his stomach were escaping through his throat.

When the retching ended, he leaned against the truck. "I'm never eating Disco's soup again."

I blinked. "Something tells me it was Callaway's secret ingredient and not Disco's soup that did this to us. Besides the two people who didn't eat it, we all got a dose of Montezuma's revenge."

"I think you may be onto something there."

The forest ranger and Disco helped us aboard the chopper, but Mongo proved to be a handful. In his semiconscious state, his three hundred pounds must've felt like a ton. Singer lent a hand, albeit a hand fettered by a crutch wrapped in green hundred-mile-per-hour tape.

"Nice camo job," I said, motioning toward the crutch.

He smiled. "Yeah, shiny silver has never been my color."

Although I couldn't see him from my position on my back in the helicopter, I assumed Disco was at the controls and pushing the machine to its absolute limits. It felt like a lifetime, but the two-hundred-mile flight only took fifty minutes.

As I expected, the reception party on a secluded apron of Boise Airport had little concern for the wounded operators lying throughout the helicopter's interior. Their only concern was Hannah June. After a brief examination, the medical team released her to the Secret Service, and she was spirited away to points unknown aboard an unmarked, officially non-existent Learjet.

With time and rubber gloves on their hands, the emergency medical team climbed aboard and probed our arms with IV needles and shined penlights into our eyes.

Mongo floated in and out of the spirit world, cursing and mumbling every time he returned to the land of the living. I wondered what was happening inside the big man's head, but I had a feeling I knew exactly how he felt. I'd been there. I'd *also* hated the Russian who shredded my heart, so for the sake of his sanity, I hoped he would fall asleep until the ordeal was over.

A trio of ambulances whisked us the fifty-mile trip down Interstate 84 to the hospital at Mountain Home Air Force Base.

I don't remember much about what happened there, but I'll never forget the visitors I had in succession the next afternoon. At least I assume it was my second day in the hospital, but I'll never be certain.

The unmistakable voice and wild hair of my beautiful wife poured through the door of my room. Concern replaced elation in her voice when she saw me lying in the bed, attached to traction devices at both ends, and a spiderweb of hoses and wires crisscrossing my body. She squeezed my hand as tears rolled down her freckled cheeks. I'd known her for four years and loved her since the first second I saw her, but I never remember her being utterly speechless. She didn't have to speak, though. Having her hand wrapped around mine and feeling her next to me was the only conversation either of us required in that moment.

Perhaps she sat on the edge of my bed for days, or maybe only minutes, but my second visitor splintered the beautiful silence Penny and I were sharing.

Skipper stood a foot from my bed, her glasses sliding down her nose, and a massive file in her arms. "You look good, Chase."

"No, I don't. I look like a mummy trapped in a hangman's gallows, but you're sweet to lie to me."

"Are you ready?" she asked as she bounced on the balls of her feet.

I hoped she'd never lose that energy and girlish excitement about our work. As an analyst, she was talented beyond measure, but away from her computers and satellite comms, she was one of the most delightfully high-energy personalities imaginable.

"I doubt if I'm ready, but I can see that's not going to stop you, so let's have it."

She dragged a heavy military surplus chair across the floor and plopped down on the tattered cushion. "So, it went like this. Al Brown, the Montana team leader, put it all together, and he called a team meeting to confront his men about the treason they'd committed. Instead of cooperating with their team leader and turning themselves in, they attacked him, but not before he did a little damage of his own. He put three forty-five rounds into Gabe Lovell, the team's medic, but that's not all. He took a knife away from Aaron Copeland and sank it in his thigh a few times."

"Wait a minute," I said. "Copeland was at the compound. He was the shooter on the roof."

"Will you shut up and let me finish? Yes, he was there, but he wasn't healthy. It takes a long time for multiple stab wounds to the thigh to heal. That explains why his marksmanship sucked so badly."

"Okay, I'm sorry. I won't interrupt again."

She rolled her eyes. "You just did, but never mind that. Here's the rest. The remainder of the team—the ones Brown hadn't killed or stabbed—jumped him and beat him to death . . . or so they thought. He turned out to be a little bit hard to kill, but we'll come back to that part. Am I going too fast?"

I shook my head and felt bolts of lightning shoot down my spine. "Would you slow down if I said yes?"

"Probably not."

"That's what I thought. So, keep going."

She rifled through some papers in her file. "Do you remember when Clark said he thought there must be some connection between the cult and the team? Yeah, I know you remember. Well, his gut instinct was right. Callaway and the others were working off-the-books private security for the cult, and they had been for several months."

"Clark's rarely wrong," I said.

She thumbed through another stack. "Duh, everybody knows that. So, anyway, when you captured Callaway, he cooked up a scheme to infiltrate your team—*our* team—and he pulled it off perfectly by all indications. He was apparently communicating with his team of traitorous assholes the whole time. The Bitterroot compound was a setup all along. It was an ambush from the jump. We didn't have a chance."

I felt the smile that came to my lips that time. "Apparently, we did have at least a little bit of a chance because Hannah June is safe and sound."

"Yeah, whatever. We'll get to that part later. Right now, we're going to talk about the day before the raid—the day the livestock agents found Brown. Apparently, the rogue team got word that Brown wasn't dead and that he was coming after them. They knew he'd drive his Land Cruiser when he came for them, so they ambushed him in his barn and tried to make it look like a suicidal overdose. They pumped him full of enough dope to kill an elephant, but Brown wouldn't die. He kept hanging on. When the agents found him after a neighbor reported repeated gunfire coming from the vicinity of the barn, they said he was drifting in and out of consciousness with his forty-five in his hand and apparently shooting every time he woke up. They found six empty magazines and only one round left in his pistol when they got there."

She paused and pulled a stack of papers from the back of her file. "He survived, Chase. That guy must be made of hardened steel and kryptonite. I've never heard of anybody hanging on like that. He's still in the hospital in Bozeman. They say his kidneys were failing from all the drugs they pumped into him, but they put him on the transplant list, and you'll never believe the poetic justice. Check this out. Mongo didn't kill Copeland when he threw him around after the thing with the grenade. He was still alive, and he ended up in the hospital in Bozeman clinging to life until his lights finally went out."

"I don't get it," I said. "How's that poetic justice?"

She glared at me. "Stop interrupting me and listen. Copeland and Alvin Brown both have AB-negative blood type. Do you know what the chances are of that? No, of course you don't, because you're not as smart as me. Only one percent of Caucasian men are AB negative. That means not all of Copeland is dead. His kidneys are now permanent passengers inside Alvin Brown's gut. Can you believe that?"

She closed the file and looked up. "Oh, I almost forgot. Remember the forest ranger who fed you coffee and snacks before the raid? Well, he's not a ranger. He's a CIA case officer. It still freaks me out when pretend spies stumble into us real ones."

"We're not spies," Penny and I said in unison.

Before Skipper could huff, someone knocked on the door to my room and pushed it open before I could answer. The man who knocked looked like someone central casting had sent over to play a Secret Service agent in some Hollywood low-budget production.

He said, "I'm going to have to ask everyone to leave the room for security reasons."

Penny squeezed my hand, and Skipper wrinkled her forehead. "Security reasons? What kind of security reasons?" Skipper demanded.

"I'm sorry," the man said. "But you have to leave the room . . . now."

With defiance written all over her face, Skipper stood. "I'll get to the bottom of this. Just wait here."

Before she took a step, the man pushed the heavy oak door open until it struck the wall, and the president of the United States stepped into the room. He laid a hand on the man's shoulder. "It's all right, Jeff. They can stay."

Every muscle in my body wanted to get on my feet and shake the president's hand, but no matter how badly I wanted to be standing, my injuries and the traction devices made it impossible.

The president crossed the room with the confidence and swagger the leader of the free world should display. He put his hand in mine. "Well, Chase. You've done it again. You pulled yet another of the former president's family out of the flames, and the White House is running out of ways to say thank you, but try this one on for size. I'm hosting a state dinner at the White House in seven weeks. They tell me you'll be back on your feet and ready to dance the jitterbug by then, so I'd like to extend an invitation not only for you, but for your entire team to grace us with your presence."

"I don't know what to say, Mr. President."

"Say yes, Chase. That's what people do when the president extends an invitation to a state dinner. But that's not all . . . The Lincoln Bedroom just happens to be vacant the night of the dinner, so I'd be honored if you and Miss Penny would stay the night."

I don't remember what I said, but it must've been something resembling yes.

The president turned to leave, but before he reached the door, he turned back and raised a finger. "Oh, there is one more thing. I almost forgot to mention that we've got a little thing called a black ops budget, and those purse strings have recently fallen open. The damage to the floats on your airplane couldn't be repaired, but they're being replaced with shiny new carbon fiber floats. They're half the weight and twice the strength . . . or so they tell me. And while the purse strings were open, I authorized the payment to cover the check you wrote for your new helicopter, as well as a little something extra to put some good radios and instrumentation in that old, worn-out panel."

The Secret Service agent closed the door before I could offer thanks, and Penny and Skipper sat in wide-eyed disbelief, both of them in silent awe.

Epilogue

I was starting to wish someone would install a revolving door to my hospital room by the time another knock landed on the door. Much like the previous knock, that one was followed by a man pushing the door to its inward limit.

Clark Johnson led the parade of warriors who made their way through my door in various stages of mobility. With an enormous bandage on his thigh, Hunter hobbled just behind Clark. Singer clumped across the floor on his single camouflaged crutch and one good foot. Mongo rolled himself through the door in the biggest wheelchair I'd ever seen. And finally, Disco stepped inside and closed the door behind him.

The reunion lasted half an hour as we retold the adventure six different times from six different perspectives. We were all wrong while at the same time, all perfectly correct in our telling of the experience.

When the laughter and celebration finally came to an end, Clark sidled up to my bed and gave my shoulder a slug. "So, College Boy, have you figured it out yet?"

"What's that?"

He gave the team a long look and then put on his crooked smile. "Have you figured out who Rabin was talking about when he told you there's someone close to you who isn't what you believe him to be? We figured it out a long time ago, but you seem to be a little slow on the uptake."

I felt a lump rise in my throat as my team waited for me to answer. "Yeah, I think I may understand it now. It was me. I'm not at all what I believed I was. I thought I was a baseball player and a lost soul stumbling around in a world where I didn't belong, but the people in this room have made me believe and understand that I'm none of those things. Even though I've never worn the uniforms all of you once wore, I'm a warrior nonetheless, and your faith in me and willingness to follow me into the pits of Hell make me understand and believe I'm exactly where I belong, doing exactly what I'm meant to do."

Author's Note

First, let's talk about the cult so we can get that ugly business out of the way and have some fun. The Temple of Truth cult in this work of fiction is entirely the product of my imagination and based on nothing. The location for the cult is, however, based extremely loosely on the approximate location of the Church Universal and Triumphant compound near Gardiner, Montana, established in 1981. (Gardiner, Montana, wasn't established in 1981, the church was.) When I learned of the existence of such a compound, I gave no thought to the teachings of the group; instead, I grew fascinated with the location. What better spot for an isolationist extremist compound than the wilds of southern Montana? I still have no idea what the Church Universal and Triumphant believed, taught, or practiced, and I don't particularly care. Here in the South, we may take up a serpent or two and occasionally speak in tongues, but in general, people like me aren't interested in communal living and drinking the Kool-Aid. My fictional cult doesn't, and to my knowledge, has never existed in Montana or anywhere else. My references to incidents in Waco, Texas, are meant only to provide a fictional link to real-world historic events. I make no public praise nor condemnation of the Branch Davidians of Waco or the tragic loss of life in April of 1993. Ultimately, my cult does not exist, never has existed, and is

based on nothing other than my imagination. After all, my imagination is why you were willing to pay $4.99 for this book.

Now that we have that out of the way, let's talk about Montana. Like many of you, no doubt, Melissa and I are big fans of the
television series *Yellowstone*. The breathtaking scenery shown
throughout the series sparked a fire in us to go take a look for ourselves. So, that's what we did, and we were mesmerized from the
moment we stepped off the airplane. The only thing that rivals the
awesome scenery of the area is the kindness and cordiality of the
people of Montana. We spent five days exploring Yellowstone National Park, Beartooth Mountain, Bozeman, Big Sky, and some
magnificent parts of Wyoming we discovered while completely
lost. (By lost, I mean both physically and metaphorically. We had
no idea where we were, and we didn't care.)

I'm a novelist. I can't draw, sing, play any instrument, paint,
sculpt, create poetry, or perform any other task falling under the
enormous umbrella of art; however, I did take the photograph
that ultimately became the cover of this novel. I don't know the
name of the mountain peaks, and in my opinion, anything as
beautiful as those mountains doesn't need a man-given name. I
took the picture from a trail off Beartooth Pass, but I can't honestly say I knew what state we were in. For those of you who are
photographers, I'll give you the details of the camera, settings, and
technique I used to capture those gorgeous mountain peaks: I
stood relatively still and snapped it with my iPhone. Perhaps
beauty like the landscape of Yellowstone and the surrounding area
transcends technology and skill. Sometimes beauty simply is.

The five days we spent in southern Montana burned such an
impression into our minds and hearts that I've been dreaming of
setting a story in those magnificent mountains since our plane
touched back down on the Gulf Coast of Florida. Most of my
books have been branded as belonging in the sea-adventure genre.

I must confess that not even the most talented sea-adventure writer can believably put a fifty-foot saltwater sailing catamaran in Montana. (Okay, the late great Clive Cussler probably could've pulled it off.) I didn't try, but I hope you'll forgive me for departing from the sea long enough to create this novel. I'll never have the skill or talent to capture Montana with mere words—I'm not sure anyone does—but I hope I've given you a look at the region through fascinated, awestricken eyes. For me, the area became as much a character in this book as Chase, Clark, and the gang. The terrain played a major role in every action sequence of the story and captivated Chase every time he looked out the window. My most sincere hope is that I've inspired you to go see those astonishing mountains and meet those unforgettable people of southern Montana. You won't regret the experience, and if you're anything like me, you'll forever feel the longing to return to the Montana Rockies.

A great many novelists fell in love with Montana like I have—most notably, of course, was Ernest Hemingway. Good ole Papa wasn't the only one, though. Debra Magpie Earling, creator of *Perma Red*; Norman Maclean of *A River Runs Through It*; Stanley Gordon West, the genius behind *Blind Your Ponies*; and the incomparable James Welch, who wrote *Fools Crow*, all discovered Montana through the eye of the wordsmith and gave in to the little piece of the area that will forever live inside their hearts. I wouldn't dream of comparing myself to any of these greats, but I have felt the same magic and been touched in ways no other place has ever done. I'll always love the sea, even when she's angry and murderous, but Montana is a love affair all her own.

Let's talk about the airplanes now. I would suspect there's a better-than-good chance this isn't the first of my books you've read, so you've been with me long enough to know I'm in love with every machine that is capable of taking flight. The earliest childhood memory I can recall is staring in the sky as those magical flying machines roared overhead, and wanting nothing more than to be one of the incredible people who were blessed to sit in the front seat and command those magic carpets. My first ride in an airplane was a flight lesson. It was in the left seat of a Cessna 150 at the Gatlinburg–Pigeon Forge Airport in East Tennessee in the 1980s. I'll never forget the shiver that ran down my spine when the wheels left the ground and I was flying. I've owned several aircraft and logged thousands of hours over the years, but I've never left the ground in any of those wonderful machines without feeling that same shiver. I pray and believe it will never go away. I damaged Chase's gorgeous amphibious Caravan in this novel, but I made up for it by installing a shiny new pair of carbon-fiber floats. We got to spend a little time in the Citation, but only because of the distance from Saint Marys to Montana. I love the Citation for its astonishing capabilities, but I'll always prefer the stick and rudder skills of flying low and slow. I am not Chase Fulton, and I have no illusion of ever having been him, but his passion for aviation is purely mine. I hope you can feel my love of all things aeronautical when you read my fiction. After all, passion is what good fiction is supposed to be about.

It's now time to discuss Mongo. As the late, great Lewis Grizzard would say, they ripped Mongo's heart out and stomped that sucker flat. That's what beautiful former Russian spies do. Please don't hate Anya for breaking Mongo's gigantic heart. It's not her fault. I did it. Besides, there are lots of other reasons to hate (and love) Anya. It's easy for me to forget that these characters aren't real because they've become such an enormous part of my life. Mongo, the gentle giant, blows off a little steam and almost flails the life out of poor old Aaron Copeland in the Bitterroot Mountains. He also mumbled a few less-than-complimentary things about our favorite Russian assassin during his semiconscious period. If he were real, he would only be human, and as such, he would be susceptible to all the same emotions, sorrow, and bitterness the rest of us experience. I've written his character to be above those faults in previous novels, but I let his humanity and anger rise to the surface in this book. We all need to vent from time to time, and this was Mongo's time. Please don't think less of him for being human.

I'm often asked, "What is the overall theme of your work?" Perhaps for serious artists with some social or political agenda, that question may open the door for them to preach ad nauseam about injustices, unfairness, or some other catchphrase they love, but I'm not a serious artist. I'm a storyteller. I have only two agendas: First, I want to entertain the stuffing out of you with my larger-than-life stories. Second, I want to pay homage to the astonishingly brave men and women who stand with their backs to us and their faces to our enemies and raise their swords so we don't have to. We owe these warriors a debt of gratitude we will never be capable of repaying, but they don't ask us to. They simply pull on their boots every day and keep this, the greatest nation on the planet, free for one more day.

Thank you from the depths of my heart for reading and supporting my work. You've given me the greatest gift any man could ever hope to receive. You've made my dreams come true, and I will never take that for granted. I love every second of being your personal storyteller, and I never want to be anything else.

-Cap

About the Author

Cap Daniels

Cap Daniels is a former sailing charter captain, scuba and sailing instructor, pilot, Air Force combat veteran, and civil servant of the U.S. Department of Defense. Raised far from the ocean in rural East Tennessee, his early infatuation with salt water was sparked by the fascinating, and sometimes true, sea stories told by his father, a retired Navy Chief Petty Officer. Those stories of adventure on the high seas sent Cap in search of adventure of his own, which eventually landed him on Florida's Gulf Coast where he spends as much time as possible on, in, and under the waters of the Emerald Coast.

With a headful of larger-than-life characters and their thrilling exploits, Cap pours his love of adventure and passion for the ocean onto the pages of the Chase Fulton Novels and the Avenging Angel - Seven Deadly Sins series.

Visit www.CapDaniels.com to join the mailing list to receive newsletter and release updates.

Connect with Cap Daniels

Facebook: www.Facebook.com/WriterCapDaniels
Instagram: https://www.instagram.com/authorcapdaniels/
BookBub: https://www.bookbub.com/profile/cap-daniels

Also by Cap Daniels

The Chase Fulton Novels Series
Book One: *The Opening Chase*
Book Two: *The Broken Chase*
Book Three: *The Stronger Chase*
Book Four: *The Unending Chase*
Book Five: *The Distant Chase*
Book Six: *The Entangled Chase*
Book Seven: *The Devil's Chase*
Book Eight: *The Angel's Chase*
Book Nine: *The Forgotten Chase*
Book Ten: *The Emerald Chase*
Book Eleven: *The Polar Chase*
Book Twelve: *The Burning Chase*
Book Thirteen: *The Poison Chase*
Book Fourteen: *The Bitter Chase*
Book Fifteen: *The Blind Chase* (Fall 2021)

The Avenging Angel – Seven Deadly Sins Series
Book One: *The Russian's Pride*
Book Two: *The Russian's Greed*
Book Three: *The Russian's Gluttony* (Winter 2021)

Stand Alone Novels
We Were Brave

Novellas
I Am Gypsy (Novella*)*
The Chase Is On (Novella)

Made in the USA
Coppell, TX
25 February 2024

29327146R10152